Forget Everything & Run

By Eliza Murphy

Forget Everything & Run
by Eliza Murphy

Book cover design by Abi Eneman. Cover image used with permission from rights owner.

Thank you so much for supporting this work.

Dedication

For Patrick, Derek, Mairead, and Cornelia with love.

FORGET EVERYTHING AND RUN

Prologue

Forget everything and run or
Face everything and rise.
The choice is yours. - Zig Ziglar

I have been running since 1969 and I haven't forgotten anything. That's nearly seventeen years. The worst part is I'm not the only one who remembers.

May 15, 1988, will be Maizey's eighteenth birthday. She's already bugging me for a party – in fact we've had quite a few spats over stuff in the past few months.

I hope I haven't run out of time and I'm one step ahead of those who know the truth. They're wrong. The truth can hurt.

I just hope we can make it to her birthday. All I want is two more years.

Part One

Chapter One

Jenny: Tuesday, January 28, 1986

If ever there was a day for my head to explode, today would be it. It started with the slam of the apartment door at 7:10 am. I keep telling myself that she is just an average teenager, and that I should expect it. However, today there is electricity in the air and the nerve endings in my brain can feel it.

I get dressed quickly and throw water on my face, not wanting to make eye contact in the mirror. The crow's feet around my eyes are mocking me today. They are like the small cracks that bring down a huge wall, a perfectly constructed wall that is beginning to sag.

Out into the kitchen, where I see the empty cereal bowl in the sink and the spoon sunk into the dirty water. I rinse them both, and put them in the strainer. I go to the junk drawer to find some aspirin and take three. It's too late for me to make coffee so I'll get some at the office and get a pastry for breakfast. I'm sure the caffeine and sugar will do nothing for this headache.

There's something wrong in the room. Something different, I cannot put my finger on it. I know I'm always paranoid but today feels different. If I felt auras, I suppose I'd feel one this morning of impending doom. I see the note from Maizey, telling me that she's going to Chorus practice after school and could I pick her up after work. Deep sigh. I'm losing her. What will she do when she finds out the truth? I wonder if she'll hate me but I can't think of that now because I'm beginning to run late for work.

I gather all my things together and start to open the locks on the outside door when I bump into a package on the inside of the door. Maizey must have put it here on the way out.
It's plainly labeled in neat block letters.

To:
JENNIFER MORALES
345 DESERT HIGHWAY
PHOENIX, ARIZONA
APT12D

I pick up the box and shake it. A feeling of dread comes over me, like it's Pandora's box. I can't leave it here and open it when Maizey sees it. I have to open it now. I have to see what's in it. My gut is telling me to just throw it in the dumpster, but I cannot. My paranoia needs to know that it's not right. Today is like every other day for the past fifteen years.

I open the package expecting a real bomb to go off, but instead the bomb goes off behind the wall of my brain. I just see the Santana 45 record and I go blank. I slide down along the wall. I can't look beyond that because this can only be from him.

I rub my eyes, pick up the box and walk to my car. I have this intense feeling that someone is watching me, so instead of throwing the box in the dumpster, I open the passenger door of my car and put it in there.

My hands are shaking as I'm starting to pull out of the apartment parking lot and onto the familiar road to work. Normally it takes thirty minutes to get to the other part of Phoenix. I'm going east and I forget my sunglasses so the sun is right in my eyes. I turn on the radio and they are talking about Commander Scobee and the *Challenger* launch. He went to the University of Arizona, so the broadcasters are gushing about him. It's 8:35 and they have broken through the radio station to give the countdown of the launch. All systems are a go.

I'm at a red light as I see a black sedan two cars behind me. I recognize that sedan. I decide to make a right-hand turn to get out of the east-facing sun. I see the black sedan make the same turn. The radio's just background, but they have achieved lift-off. In my rearview mirror, I see the black sedan speed up. I'm just about to speed up, too, when I hear the *Challenger* has exploded and the car in front of me abruptly stops.

Everything goes in slow motion. I hear the silence, I brace for the crash, and the contents of the package spill out on the floor of the Impala.

I'm drifting in and out of consciousness. I hear the sirens; I see the lights. Someone asks me, "What's your name?"

I mumble – "Jenny La Chance."

All goes blank. I feel the seatbelt and I want to unclip it but I can't. I can't seem to move my hands. I open my eyes to the morning sun still in my eyes, facing east. Always facing east. There must be steam coming off the engine because I can smell the moisture in the dry heat.

Where was I going? I don't know. My head is pounding and I think I must have hit the dash. I'm sure there's blood on my face but the rearview mirror is tipped away from me. I feel jammed into the driver's seat metal pressing into me in places that it probably shouldn't.

Time moves slowly and I shut my eyes. I move the fingers of my right hand. I can wiggle them. I make a slight movement and feel something sticky. Oh God, blood is supposed to feel sticky. My brain is slow to process and make me aware of all the senses. Then there is a smell, an old familiar smell: maple syrup. I'm relieved that it's not blood but I wonder why there's maple syrup in the car.

The shattered glass bottle is in the shape of a maple leaf. There's something very familiar about it. I'm starting to shake and feel cold – even in the desert sun, you can feel cold. Someone is talking to me telling me to open my eyes. They shine a bright light and ask me my name.

"Jenny," I groan.

I hear another male voice in the background saying that the car is registered under the name Jennifer Morales. The first voice starts again. "Ok, Jenny. You've been in a car accident. We are going to get you out of the car and get you medical help. I want you to tell me if anything hurts when we touch you, okay? My name is Kevin. I'm a firefighter and EMT."

I turn my head slightly to look at him. I see brown eyes with long lashes, kind and concerned. He looks familiar to me. Kevin's voice is soothing so I close my eyes and follow his instructions, which is to just let them do all the work.

When I open my eyes, I see Johnny's brown eyes staring at me.

"Johnny, I knew you'd come back." I start to sob.

Johnny speaks. "Jenny, take a deep breath and hold it for me." I do what he says. I feel the seat belt loosen around me and then shooting pain. I cry out.

"Okay, Jenny, I am going to touch your stomach, lay you back, and put this brace on your neck. Ready?"

"Okay, Johnny," I mumble.

I feel myself being lifted from the car by strong hands and am placed flat on a stretcher. I am wheeled over to the ambulance. The medical equipment is beeping. I can hear the dispatch speaking – "An adult Hispanic female with possible head injuries and unknown internal injuries due to an auto accident, stabilized on a backboard, BP weak, heart rate elevated. Displaying symptoms of shock. Fades between unconscious and consciousness. Able to give the first name as Jenny. Now ready for transport." Then to me, "Dispatch says waiting for your arrival. Estimated time of arrival is eight minutes."

I'm moving fast now. I feel like I'm flying down the hill on the toboggan with Johnny. I can hear him talking. He's not talking to me but I feel better knowing he's there. I shut my eyes and relax. Johnny's here and he'll take care of me.

* * * * *

The next time I open my eyes I'm in a hospital bed. I'm groggy. I can see out the window that the sun is going down across a flat horizon. A nurse comes in.

"Oh, you're awake. Just have to take your blood pressure." She unwraps the blood pressure cuff and I feel a tightening on my arm.

"Good," she says as the ripping sounds and the pressure eases. She tells me, "My name is Donna. I'm going to be your nurse today." I try to sit up. She says, "I can move the bed, so don't you try to move." She smiles at me and continues, "I bet you've got some questions for the doctor. He was doing rounds and I'll catch him before he takes off to the next room."

She hurries off, and I'm left in the hospital room with the hum of all the medical instruments. I hear a light rap on the door. A slightly older man with a white coat comes into the room. He takes the clipboard from the end of the bed.

"I'm Dr. Jones, the doctor on duty tonight. You are Jennifer Morales, right?"

"Jenny."

He says, "Okay, Jenny. I bet you're wondering what happened."

I try to shake my head but I can't.

He continues. "You were in a car accident this morning. You are very lucky that both the X-rays and MRI show that it looks like you only have a broken right arm along with a head injury. We won't know for a day or two how serious. We have to wait for the swelling to go down, but for the moment there doesn't seem to be any issues with your spine or neck. You can thank Kevin Strickland for his experience with moving injured people."

I mumble to myself, "…Kevin?"

"Yes, he treated you at the scene and transport."

I'm confused as I think to myself: "Where's Johnny?"

I must have said it aloud, too.

The doctor looks at the papers on the clipboard. "We have Carlos Peña listed as your emergency contact from when you had some blood work done three years ago. I'm going to ask the nurse to sort out your contact information later, and you have something to drink. We have you in a neck brace just for the night until we can assess the swelling, so sorry, only liquids for tonight."

He continues: "I'm giving you some pain meds so that you'll get some rest. Nurse Donna will be back in a few minutes with something to drink. She'll explain how to move the bed and the call button. I'll check back with you at the end of my shift."

Nurse Donna comes back in with a glass of water with a bent paper straw.

She tips it back to me, and I take a sip. I didn't realize how thirsty I was. My lips are parched but I take the cup. Nurse Donna returns and she changes the dressing on my head. She says, "You got quite a bump here, but other than a broken arm your tests are coming back good. I think you'll be out of here in no time. I don't think you've got any wiggly teeth, so we can try some soft foods in the morning. The doctor wanted me to tell you all that. He was called away for an emergency. Do you want me to call anyone? I tried the number here on your admittance form but it's been disconnected."

I look back at her. I don't know who I would call.

"Jenny, can you tell me what happened?"

I say slowly, "I was in a car accident." I blankly look at her.

"Do you know where you were going?"

"To the fair maybe."

She writes this down. For some reason, I feel slightly agitated. My head hurts and I don't want to answer her questions. I'm getting tired and when I shut my eyes she's gone. The first thing I've learned is if I shut my eyes, they will leave me alone.

I try to think. Where was I going? Was I going to the fair with Johnny? I want to be going to the fair but inside my mind I knew I wasn't. Why am I in the desert? Everything's jumbled. If I'm going to find Johnny, I better play along.

I fall asleep and dream. I am flying in the sky and there's an explosion. I fall to the earth slowly and I hear a baby crying. I try to reach for the baby but it falls faster and it grows up to be a teenager and lands in a cornfield. It's a girl. She waves to me and walks into the corn maze. I land later in the mud of the corn maze but I'm terrified to open my eyes. I scream. I must have really screamed, because Nurse Donna arouses me and says, "Jenny, are you okay?"

"I was dreaming. I was falling from the sky after an explosion," I say.

Nurse Jenny writes it down. "The *Challenger* exploded yesterday about the same time you got in your accident."

I take a deep breath, I can hear the radio and then slamming the brakes. I am certain my memory is all mixed up because I can't focus. I wonder if it's the pain meds or if it's me. I've been here less than a day.

Is someone looking for me?

Chapter Two

Maizey: Tuesday

If ever there was a day to be excited, today would be it. I got up super early because I wanted to make sure I liked my outfit. I tried on at least seven outfits before deciding. It's not every day you get Beto as a lab partner in Chem class. Mr. Alvarez paired us up together last class, but he's not going to make us do a lab today because of the *Challenger* rocket taking off during our lab period. He said it was because we would talk about rocket fuels and the chemistry behind the launch after, and he said that we should watch because it was history. All week we've been hearing about the old guy Commander Scobee, who went to the University of Arizona. Pride of Phoenix. I don't think he was born here but that doesn't seem to matter to anyone. We all think it's cool that there's a teacher on board. She's from New Hampshire.

Jenna and I wonder what it would be like to be her students, now that she's famous. She seems nice enough, and we'd be proud. Some of them even got to go to Florida to Cape Canaveral to watch in person. I think that would be cool. I've never been to New Hampshire or Florida. All I have seen is the desert, dry and dusty. But our senior trip next year is to Washington DC. I can't believe Mom is going to let me go. She never lets me do anything. She's kinda strict but in a weird way. I don't want to think about my mom, though, because I'm annoyed with her from last night.

We had another one of our Mom fights about eyeliner and crop shirts. She sounds so old when she says things like, "If everyone was going to jump off a bridge would you?" She's going to be thirty-six this year. I wish she'd find a guy. Carlos doesn't count. He's more like a brother to Mom than anything.

I'm going to eat a bowl of cereal before I put on my lipstick. Thank God I have a mirror in my locker so I can check it before Chem class. I grab a bowl from the cupboard and pour in the cornflakes. I have to eat them fast before they get soggy. I want to get my things and get out of here before Mom wakes up. I'm just too happy right now to see her. I don't want anything to spoil my mood. I drop my bowl in the sink, and grab my purse and backpack. I open the door – there's a package addressed to Mom. I put it down by the door. I write a quick note about chorus practice and leave it on the counter by the cornflakes box. I almost forget my perfume. Linda and Jenna heard that Beto said he liked Angel. I run back into my room to get it and realize that it's almost 7:10 – the bus comes at 7:15, and today I can't miss it.

I slam the door and say "Sorry!" 'cause I know this will wake up Mom. I'm too happy right now to care whether she's still mad at me. I'll give her a hug and we'll be good. I just wish she wasn't so protective all the time. I mean, I am sixteen, going on seventeen.

I run outside the apartment complex and luckily the three other kids are still waiting for the bus. The annoying kids from Apt 10. They always are doing stuff to the old people in the building and causing trouble. They give me and Jenna a bad reputation with the neighbors living in this complex.

The sun is just coming up but it's already hot and you can smell the dry dirt. I look for Jenna and I see her walking toward the bus stop. She hurries by an unfamiliar black sedan. The Jones brothers smirk and say, "Guess they didn't want her!" meaning the car was kinda out of place and creepy. I'm angry because they've kind of insulted my best friend. I yell over to them, "Shut up, you morons!"

Jenna comes over to the group.

"Weird," she says, tipping her head to the car.

"Yeah. I know."

But before we get too much into it, the bus arrives. We make our way to the middle and pull out of the parking lot, leaving thoughts of the black car behind.

Jenna and I made a pact never to discuss anything on the bus ride. One time Ashley did, and it was spread all over the school. So, we sit quietly next to each other for the rest of the ride to Moon Valley High School. Jenna and I are both in the same homeroom, but she doesn't have Mr. Alvarez for Chemistry. She's got Spanish that period. The bell rings to pass between periods. We got four minutes. I can get there in two, so Jenna and I go to my locker. I put on some more lipstick, and a dab of Angel. Jenna inspects me and wishes me good luck: "Buena suerte!"

I walk down the hall to Chem class and peek in. Beto is already sitting in his chair. I see my empty chair next to him. I try to look natural but underneath I'm sweating and nervous. He sees me coming and he smiles.

Oh my God, this is the best day of my life. Beto smiles at me.

I get to my chair and put my stuff down.

"Hi," I reply.

"Hi." I look down at my books. God, I'm already blowing this.

The bell rings and Mr. Alvarez wheels in a TV so we can watch the *Challenger*'s liftoff.

It's 8:15.

Mr. Alvarez is having trouble getting the TV to work. One of the kids in the back who does the lighting for the plays gets up and pushes a button on the back of the TV. Now we can see the TV. Mr. Alvarez is talking. I'm looking at him but I can't concentrate because I can feel Beto next to me. His arm is almost touching mine. It's like electricity.

I hear Beto start counting down, and then the boys in the room all cheer, "And there's lift off!" like it was a winning touchdown. They pan to the crowd. I see high school kids from New Hampshire watching their teacher go into space. I look at Mr. Alvarez. I look at the TV. Beto's arm brushes mine and I look at him. He winks at me. I feel my face blush.

The door to our room is open. I hear the explosion on the TV and then the kids in the back say "Holy shit" and swear in Spanish. I hear the class across the hall swearing too. Mr. Alvarez is stunned. Beto looks at me. I'm wide-eyed. He says, "That can't be good." "No," I say, trying not to explode myself.

I let out a small gasp. Beto takes my head and puts it on his shoulder. I feel like crying. I don't know why. Maybe I'm thinking of all those New Hampshire students who just watched their teacher get blown up or that Commander Scobee won't be able to come back to Phoenix or that I had a fight with my mom or that I was so happy and now everyone is shocked and sad.

We all sit quietly thinking about whatever we are thinking and watching the TV. Mr. Alvarez gets a call from the office. He's speaking in hushed tones but you can tell he's shaken up. He says I think school might get out early today. No one cheers, not even the kids in the back.

I know I shouldn't think this, but I don't want to move. It feels like it has been a long time since my head has been on Beto's shoulder, but I look at the clock and it's only been about two minutes since the *Challenger* blew up. The class is starting to get restless and Mr. Alvarez doesn't know what to say. He's a science guy so he probably had all this chemistry rocket science planned for today. That isn't gonna happen now.

Finally, the boys in the back break the silence. "Hey Mr. A., are we getting out of class early or what?"

"I don't know, they'll tell us over the loudspeaker soon," he says, shaken.

He gets up and goes to the board. He's looking down at a piece of paper. He starts to write some names and numbers on the board. He tells everyone to open up their notebooks.

I have to move my head and sit up straight. My contact with Beto has ended. I grab my notebook from my backpack and open it to a blank page. After the second name, I realize we are writing the names of the people who were on the *Challenger*.

I wonder, if Mr. Alvarez had been on the flight, would other high school kids be writing his name in a spiral notebook? He's a decent guy but I'm not interested in chemistry, only that I got a chance to be Beto's partner. It's stupid, I know. My mom was mad at me because she says I don't apply myself and I'm smarter than that. She shakes her head at me and calls me boy crazy. I yell back at her she must have been sixteen once. That stops the fight every time. I know I'm mean about that 'cause I can see something behind my mom's eyes, something she's hiding. Something bad happened to her. Something she doesn't want me to know.

Mr. Alvarez starts up again. "This is your homework for the rest of the week. We've talked so much about Commander Scobee, and a little about Christa McAuliffe, but for the rest of the week, I want you to read the newspapers or watch TV and write a 250-word essay on each of the other five astronauts. You can work together with your lab partner or by yourself. I just want to emphasize that this is an assignment of *integrity* and *honor*. I want you to do your best work. Seven people have died in the name of science and I want you to remember this day."

Mr. Alvarez hears the groans in the back. He's getting his teacher's voice back. "Gentlemen, if this assignment doesn't work for you, I'm sure I can assign some memorization of the periodic table."

Beto snickers, "That'll show them." He turns his big beautiful brown eyes to me and says, "You okay with working on this together? I mean, if you want to?"

I'm going to remember this day for sure because now I've got Beto's attention for the next couple of days. I have such mixed feelings: I'm super excited but I'm super sad too.

"Yeah, I think it would be easier to do it together." He grabs the pen out of my hand and writes his phone number on my notebook page with his name. *BETO*. I drop the pen (on purpose) so I can put it away for later and grab another one. I start to write in his notebook but the pen has gone dry. Beto grabs his pencil and tells me to take it. My fingers touch his, and the chemistry hits my hand. I jot down my phone number and put down my full name: Maizey Morales. There aren't any other Maizeys in the school, but in case he comes across one this week, I've got to be sure.

Beto says, "Okay. I'll call you tonight after dinner, say around 7:30. We can figure out when to get together. I've got track this afternoon."

"I've got chorus," I say.

"Oh yeah, I went to the concert at Christmas." He starts to say something else, but the loudspeaker squawks on. The principal gets on and starts to speak:

"By now you all know the *Challenger*. Many of you were watching it on TV. The guidance counselors and I have decided that we will have a special assembly after lunch. Periods 5 and 6 will be canceled, and everyone should report to their homerooms after lunch for further instructions. If you feel like you need to talk to someone beforehand, please get a pass from your teacher to come to the guidance office. Periods 2, 3, and 4 will stay on the same schedule for today."

Ms. Gomez, the bilingual teacher, gets on and repeats the message in Spanish. She only does this when it's something important like early dismissal. Most of the Mexican kids have excellent English but she always wants to make sure no one has an excuse to say they didn't get the message.

Mr. Alvarez faces us all. "The bells are going to ring any minute now. Does anyone have any questions?"

Becky the quiet girl raises her hand.

"Yes, Becky."

"Mr. A, how could this happen? I mean, all those kids watching the rocket blow up."

Mr. Alvarez sighs. "I don't know, Becky. It's a good question. As scientists, they will do a thorough investigation. We'll be hearing about it over the next week or so."

Becky says, "What about the kids?"

Mr. Alvarez rubs his eyes. I can see that he's trying not to cry. He takes a step forward. "That's when we look to God for answers. I pray for those children and their families. I am a scientist but I also believe in God. I think that's the only honest answer I can give you."

Becky says, "Thank you."

"Anyone else?"

I sit there uncomfortable because Mr. Alvarez feels like a real person now, not just the teacher who blabs about the periodic table. I look at the second hand on the wall clock, and when it hits 12 the bell rings. We shuffle out of class. Beto says, "7:30?"

"Yeah, 7:30," I reply.

The hallway is a mix of kids just wasting time. Some you can tell couldn't have cared less about the rocket, but are happy not to have to go to the last two periods. I scramble to get to my locker, hoping that Jenna will be there. I'm in shock about having Beto's number, him winking at me, my head on his shoulder, and the *Challenger* blowing up. I'm staring at myself in the mirror, but Jenna doesn't get there in time, so I slam my locker shut.

It reminds me of this morning when I slammed the apartment door shut on Mom. I wonder how Mom is taking the news of the *Challenger*. She's about the same age as Christa McAuliffe. She is always worried about things happening so I bet she's freaking out. I bet she's worried about me. I bet she's going to try and get to chorus practice before it starts so she can check on me.

I'm walking to my next class when I pass Jenna in her seat talking to Lou. She looks over Lou's head and I give her an air high five. I get to my next class, which is English, and take out the pen Beto used to write his name. The teacher tells us that we can get out our copies of *To Kill a Mockingbird* and have some silent reading. I think it's because the adults are so distracted by the *Challenger* explosion. That's fine by me.

Three themes of the book are written on the board: courage, family life, and prejudice. I write them in my notebook. We have to answer one for tomorrow. Five-hundred-word essay. I pick "courage" because it seems like a theme today.

Finally, it's lunchtime and I get to our usual table. Jenna is waiting for me.

She looks at me and says, "So?"

I pull open my notebook and show her Beto's phone number in my green spiral.

She's like, "Wow, Maizey. Wow."

"He's calling me at 7:30 tonight. Mr. Alvarez gave us the assignment to work on with our lab partner. I put *my* number in his science notebook!" I paused. "I hope my mom's not going to freak out. You know how she is."

"It's just homework," Jenna reassures me.

I smirk and say to Jenna, "Yeah, it's just homework."

We get to talking about the *Challenger*. "That was horrible this morning. I thought Mr. A was going to cry."

"Yeah, same with Señora Lorenza. She even swore in Spanish and then I heard her saying Hail Marys under her breath."

"God and science, that's what Mr. A said."

"Well, God was looking out for you today."

"Jenna, I put my head on Beto's shoulder and he winked at me!"

"All good signs! I think he likes you."

"I think he does too."

Grown-ups always think they know what's best for kids. It's like they say "Hey, I've lived longer than you, so you gotta follow me." Sometimes, they're just awkward. That's the feeling I got walking into the auditorium for the afternoon assembly.

We sit together with our homerooms. Lucky for me, I had Jenna to sit next to. We're always strategic, and try and get the end seat so we only have to sit next to one other person. Jenna lets me sit on the end in case Beto can see me. I can't find him in the crowd without it looking like I was *really* looking for him. It doesn't matter now though, because I got his number and he's going to call me tonight.

All the science teachers and the principal are on the stage. They have a projector screen pulled down and the mic on. There was some confusion among the adults about the mic. The same kid who works in lights from this morning walks over to the stage, and does something down under the podium. He goes up to the mic and taps it. His voice rings out over the talking. "Check, check." The adults look relieved and they pat him on his back. You can see that makes him clearly uncomfortable, but they don't notice that and as he's walking off the stage he hears his name and puts his head down. There's always one or two smart-asses in the group and they mock him as he goes by. I can strain my neck to look around. I see Beto whispering to Daren. I hope he's talking about me, but I don't want to get caught looking at him. Jenna says, "That guy Larry's hot. Look at him with that tighty white."

I say, "But he's a jerk!"

Jenna says she knows, but "I can still appreciate a fine guy!"

"I swear, Jenna, if you go after him I'm not going to sit with you on the bus anymore. You're full of it, you'd have to sit with those creepy Jones brothers. I mean it, though, stay away from tighty whitey."

She rolls her eyes at me, and we hear Mr. Cummings start to say "Okay everyone, settle down." No one's listening. He raises his voice again into the microphone, and it pierces with a shrill noise. Everyone grumbles and puts their hands over their ears. My ears hurt and I have a weird thought: Is this what those astronauts felt?

Mr. Cummings has got control of the room now. All eyes are on him at the podium. The American flag and the Arizona state flag are set up on the stage. Mr. Alvarez and the other three science teachers are sitting in blue metal chairs behind him.

"Good afternoon, Moon Valley High School. Today is a tragic day in United States history. I want to start today's assembly with a minute of silence for the brave astronauts who perished today. So in ten seconds, we'll start. If you feel like you can send a silent prayer to their families, then do so. If not just, think of their scientific contributions. The silence will begin now."

I shut my eyes. God and science, there it was again. I say a Hail Mary for each one of the astronaut's families. I think, *Was it worth it to them?* I guess they knew the risk, so in the name of science they'd be okay with it logically.

That's the thing about bad things. Logically, it can seem okay and you can tell yourself a reasonable explanation. Deep down though, there's the emotion behind it. I'm not sure if they weren't praying to God at the end and were sad about leaving their families.

I open my eyes and see ten seconds left on the clock; I think I jammed a lot into a minute. Maybe adults do kinda know stuff.

Mr. Cummings comes back on and says he's handing the mic to Mr. A. Mr. A gets up and rotates his shoulders, maybe to ward off all his heavy thoughts. He gets to the mic and starts to talk.

"Your science teachers and I have chosen a video for you to watch. It takes about an hour." He pauses.

"I just want to say to all of you, that this is one of those events people will ask you about for the rest of your lives. Where were you when you heard the news of the *Challenger* explosion? Think of it like President Kennedy's assassination. Treat this afternoon with respect because you'll always have to answer this question for yourself. How did you handle yourself when unexpectedly bad things happened?"

Mr. A is so deep. The lights go out, and we start to watch a documentary on space travel. Some of the astronauts who were on the *Challenger* come up on the screen, smiling and floating in the air. I start to zone out and think about floating in the air 'cause I can relate to that. It's how I felt this morning when I sat down next to Beto.

In my mind, I think I should feel sadder – but I'm excited about Beto.

I can't lie. I think I'm selfish but I start thinking about losing my family. I wonder if any of them fought with their children before they got in the rocket. Probably not.

I wonder where my mom is. What is she thinking about this? Is she sad? Does it remind her of other bad things? Like, President Kennedy. Or that Christa was about her age. I think about losing my mom now. What would happen to me? I suppose I'd go with Carlos. I'd be an orphan. I start to cry a bit. This morning has been too much. Maybe I'm getting my period. I just want to get out of here and find my mom. I guess I'm not all grown up yet. I still need my mom.

The lights go up in the auditorium and the room stinks. It feels like the AC might have broken during the video because only Mr. A is left on the stage. He gets on the mic and says, “Ladies and gentlemen, we are going to release you ten minutes early because the AC just shut down. I am only going to say this once. If I hear of anyone, and I mean *anyone*, doing anything in those ten minutes, You’ll have detention with me after school for a week. No excuses.”

There’s some groaning in the back and mumbling. Mr. A must have supersonic hearing because he says, “For you in the back, yes it does involve sulfur experiment cleanups. Remember you’ll always have to answer the question, what did do on the day the *Challenger* exploded? I know it’s hard to believe, but one day you might have to answer your teenager, and what are you going to say? Make your future self proud.” Kids are already moving to get out of the room.

Jenna whispers to me, “Is he always that deep?”

“Yeah, that’s kinda his thing. Maybe it’s all those chemicals.”

“Haha! Now let’s see if I can see Tighty Whitey, he’s coming up the aisle. Maybe I can get a better look at his backside.” She pushes me out into the aisle and I bump arms with Loreinda. She tells me, “Watch it!”

She pushes me back. Jenna knows she’s been outplayed and they are both looking for the same view. Larry must have eyes in the back of his head ’cause he gives his butt a little wiggle. Jenna says, “Never mind, he’s a jerk.”

"Told you." I looked up to where Beto and Daren were sitting, but their seats are empty.

We get out into the courtyard and I squint my eyes and finally take a breath. I didn't realized I was warding off the perfume and sweat smells. Jenna says, "It's good to be done with this day."

"We're not done yet, we got Chorus practice at 3."

"Right. Do you think we will have to learn some new songs because of the *Challenger* explosion? I mean, I just want to go to D.C. I don't really care what we sing."

"Are you signed up to sell candy bars?"

"I almost forgot about that."

"I don't know why your mom probably won't let you go door to door."

"Yeah, but I think she'll take them into her office and sell them for me. She's always bringing home Girl Scout cookies and lame candles."

"Do you think your mom will give me a ride home too? I don't want to take the after-school bus."

"I think she will."

"Better just to ask when she gets here than to call her now and have her say no."

We go to the vending machines and I get some peanut M&Ms and a Sprite. I think I must be getting my period. Jenna swipes the green ones, but I say, "Stop it! You don't need these. *I* do."

She's the boy-crazy one. I'm *Beto* crazy.

I look up at the sun and think, *You almost got there.*

Chorus practice goes by without a hitch. It's close to 5:30 now. Only two hours until I can talk to Beto. Jenna and I gather our stuff and go to the parking lot. I don't see my mom's car.

Jenna notices too. "Where's your mom?"

"I don't know, I left her a note this morning. Maybe she didn't see it?"

"Your mom knows your schedule by heart, maybe she's caught in traffic."

"Yeah, maybe."

I used up all my change in the vending machine. I don't have a quarter left.

Wait. I go to the bottom of my purse and in the side pocket, there are four quarters. Mom had given me it in case of an emergency.

Jenna keeps talking. "I'll run over to the bus driver and ask her to hold the bus. I think we got like, ten minutes." I run to the closest pay phone. I plunk in the quarter and dial my mom's office. Five rings, and click: Phoenix Payroll. I hear my mom's voice.

"No one is here right now to take your call. We are open nine to five Monday through Friday. Leave a brief message and your phone number and we'll get back to you on the next business day." I hang up without leaving a message.

I'm about to call the apartment when Jenna rushes over to me. "She can't hold the bus any longer." I drop the receiver and it's just left dangling there. We rush over to the bus and hop on. I still don't see my mom in the parking lot. Maybe she is mad at me?

"Your mom will probably figure you took the bus back if she gets here and you're not here."

"Yeah, but she'll be pissed."

"Right now, we got to get you home before 7:30."

"Yeah." I look around. There's probably twenty other kids on the bus, so it's going to take a solid forty-five minutes.

I can't miss the call. Jenna and I watch the sun setting in over the cacti. When we get to the apartment complex, my mom's car isn't there.

Jenna sees me look confused. "Maybe she just went to the grocery store on her way home?"

I say "Yeah," but I know she always goes to the grocery store on Monday.

Jenna and I hop out and the bus makes a U-turn to head east. In the corner of my eye, I see a black sedan at the light. It has its turn signal on to come into the parking lot. The bus driver wants to merge onto the road so she blows her horn for the driver to turn, but instead the driver decides to go straight. Something's not right.

I have my key and I put it in the lock. The apartment's dark. I turn on the light and see the cereal bowl in the kitchen strainer. I put my stuff on the chair. I go into every room, turn the lights on, and call out "Mom?" I don't know why I do this, because I know she's not here. I sit down at the kitchen table and start to think. Where could she be?

The phone rings! It catches me off guard. I look at the clock. It says 7:20 pm, but I know it's only 7:05 pm because my mom likes to make sure she gets out of the house on time. After the third ring, I pick it up. Maybe it's Beto and he's calling me early.

The person on the other end is a woman.

"Jenny? Jenny, is that you?"

"Who is this?"

"Oh, Maizey, it's Lisa, from work."

"Oh hi, Lisa."

"Is your mom there?"

"No, she's not back from work yet. I just got home from school."

"Maizey, your mom isn't there?"

"No."

"Honey, I don't know how to tell you this – but she didn't come to work today. I've been calling the house all day. No one here's heard from her."

"What? What are you saying? I left for school and she was getting ready for work and her car's gone."

"She didn't call, and she didn't come to work."

"I – I could call Carlos. Maybe she went down to see him."

"I want you to call Carlos and then call me back, okay?"

"Yeah, sure."

"It's not like your mom to just disappear."

"She was supposed to pick me up at school."

"That's definitely not like her. Let's not jump to any conclusions yet. Maybe she just needed a day off, especially after what happened this morning. A lot of people are shocked and sad."

"But my mom wouldn't just leave, would she??"

"I don't know, honey. The best thing you can do is make the call to Carlos. Let's say she just had a hankering for some real empanadas and we'll yell at her when she gets back."

"Okay, Lisa."

"Do you have a pen?" I get the pen Beto touched in Chem class and write her number down. I hang up the phone on the wall. Staring at the door, willing it to open. I swear to God, Mom, you better be okay.

The phone rings again. This time I answer and I hear Beto's voice. It's kind of tinny and far away because I'm far away. Beto asks, "Maizey?"

"Yeah, this Maizey."

"Hi, it's Beto from Chem class."

"I…"

"You sound like you don't want to talk to me – I can work on the project by myself, it's okay, I just thought..."

"No, Beto, that's not it. It's…"

"You got someone else."

"No, that's not it either. Beto, listen. My mother is missing." I said those words. "I just got home and her work called. She didn't go to work."

He's silent.

"I got to figure out where she is because her car is not here."

"Maizey?"

"Yeah, Beto."

"You'll find her."

"Beto, thanks."

He goes on, "We can figure out something tomorrow in Chem class."

"Yeah… I got to go."

"Bye, Maizey."

"Bye, Beto." I stare at the receiver and say out loud, "I like you!"

I know Carlos's number by heart. Something my mom made me memorize. I punch those numbers in. The phone rings six times and I'm just about ready to hang up when I hear a familiar breathy voice.

"Hi, Carlos."

The voice brightens. "I just ran up the stairs to catch the phone. Maizey girl, are you still there?"

"She's not here." I'm holding my breath. Carlos can hear it through the phone line.

"Who? Your mom?"

I let out a long sigh. "Yeah. Is she with you??"

"No, she's not here. I haven't heard from her since you both came down to Yuma for the empanadas. Maybe she's late from work?"

The words just come out in a rush, all fast and choppy.

"She was supposed to pick me up from school, but her car was gone, but then Lisa called from her work, and she said didn't show up today, and we had a fight last night!"

"Whoa, whoa. Slow down."

"She's disappeared."

"You don't know that yet! Maybe she'll walk through the door any minute and we'll put her in time out?"

He's trying to make me laugh but I hear the worry in his voice.

"Lisa wants me to call her back."

"Yeah, you do that and maybe have Jenna come over, unless you got some boyfriend hiding under the couch."

"You know my mother would not allow any boys in the house."

"I won't tell if you won't tell."

"Carlos, I'm scared."

"Yeah, I know. I'm going to come by as soon as I can. I'll call you when I leave. Should take me about two hours."

"Okay, I'll call Jenna and see if she can come over."

"Don't forget to call Lisa and tell her I'm on my way."

"Thanks, Carlos."

"Anything for you."

I hung up the phone. I decided I'd better call Lisa first.

I dial her number and she picks up right away on the first ring.

"Maizey?"

"Yeah." She can hear something in my voice. Fear and disappointment.

"She's not with Carlos. He hasn't seen her today."

There's a long pause.

"He's coming up from Yuma. He said he'd call me when he was leaving. I'm going to call Jenna and see if her mom will let her stay with me until he gets here."

"That's good."

"I don't want to stay on the phone too long in case Carlos tries to call."

"Okay, honey. You had dinner yet?"

"No."

"I'll come by and bring you a pizza, alright? Cheese, or something else?"

"Cheese is good."

"I'll see you in about a half hour. Maizey – don't answer the door unless you see the person through the peephole, okay?"

"Yeah, I know. My mom says that all the time."

"Okay, be there in a half hour or so."

I hang up and dial Jenna.

She picks up on the second ring.

"So?"

"Jenna," I start to cry.

"Beto better to have not messed with you."

"No, it's…"

"God damn nice looking, fine boys."

"No, it's…"

"Good thing he's on track. He's going have to run fast to get away from me."

"Jenna, stop!" I scream. "You're not listening. My mom's missing."

"What?!"

"My mom's missing. Can… can you come over and stay with me until Carlos gets here?"

"I think so. Let me just ask my mom."

She puts the phone down and I hear her run into the other room.

"My mom says okay. I'll be over in like two seconds."

I hang up the phone. I go back into the kitchen and see the dishes drying in the sink. I touch them, trying to feel my mom there. They just feel like warm ceramic. There's furious banging at the door.

"Maizey, it's me, let me in."

I open the door and let Jenna in. I lock the chain bolt behind her.

She says, "Tell me everything."

I think I'm going to crack, but then I explode into laughter. Jenna has those stupid curlers in her hair and her hair is sticking out all over the place.

"Oh God. I didn't even think, I just ran over!" she says as she sees her reflection in the mirror.

I start to calm down, but then I go from peals of laughter right into heaving sobs. Maybe it's all the tension of today, the *Challenger* explosion, Beto, my mom missing, or maybe I'm getting my period.

Jenna starts pulling all the curlers out of her hair and says, "Tomorrow is a baseball cap day. Thank God no one saw me."

I tell her everything from the beginning. When I'm done, she looks right at me. "We'll find your mom. It's not like she's disappeared before."

"Yeah, you're right."

"Let's turn on the TV, and wait for the pizza."

She gets up and turns on the TV.

The first station, special report on the *Challenger* explosion. The second station, special report on the *Challenger* explosion. The third station, a special report on the *Challenger* explosion.

She's looking down under the TV and VHS player.

"Hey, let's watch this instead." She holds up my new VHS copy of *The Breakfast Club.*

She pops the tape into the VCR. The screen jumps alive, and we're watching as the opening credits play. "Don't You Forget About Me" comes on. Why can't the movie just be a movie? I won't forget about you, Mom.

In the opening scene, glass explodes. God, Mr. A is getting to me. This is all too much. I'm thinking about all these things, while Jenna is just watching for Emilio to arrive.

Another bad boy. "Damn, he's hot." She's right of course, but he's not my type at all. Beto's not in the breakfast club.

Jenna is looking at me. "What?"

"Well, I'm just dying to know. Did you talk to him? Did he call?"

I'm struggling again with being excited and scared.

"Yeah, he called, I think right at 7:30."

"So?" She moves closer. "What did he say?"

"We'd figure it out tomorrow in Chem class. He called me right after Lisa did. So I think I was in shock. He almost thought I didn't want to work with him on the homework. I told him about my mom being missing, and he said he was sorry."

"Beto's a decent guy. I don't think he'll say anything to anyone. He doesn't seem to get caught up in the drama."

"Yeah." I didn't even think about what the school would think. Two weeks ago, Mary Ellen's dad ran a red light and hit a pole. He wound up being ok, but the kids at school were *relentless*. Mocking her with "red light, green light" chants.

That whole big group that the Jones brothers were a part of. My mom was always nice to them, though. Giving them cookies at Christmas and on their birthdays. She always told me, "You never know what someone's going through."

There's a rap at the door and Jenna jumps up. We hear a call from outside.

"Maizey, it's me, Lisa."

Jenna slides the chain lock and lets her in. Lisa is your average middle-age person who never married. She looks older than my mom, and acts like it, too. She sweeps me up and puts the pizza box on the coffee table.

She looks at the TV. *The Breakfast Club.*

"Oh, I never saw it."

She goes to the cupboard and takes out some plates and gives them to us.

"Eat first, and then we'll talk."

I didn't realize how hungry I was, but I plow through two slices and then sit back on the couch. Jenna picks at her first slice. I'm thinking she probably had dinner already with her family. She is on a strict calorie-counting diet.

Lisa starts up again. "Okay, Maizey. Did your mom say anything to you about where she might go?"

"Nothing."

"*I* think we should call the police."

"The police? Can't we wait a little bit longer? Until Carlos gets here?

Lisa looks at her watch. "It's close to 9:15. I suppose we can wait like, 45 minutes more, but I think at 10 we should absolutely call the police."

It's funny how adults set these stupid time things. Like if my mom walks in at 9:59 it will be okay, but if it's 10:01, the cops will be on their way.

The phone rings. I ran to get it. *Mom.*

"Oh, Maizey, this is Jenna's mom."

"Oh hi, Mrs. Garcia."

"No word on your mom yet?"

"Nothing yet."

"Well, have faith. You'll find her."

"Thanks, Mrs. Garcia."

"May I speak to Jenna?"

I hand her the phone. She gives her mom an update on the situation.

"Yeah, Mrs. Morales's friend Lisa brought over some pizza and we're waiting for Carlos. He's coming up from Yuma. Lisa wants to call the police. Maizey wants to wait until Carlos gets here."

She hangs up the phone, and says, "My mom said I can stay until Carlos gets here, and then I got to go home. She said you might want some privacy."

Privacy – from what? I think.

The clock ticks away. It's 9:55, and Carlos arrives with five minutes to spare.

Lisa opens the door and he scans the room. We make eye contact. He looks at me deeply and doesn't shut his eyes until he has me in one of his big bear hugs.

I release all my built-up tension. Carlos absorbs it. Holding me tighter.

I don't know how long it lasts, but finally, he says, "Mi hija" and squeezes me on my arm. I'm not his daughter, but he's the closest thing I have to a dad.

"Hi, Lisa. Hi, Jenna."

He smiles a big smile and it melts the room.

Jenna says, "I got to go home now. My mom said I could only stay until you got here."

Carlos says, "I'll watch you from the door."

Jenna grabs her stuff and hugs me. "You'll find her."

"See you tomorrow. Yeah, in the morning."

She leaves and Carlos watches after her.

He shuts the door, and I know that Jenna is at her place.

"She didn't show up for work?"

"No."

"She didn't call?"

"No. We started to worry about her when it got late and she didn't show up. We were distracted by the *Challenger* explosion and we weren't watching the clock. By 10:30, I started calling the house. No answer. By mid-afternoon, I figured maybe she just needed a day off. It's been kind of stressful at work, and we all need a break every now and then. I mean, last week Susan went missing in the afternoon, after lunch." Lisa continued, "We joked about it. Wouldn't it be great just to get out of here and not have anyone know where we were? Well, I joked mostly."

Carlos has mixed emotions on his face like he's taken a bite of lemon and is trying not to spit it out.

Lisa continues, "So I tried a couple more times, and it wasn't until I got Maizey here after seven that I heard anything."

Carlos looks at me.

"She was supposed to pick me up after school and never showed," I say. "I wound up taking the late bus. I started to wonder, because it's not like her to just, you know, *not* show up, and her car wasn't in the lot."

"Maizey, did your mom say anything to you this morning?"

"No." I start to cry. "We had a fight. A fight the night before, about my birthday. She didn't want us to go to bed mad, but I locked my door and put my Walkman on. I was *really* upset. I didn't have a quinceañera, or a sweet sixteen. I want a *real* party for my eighteenth birthday. She said 'We'll see.' Which usually means no."

Carlos was thinking while I was talking.

"Anything else happen this morning?"

I shut my eyes. "There was a package outside the door addressed to my mom."

"I put it here." I point to the spot by the door. Carlos goes over and picks up a scrap of brown paper. "Looks like it's not here now."

He doesn't think I see him pick up the paper, but I do.

Lisa said, "Well she must have taken it with her in the car. That's what I would do."

Carlos looks at his watch.

"It's been more than twelve hours. I think we need to call the police."

Lisa shakes her head in agreement.

Carlos calls the Phoenix police. He wants them to come to the apartment, but asks them not to put their lights on. He lets them know that she hasn't been seen since this morning. He hangs up the phone.

"I'm going to stay with you tonight. I already told Maria when I left. Let's talk to the police and see what they know."

"Lisa, we'll let you talk first so you can go home."

"Carlos, thank you. I know everyone's worried about her at the office. It's not like her to just *disappear*."

Carlos just nods his head but looks away. It seems like he's fighting not to say something. Carlos and my mom have known each other for almost twenty years, I think. At least, longer than I was born.

Twenty minutes pass and there's a rap at the door. Phoenix police.

Carlos answers the door to two cops, one male and one female. He shakes the male cop's hand and ushers them in.

They scan the place and the female cop gives him a raised eyebrow.

The male cop takes charge.

"Okay, Mr. Peña, can you explain who is missing? "

"Jenny Morales."

"And you are to her –?"

"Longtime friend, and guardian of her daughter here, Maizey."

"Okay, why don't we start at the beginning."

Lisa tells them her part. I tell them my part, and Carlos gives them a description of her car. The female officer asks for a photo of my mom.

The quickest one I can see is on the fridge. My mom and I smile out at me from the picture.

The female cop looks at me. She tells me, "I'm going to take it now, but I'll make sure you get it back."

The cops tell Lisa she can go home. They say they will call her at work tomorrow if they need anything. She hugs me and then leaves.

The male cop says technically Mom's not missing because you have to be gone for more than forty-eight hours. "But what I'm going to do is go down to the station and see if her car has been ticketed anywhere or towed. We'll call the hospitals and see if anyone matching her description has come into an emergency room." He continues, "We'll find her. I promise. The best thing you can do is get some rest."

"Mr. Peña – can I speak to you privately?"

The cop has his back to me while they talk, but I can see Carlos shaking his head and he finally shakes hands with the cop. The female officer leaves a business card for me. They both leave.

Carlos turns back to me. "We're alone. Let's have some hot chocolate, and then it's bedtime. I'm going to sleep in your mother's room in case the phone rings in the middle of the night. Now, I want you to come here, and let me tell you, we'll find her, and we'll give her *hell* when she gets back. I am going to *personally* get you that party you want. She's going to pay." He mumbles something in Spanish that I don't understand. He's being silly, but I know he's worried. So I play along.

I get into bed and hope to dream of Beto.

Chapter Three

Jenny: Wednesday, January 29

Nurse Donna comes in and wipes her name from a whiteboard in my room, replacing it with the name *Michelle.* She turns to me. "This here will tell you who's on duty," she says, pointing to the board. "It's almost midnight, so I'm going home for the night. Michelle will take over and then a day nurse will be here at seven. I'll be back tomorrow at three. You probably won't see Michelle – the doctor ordered a mild sedative to help you sleep. They'll be taking you in the morning for tests."

"Thank you."

"Okay, Jenny. Be well."

I can feel the meds taking over and I close my eyes. This time, I don't have any dreams. I just sleep and sleep and sleep, and I don't wake up until the sun is coming up.

There are two nurses in the room now. One looks tired, and one is wide awake.

"Can I have some water?"

"Oh, of course. We didn't realize that you were awake. Jenny, I'm Sarah. I'm the day nurse. This is Michelle, she was the night nurse. I'll be taking care of you today."

"First off, we have to get you ready for the CAT scan. After that, you can come back and have something to eat. I bet you're hungry. Maybe you could try some toast and scrambled eggs?"

"Sure," I say.

"Jenny, does anything hurt right now?"

"About the same."

"Let us know when we move you if anything hurts."

"I need to use the bathroom."

"Well, for the moment, you've got a catheter so it'll take care of it. *Buuuuut*, if your tests come back good, you'll go to the bedpan. Something to look forward to."

I do laugh. I like Sarah.

"Okay, looks like you haven't lost your sense of humor."

She rolls me to my side and I feel a draft. I'm still trying to figure out my surroundings. I can see out the window – a flat sky.

"Jenny, okay, ready."

The nurses pick me up and put me on a stretcher. They talk between themselves. I can't move my right arm. I can see it's in a soft cast. As they push me down the hallway, I can see bits and pieces. I read the sign over the door that reads *Phoenix Memorial*.

"So I'm in Phoenix," I muse to myself. I'm still trying to remember where I was going. I just come up blank.

I do as I'm told, holding my breath and moving whichever way they want. It's a relief to get back to my room. As promised, there's toast with jam and scrambled eggs.

Nurse Sarah pushes up the bed. "You're all clear for soft food. I made the toast the way I like it, with strawberry jam and butter. I hope it's okay."

She gets me into position and I pick up the toast with my left hand. It feels awkward.

"So you're a righty? Okay, then I'm going to help you with the eggs this morning."

It's tough being an unexpected lefty. We finish eating and I drink some apple juice from the bendy straw.

"Jenny, now that you're settled in, I have to ask you a few questions. Okay?"

She's looking down at the clipboard. She grabs it from the end of my bed and continues: "Your address was wrong on your admittance slip and your car registration. Did you move in the last eighteen months?"

"I think so."

"Do you know your address?"

"No."

"Does this address sound familiar?"

She reads off the address. 435 Desert Highway, Apt 12D.

"Sort of," I lie. I think Sarah knows I'm lying but she doesn't let on.

"Here on your contact info, it lists a Carlos Peña." It triggers a memory. I can see Carlos, like in a movie clip lifting me out of the mud. I recognize that name. I know him.

"He's your contact person. We found him last night. Everyone's been worried about you. The police contacted him in the middle of the night and told him you were here resting comfortably. He's been calling the nursing station every hour asking if you're awake yet and if he can come and see you."

"Do you want any visitors right now?"

I think for a moment. And then I ask, "Has anyone else been asking for me?"

"Not yet, but usually when people find out about something like this, they start calling and sending flowers."

"Okay." *I'm a little disappointed that Johnny hasn't called,* I think to myself.

"Jenny, do you want Carlos to come to see you?"

"Yes, I'd like to see him," I say, and think that maybe he knows where Johnny is.

"Jenny, Carlos asked if he could bring Maizey."

Maizey? I think of the baby in my dream.

"Maizey, she's your daughter."

"My daughter?"

"Do you remember?"

I start to cry. "No, I don't remember." I think I must be a terrible mother since I can't remember my daughter.

"Jenny, you got quite a bang on your head. Sometimes it takes a while for everything to make sense. Do you think you'd be up for a short visit this morning?"

"Yes."

"Okay, I'm going to set it up with Dr. Smith. He might come by afterward. Jenny, is it okay if I stay in the room while they visit?"

"Yes," I respond.

"Okay. I'll call them and let you know when they are coming. We'll change your dressing gown and wipe your face before they get here."

I think Sarah is an angel.

Chapter Four

Maizey: Thursday, January 30

I wake up to the smell of scrambled eggs and Carlos whistling "Evil Ways" by Santana. Carlos used to be a roadie for Santana when he was younger. He says these notes were blasted into his mind.

"Good morning," he says as he comes over and hugs me. "Your mom had a car accident – she's in Memorial Hospital. It seems like your mom hadn't changed her car registration or her license from your last apartment, so no one knew who to contact. She hadn't been to that hospital in three years, so my contact information was all wrong too."

"She's forgetful like that. Can I call her?"

"Not yet. I have been calling the hospital nonstop. I think those nurses must be sick of me." He flashes me a quick grin before continuing. "She's sleeping, so as soon as she wakes up they have to get her permission, both for visitors and to tell us anything about what happened in the crash."

"Is she okay?"

"They say she's okay," he continues, "I think she must be okay enough to get visitors, so that's good. I'm going to have to go today and see if her car can be fixed. I'll have it towed to Yuma so I can get Gregg to work on it." He pushes the plate towards me. "Eat up," he says, and he kisses me on the top of the head.

The eggs have gone cold but I force them down with the orange juice.

The phone rings and it's Jenna. "Hey."

"Hi, they found my mom. She had a car accident."

"Oh my God, that's so scary! Is she okay?"

"I'm not sure yet. We have to wait to hear back from the hospital. Jenna, I won't be able to go to school today. Carlos is going to call to get me excused. What do I do about Beto?"

Jenna's quiet for a minute, but finally says, "I know! I can give him a note from you."

"What will it say?"

"Short and sweet. I'll be over in ten minutes. Riding the bus without you is going to be torture, though."

"Okay, I'll see you in ten."

Carlos is looking at me with mischievous eyes. "Beto?" I straighten up and say he's my lab partner, and that we were supposed to work on a homework assignment together.

"Homework? Just homework."

"Yeah, *just* homework," I say exasperatedly.

"Well, I'd like to meet this homework boy."

"I don't think we'll be doing the assignment today."

"Not today, but maybe tomorrow. I can stay another night and make my famous empanadas."

"Maybe, I …"

Carlos smiles and sings, "Maizey and Beto / Sitting in a tree."

I blush. "It's not like that."

He winks. "It's not like that, yet. You think Old Carlos will embarrass you?"

I say nothing.

"Maria would make me sleep on the couch if I did."

There's a rap on the door. It's Jenna. I haven't even written the note.

I write Beto:

My mom's in the hospital.

I won't be in school today.

Please don't say anything to anyone.

I hope we can do some of the homework together.

Maizey

I give the note to Jenna. The bus is going to be here any second.

"Call me later!"

Carlos watches after her. He sees the Jones brothers and swears in Spanish. "Punks." I watch the bus pull up, and stay by the window as I see Jenna and the Jones brothers step up inside. That's when I notice it: that creepy black sedan.

Carlos notices my worried expression. "Relax, I'm sure Jenna will get the note to Beto."

"That's… not it. We must have a creepy new neighbor, 'cause that black sedan is parked in the same spot as yesterday."

"That one?" asks Carlos, pointing at the sedan. I nod my head. He goes ahead of me, about to walk out the door, when then the phone rings.

I pick it up. "It's for you, it's the hospital." He shuts the door and picks up the phone.

"Yes, this is Carlos. That's what I wanted to hear. Okay, we can come for 8:30. I understand. Okay. I see. We will ask for Room 304 when we get to the nurse's station."

He hangs up the phone.

"We can go and see your mom at 8:30. First, though, we have to meet the doctor. I told you we'd find her."

I'm relieved; I start to allow myself to think about my note, traveling on the bus to school with Jenna. I imagine she'd be outside Mr. A's class waiting for Beto to arrive. I imagine her saying Beto's name and putting the note in his hand. Making it light for everyone who's watching. Something about "your Chemistry homework from Maizey." I imagine him putting it in his chemistry book and saying thanks. I imagine Jenna just making it into Spanish class before the bell rings. I imagine Beto opening the note and looking at the empty chair next to him. I imagine hard that he touches the back of the chair like he misses me being there.

Carlos and I go out to his car. He looks around.

"That black car, it's not here now." I think out loud to myself. "Maybe it's just a random black car that looks like the black car from yesterday."

"Well, it's gone," he says, before continuing, "I think we need to listen to some upbeat music," which generally means Santana. He pops in a cassette and "Soul Sacrifice" comes on. He starts hitting the steering wheel and grooving to the music. He looks at me and says, "Did I ever tell you I was a roadie for Santana?"

I'm feeling more and more relaxed, so I can tease him back: "Only every chance you get."

"Ah, there's my little Chita. See, it'll all work out, and I haven't forgotten. We'll get that eighteenth birthday party for you from your mom." The music changes the mood in the car and I find myself rocking to the drum solos.

We arrive at the hospital and park the car. I've only been to a hospital once before, when I broke my finger and had to have a splint put on my hand. It looked the same and smelled the same, like bleach and cherry soap cleaner. Carlos goes up to the reception desk to check in, and the receptionist tells us that our meeting with Dr. Smith will be in Conference Room A on floor three. We get in the elevator and follow the signs to Conference Room A. We peek inside, but there is no one in there but a single nurse. She comes over to ask us, "Can I help you two with anything?"

Carlos lets her know we were supposed to meet Dr. Smith at 8:15, and then see Jenny Morales in room 304.

The nurse looks us both over. "Why don't you go in and make yourself comfortable? Can I get you a drink? Maybe a Coke or a coffee." We both shake our heads no.

As we sit down and I think more about the Coke, I realize that we haven't called Lisa. I remind Carlos.

"Ah, I knew there was something I was forgetting. Well, we'll call her once we see your mom. There must be a pay phone somewhere on this floor."

I sit there in a standard-issue chair. Plastic arms and seat, me chewing on my lower lip. Carlos paces around the room like a caged animal. He's good at keeping things inside, but he's worried. The clock on the wall moves slowly. It's past 8:30, almost 8:40.

Yesterday at this time, Beto was winking at me. He must have gotten the note by now. Chemistry class would be going on. I wonder what Mr. A would be talking about. I wonder how those New Hampshire kids feel today.

There's a quick swish of energy in the room, and Dr. Smith with his stethoscope around his neck and clipboard in hand hurries in. He stops short when he almost hits the conference room table and apologizes to the table. He looks at Carlos.

"You must be Mr. Peña. I'm Dr. Jones. I've been the doctor looking after Ms. Morales since she arrived here yesterday morning." He shakes Carlos's hand, and motions for us to sit down in the oversized chairs by the table. He takes the one at the head of the table, while I sit next to Carlos.

"You must be Maizey."

"Yes," I say.

"It took us a while to figure out how to get in touch with you. The information we had wasn't correct. I want to tell you that we treated Jennifer as we would treat any patient. We were always hopeful that we would find you."

Carlos interjects. "Doctor, is Jenny awake?"

"Yes, she's been awake most of yesterday, except for the times when we gave her pain medications."

"Then why didn't you just ask her where she lived?"

"Let me back up a minute here. This must be a shock to you both." He looks over at me before continuing. "I'm going to speak freely in front of you, Maizey, even though you are a minor." Turning back to Carlos, he says, "I am under the assumption that you wouldn't have brought her if that's not the case."

Carlos is starting to get mad. "Spit it out, Doctor, we are out of our heads with worry."

I look into Dr. Smith's eyes. "Just tell us how my mom is," pleading, "please."

A big sigh. "Okay, I'll start at the beginning. Your mom was admitted at 10:23 through the emergency room by EMS. She was quickly evaluated by a CAT scan as having a severe head injury with possible swelling of the brain, most likely caused by her head hitting the dashboard. The imaging test revealed that she had no other internal injuries except a broken right arm. We treated the head injury and potential neck injury with a brace, and she had emergency surgery for fluid drainage. We also put her right arm in a cast and sling to remove any pressure. We kept her on the fluid drain overnight, but tests this morning show the swelling has gone down and there is no presence of any edematous."

Carlos and I stare blankly back at Dr. Smith. I am not sure exactly what it all means. The doctor senses my confusion. He takes my hand. "Your mother has a broken arm and a severe head injury."

"Can we see her?" I ask.

"Only for a couple of minutes this morning. We'll see how she's doing, and maybe later tonight you can see her again. I can't promise anything. She really needs to rest."

He looks at Carlos, because I can tell he has something difficult to say.

"There… is something you both need to be aware of. Ms. Morales has lost parts of her memory. It's not uncommon for people with head injuries to confuse things or not remember. Most of the time, it's very temporary. As the brain heals, the memories return."

Carlos and I still sit motionlessly. Dr. Smith is looking down at his chart and then at Carlos. "She has a faint memory of you, Carlos, enough to permit you to have a visit and receive medical information about her care. The hospital made this judgment based on her past next of kin on old hospital records."

He turns his head to me and says, "Right now she doesn't remember you."

I put my head in my hands, to try and hid my face. I'm ashamed. I'm sad. My mom does not know me.

Carlos puts his hand on my shoulder.

The doctor continues, "I want you to understand. This won't be easy the first few days, but you have to let your mom come around on her own. As her brain heals, she'll start putting the pieces back together."

"Do you understand, Maizey?"

"No; I mean, yes, and no…" I'm holding back my tears behind a scrunched-up face.

"So today what we are going to ask you both to do is to just go in and say hello. Let her say what she wants. She might be tired, and she could doze off. She also has some medical equipment like an EEG, and you'll see where we shaved part of her head for the drainage tube. Her head itself is also bandage wrapped. There will be a nurse in the room with you."

"Do you have any questions?"

I fight back the tears. "Will she ever remember me?"

I can see into the doctor's heart. He wants to scream yes, all will be well! Instead, from behind his tired eyes he says, "We will be cautiously optimistic. Take one day at a time. I'm going to check with the nurse's station and see if she's ready for you. I'm here all day, so if you have any other questions for me, just let the nurses know."

He asks for Carlos's number. "Is this the best number to reach you? I see it's a Yuma exchange."

"The nurses have the number at Jenny's apartment. I'll be there for the next couple of days. Thank you, Doctor."

He hears his name over the intercom and has to rush out of the room.

Carlos and I are left alone.

"How can Mom not know me?"

"I don't know. The mind is a crazy thing. Listen, Maizey, you've got to be strong." He makes a fist. "You gotta do it for your mom. You can do this. We are just going to see her and let the doctors take care of her. We need to listen to them, you know. Your mom isn't gone. She's still here, and she's not going anywhere."

"It's like she's disappeared."

Carlos shakes his head sternly. "No, she's not disappeared, she's right in Room 304!"

A nurse raps on the door. "So, you're Carlos, and you must be Maizey. I'm Nurse Sarah. I've been taking care of Jenny since this morning. Do you have any questions for me? I know it's a lot to take in."

I ask, "Is she going to be okay?"

"Her brain needs to rest. The swelling has gone down. It might be a little bit of a shock for you to see your mom in the hospital bed. It's only been twenty-four hours."

Carlos asks, "Are you the nurse who will be in the room with us?"

"Yes."

"We will do whatever you want," he says, hanging his head.

"Okay, follow me then. We'll go slow, and plan on maybe a couple of minutes. I know it must be very hard, but the more rest she gets the quicker she'll recover."

I say okay, so we follow Nurse Sarah down the hallway.

I can see glimpses of other patients and hear TVs.

We get to Room 304 and the doors are closed.

Sarah turns to us. "I'll go inside first and check on her. It'll just take a sec."

She disappears behind the door. Carlos has his arm draped around mine and he kisses my head. I lean onto his shoulder. I don't feel strong; I feel a bit sick.

From behind the door, I hear Sarah say, "You can come in now. Best to use a quieter voice." The door to Room 304 opens slightly, and I think I want to run away. This is about to get real.

Carlos is in front of me. Sarah pushes the door slightly open and says again, "You can come in now." It's all too much for me. I stand back by the door. I can hear all the machines and I can smell the disinfectant. Just like a hospital. I'm glad we found Mom, but I don't want her here. I don't want her here and I don't want her hurt. I don't want her to forget me.

Carlos strides into the room and in two steps he's at the hospital bed. I keep my eyes on his back. He bends down and says to Mom, "Jenny, you're going to be okay." He moves slightly, and I can see her now. She has something on her head, and part of her hair is missing. I'm scared to go in. As I'm thinking about what to do next, Mom and I make eye contact.

It seems like the longest stare of my life. I don't know how, but my feet somehow move me forward. Mom raises her hand slightly and I take it.

"I love you, Mom." There must be a tear on my cheek because she reaches up to wipe it away. I'm standing there, and Sarah's pager goes off. Startled, I pull my hand away.

Nurse Sarah says to Mom, "Sorry, I got to get this. I'll be right back. I'll be right here in the hallway." We all look at each other and Nurse Sarah leaves the room. It's so quiet except for all the hospital noises.

Finally, Mom speaks. "I must look like a mess."

Carlos lets out a big sigh and says, "You look good to me." I nod my head in agreement. Carlos says, "How's the food?"

"They just let me eat this morning, so not so good."

"I'm going to bring you some of my famous empanadas," Carlos says.

"That sounds great."

I'm trembling inside. I wonder if she can see it. I feel so guilty. I feel like it's my fault somehow. I can't say this to anyone, so instead, I say, "I'm sorry, Mom. I'm sorry about the fight we had." Mom looks at me. I'm not sure if she heard me or if she understood, but she says, "It's okay. We'll work it out." I want to believe her. I don't care about my birthday party now. I just want my mom home.

Mom looks at Carlos. "Can you get Nurse Sarah?" Carlos walks to the door and goes out into the hall.

Mom says to me, "Sometimes I get these waves of dizziness, they just come over me. I am sorry."

"Don't be sorry, Mom. You have nothing to be sorry for."

Carlos and Nurse Sarah come back inside, and Nurse Sarah asks Mom how she's feeling. She says she's dizzy and lightheaded. "I'm starting to get a pain here." She points to the large bump on the right side of her head. I'm trying not to stare at the bump, but it's so big.

"Okay, Jenny, I'm going to draw the curtains now and get rid of that desert sun," says Nurse Sarah.

I can see what she is talking about. It looks hot outside, and dusty. She finishes saying to Mom, "I think it might be a good time for you to try and get a little rest."

Carlos grabs my hand and gives it a squeeze. He says we'll go now. He goes over to Mom, bringing me with him. He gives her a kiss on the cheek and says something in Spanish. I can't make it out because it's so soft.

I kiss her on the cheek and say, "I love you, Mom."

We turn to leave, but I look behind. I can see her eyes are already closed and Nurse Sarah is fixing her pillow. We shut the door behind us. Carlos moves to the wall next to the door and gives me a big bear hug. I feel the tension leave my shoulders, but I begin to sob. I can't help it. Carlos says nothing, but doesn't let me leave his bear hug. I can hear his heartbeat. Steady and strong. There's a commotion behind me, and I see a hospital worker trying to move a machine in the hall.

"Let's move down here, Maizey."

I wipe my eyes and I think to myself, thank God I didn't put any mascara on. I'd look like a raccoon. We walk down to a small seating area with a couch and a chair, and there's a box of tissues on the side table. I wipe my eyes and blow my nose. All this time, Carlos is quiet. Carlos looks at me.

"It was good to see your mom. She's strong. She'll be okay." I think he is trying to convince himself.

"She doesn't remember me."

"It'll come to her. She's had a bad bang. The size of the bump on her head."

"I know. It'll go away, right?"

"I think that's what the doctor said." He takes my hand. "Whatever your mom needs, we'll be here for her. I'm going to go to the nurse's station for a minute. You stay here. We'll have to find a pay phone to call Lisa and let them know at her office. I've got to call the police to find out what lot your mom's car is at, and I got to call Maria. Maria told her mother, and she's got all the Yuma ladies praying for her; so you *know* she'll be home in no time." He says haphazardly, "Glad not to be there with all those candles burning."

This makes me giggle.

Carlos goes on, "Ah, you remember when Juan hurt himself? He laughed at Maria's mother, but he got better, didn't he? I'll be right back."

He walks over to the nurse's station, and I see Nurse Sarah come out of my mom's room. She catches my eye and comes over. "Hi, Maizey." She sits down next to me where Carlos had been.

"Your mom's asleep now. She's going to need a lot of rest over the next few days. The first couple of days are the most important."

I want to ask her something, but I'm afraid. She says, "Do you have any questions for me?"

I blurt out, "Will she remember me ever?"

"Maizey, you have to give your mom's brain a chance to heal. I've seen this before – people's brains are amazing. We don't know yet about your mom. Time is what will help her, and rest. Don't expect too much in the next day or two. Her brain has got a lot of healing and figuring out to do."

Carlos has come back, and Nurse Sarah stands. "Thank you for taking care of our Jenny."

Nurse Sarah talks over me, like when adults want to say something in front of a kid but not involve them in the conversation. "I was just explaining to Maizey that her mom's brain needs rest and her memory is still working it out. Right. The most important thing from my point of view is to keep her calm and quiet. Let her brain rest. The doctor is going to do some more tests this afternoon. Just looking at her now, it appears to me the swelling has started to go down. That's a good sign. We'll know more later. Maizey, the waiting is the hardest. Healing goes slowly. I'll be here until three today. I'll update you in the early afternoon."

"Okay, that will be great," Carlos says, "I'll call you at the nurse's station."

He charms Sarah with his smile and says, "I promise I won't call every fifteen minutes. I can see you all have work to do."

Her pager goes off, and she says, "Speaking of work." She walks quickly down the hall.

"The nurses told me that there's a pay phone at the end of the hall. Let's call Lisa and let her know."

We walk side by side down the hall. I'm pulling on my purse because it keeps slipping off my shoulder. We get to the pay phone and I start to dig for a coin. Carlos says wait, and he puts his hand in his jeans pocket and pulls out a couple of coins. He plunks a quarter into the phone.

"I can talk to her, or do you want to?"

"I want to."

I dial the number and Lisa picks up on the third ring.

"Phoenix Payroll, Lisa speaking. How may I direct your call?"

"Lisa, it's Maizey."

"Oh God, Maizey. Where are you? I've been calling the apartment all morning. I'm sick with worry!"

"I'm at the hospital with Carlos."

"You found your mom?"

"Yes – she's had a car accident and she hit her head."

"Don't worry, Maizey, she's going to be okay. Can she have visitors?"

I'm starting to shake. I think Lisa must hear it in my voice.

"Oh, honey. I'm sorry. You said Carlos is there, can I talk to him?"

"Yes, he's right here." I pass the phone to Carlos.

"Hi, Lisa… Yeah… No. The nurse is going to give us updates this afternoon. Room 304. You'll tell her boss… Not sure. She has some memory confusion and a broken arm. Okay, we'll talk to you later. Sure, here she is," Carlos hands the phone back to me.

"I'm sorry, Maizey, but I'm glad you found your mom. That hospital is one of the best so I know she's in good hands. I'm going to bring you and Carlos something over for dinner tonight, okay? I know you like mac and cheese. I have to get back to work, but I'll talk to you this afternoon. Your mom is strong. She loves you. Just give it some time."

The recording operator interrupts the phone call. "Please deposit another twenty-five cents for the next three minutes, otherwise the call will be disconnected." I hang up the receiver. I look at Carlos. "She's going to make us macaroni and cheese for dinner."

He rubs his hands together and pushes up his eyebrows.

"I need to call Maria and the girls." He digs for some more coins. I give him what I can find in the bottom of my purse. This should do. He says, "I'll make it quick."

I stand by the wall as he dials the number. I hear "Hola" and then the rest of his conversation is in Spanish. Every once in a while I pick out a word. Mostly it's "Jenny."

I really should know more Spanish than I do, but I take French in school. It seems to come more easily to me.

I watch Carlos and my mind wanders to Beto. Would Beto be like Carlos? I think he might. I hope he will. I pray he will be. My mom was really lucky to find Carlos all those years ago. Carlos hangs up the phone and he says, "Maria's praying for you both and sends this hug." He gives me another squeeze.

"I'm getting hungry, let's get out of here." He has a mischievous look in his eye. "Let's go to McDonald's. What Maria doesn't know, right?"

I shake my head and think grown-ups are weird.

It's close to one o'clock when we get back to the apartment. Everything is so unnatural, quiet. I wonder what to do next. Carlos turns on the radio on the kitchen counter for noise. He switches it to the Spanish station.

Carlos says, "I have got to call the detective who was here about your mom's car. See if I can get it out of the tow yard. I think he said it was down by South Main Street."

Carlos uses the kitchen phone and takes the card the detective gave him out of his wallet. To the phone detective, he says, "This is Carlos Peña; we met last night about Jenny Morales. Yes. She's getting great care at Memorial Hospital. I'd like to arrange to have the car towed to Yuma. I have a friend who can work on it there and he has a tow. I can arrange something for this afternoon. Do I need any paperwork to have it released? Okay, I can sign off on that. I'll take full responsibility. Is there anything else?"

Carlos continues over the phone, "Jenny was a really good driver. I don't understand. Okay. I see. You'll let me know. I'll be here at the apartment with Maizey until we figure out what comes next."

He hangs up the phone. He says, "I'm going to call Gregg to get your mom's car out of the tow yard and tell him to pay the fee. I'll catch him later in Yuma to settle up. Detective Smith is interviewing witnesses, but it seems like the car in front of your mom's had stopped short when they heard the *Challenger* explosion. The driver thought your mom would have plenty of room, but a black car kind of blocked her way so she had to swerve and went down the embankment."

"Mom must have been scared. It probably happened so fast."

"What time does school get out?"

"2:15. That's about an hour from now. Usually, I get home about 3:30 on non-chorus days."

"Jenna will get back from school then, maybe with a report on Beto."

I feel myself blush. Carlos is tired, but he manages a small grin. "I'm going to call Gregg and then take a nap. Maybe you should take a nap too."

I'm exhausted, but the mention of Beto makes my heart flutter. It's sick, I think. It's all mixed up. I go into my room and lie down. I can hear Carlos speaking in Spanish. Muchas gracias is the last thing I hear. I have no dreams.

I wake up and look at the clock radio. It says 4:15. The door to my mom's room is shut and quiet. I go to the fridge and grab a glass of apple juice. I go over to the outside door and notice a piece of lined, folded notebook paper with my name on it lying on the floor.

I open it up:

Call me. I got your homework from school.

Jenna

I yawn and rub my eyes. I pick up the phone and call her number. She picks up on the second ring

"Hey."

"She doesn't remember me," I blurt out.

"What?!"

"Yeah, she hit her head and she doesn't remember me."

"Whoa, my mom says I shouldn't bother you."

"I want to know what's going on at school."

"Do you think I could come over? I have a lot to tell you!"

"Sure; Carlos is here, but he's asleep so now is a good time."

"My mom wants to know if you need anything for dinner."

"Not tonight, Lisa is making mac and cheese."

"Yum. See you in two," she says as she hangs up the phone.

She raps on the door and comes in.

"Man, girl, you look like a mess."

"Thanks, Jenna."

"Give me that brush and I'll brush out your hair for you, maybe put in a braid. How's that sound?" So I sit down on the couch, and Jenna sits behind me. She starts brushing out my long black hair. "Your hair is so soft and pretty, not like my curly mess."

"Stop it, your hair is fine."

"So did you give him the note?"

"Yeah."

"Tell me everything."

"Well, I was almost late for Spanish and getting outside Mr. A's room because that major bitch Susan had heard about the accident somehow. She was blocking my way."

"How'd she find out?"

"I don't know. I think her dad's a cop, maybe. Who cares? Anyway, I got her out of my way and I just saw the back of Beto's head and I called out his name. He turned to look at me. I hurried up and said, 'I got a note for you from Maizey.' I handed it to him. He said thanks and put it in his Chem book.

"I said, 'I can take a note back for you.' He shook his head. The hall bell went off. I'm thinking, 'Shit, I'm late now.' I bolted down to Spanish, but the door was closed so you know what that means," she says exaggeratedly. "Detention tomorrow. So I guess I'll be missing Chorus practice."

"You're a good friend."

"Wait here, I gotta get an elastic."

"There's a few on my dresser and a hand mirror there too."

She comes back and I can see her handiwork. French braid. Looks good.

My eyes are tired, but my hair looks good. She goes to her purse and grabs a note.

"Then Beto gave this to me at lunch." I see my name on the notebook paper and unfold the page. It reads:

Maizey, sorry about your mom. Mr. A says we can still work together if you want. He's going to give us an extra week to finish.

I don't know whether it's okay to call you. So here's my number.

Beto

Jenna smiles.

"You read it?"

"Of course I did. What if he was a jerkoff?"

"He's not."

"Yeah, I can see that he's a good one."

Carlos startles us both and says, "Talking about me again?"

I shove the paper in my purse, but not before Carlos sees. He doesn't miss anything.

"Are you staying for dinner, Jenna? I think Lisa should be here soon." He goes to the fridge. "We need something better to drink than juice. I like my Coke."

"Mom doesn't like it."

"Neither does Maria."

"I think we have some Coke at our house."

"I'll go get it," he says. "What apartment is it?"

Jenna gives him the apartment number, 14B, then calls her mom and Carlos is out the door.

Jenna turns back around to me. "How are you doing? I mean how's your mom *really*?"

"She doesn't remember me. Some of her hair is missing and she's got a huge bump on her head. It was too much."

Jenna puts her arm on my back. "I can't even imagine."

"I swear, Jenna, you can't tell anyone at school. It'll be too much."

"I think the bitch Susan has already started something. I'll take care of her."

"Okay. What was Beto like when he gave you the note?"

"Cute as usual. I know he's yours, but I can say that, right?"

"He's not mine."

"Not yours *yet*."

"I hope so."

Jenna smirks. "I'm going to start looking at who he hangs out with and maybe we can start double dates."

"I can't go there right now."

"I'm only trying to cheer you up. I don't know what to say. My mother told me to listen and stop with the silly boy talk. Don't tell her, but she may be right."

Carlos still wasn't back. I ask Jenna, "Can you look out the door and see if he's coming yet?"

Jenna pokes her head out the door and looks over towards her apartment. She doesn't see Carlos, but I hear her as she grumbles to herself that that stupid creepy car is back. "That person takes the best spot in the complex."

"The black one?"

"Yeah, the black one."

Carlos is back with a three-liter of Coke. "I might share," he jokes to me.

There's a knock on the door and it's Lisa. She is carrying a casserole dish covered in tin foil. She pushes her way over to the counter and puts the bag down on the table. "It's hot, so I'm going to put it here on the stove. I got all the salad fixings here in the bag." She looks in the fridge. "I bought salad dressing, but I can see your mom has her thousand islands. I could never understand liking that."

Carlos puts the plates and the silverware out. He asks Lisa if she's going to stay to eat, but she says no, that's okay. So we fuss around with the dinner stuff. I know Lisa wants to talk to Carlos. Sometimes, you can sense when grown-ups want to talk alone. I wish they would think the same thing about teenagers.

I turn to Jenna. "Hey, can you help me with picking out an outfit for tomorrow?"

"Sure." We get into my room. I leave the door slightly ajar so I can eavesdrop. I know it's wrong.

"Lisa wanted to talk to Carlos without us there."

"Yeah, I think so." They are sitting at the table. Carlos's back is to me, but I can tell by Lisa's face he's describing my mom's injuries. Lisa puts her hand over her mouth like to catch her breath.

Jenna says, "Was it bad to see your mom?"

"It was worse because she doesn't remember me and she's missing a huge bunch of her hair that will take forever to grow right. She'll hate that when she gets better."

"I would hate that for sure."

Jenna continues, "She'll get better right? My mom says you have to have faith and patience."

"Okay, I guess. Let's talk about something else." Jenna fills me in on the rest of the gossip. Carlos yells to us that dinner is on the table.

Lisa says, "I'm going up to the office to send some flowers to the hospital tomorrow. I hope that will cheer her up. Give her a hug for me, okay."

We sit down to eat dinner and the sun is starting to go down. It's a beautiful desert sky. We look out the picture window, and Jenna says, "The black car is leaving the lot."

I never get a good look at the creepo, because his windows are tinted. Carlos goes out the door and watches the black car drive east on Main. He shuts and bolts the door behind him.

We clean up the dinner dishes and Carlos calls the hospital. He talks to a new nurse. She says my mom is sleeping. She's had a sedative, so she'll likely be out all night; the swelling continues to go down, and she's eating better.

"Is Nurse Sarah in tomorrow?"

"Yes, 7 to 3."

"You have the number here if anything changes overnight. I'll call in the morning."

Carlos hangs up the phone. "It's probably best we let your mom sleep. We can go in tomorrow, maybe the afternoon. Do you want to go to school for a half day?"

"Yes, then I could get all my homework."

"While you're in school, I'll call Gregg and make sure your mom's car is drivable. I can drive you both to school, so you don't have to take the bus and I can talk to your principal – and maybe even see Mr. Beto."

I'm turning red. Jenna is laughing. Carlos struts away whistling.

"He's so funny."

"Yeah, a riot."

"He's a good guy."

"Yeah, he's like a dad to me."

"I'm going home now, you okay?"

"Yeah." I decide that I'm going to take a shower and go to bed. I cry a little in the shower so that Carlos won't hear me. I give him a hug goodnight, and the next thing I know I am fading out and hoping that I have a dream about Beto.

Chapter Five

Jenny: Thursday

The door opens slightly, and Nurse Sarah comes over to ask if I am ready for my visitors.

"Let me look at you." She adjusts the blanket around me and asks if I want the bed tipped up a bit more. She adjusts the bed and I am sitting up. She explains, "I'm going to be sitting here in the chair behind you during the visit."

She goes back to the door, and gestures outside saying "Okay, you can come in now." I see a middle-aged Hispanic man. He looks older than I imagined him to be. Behind him is a pretty teenage girl with dark black hair. She looks like I think I did when I was with Johnny. I don't have time to sort out my thought, because Carlos makes it to the bed in two steps.

He takes my hand and kisses it. He puts his hand up to my face and traces my jawline.

"You're going to be okay, Jenny." I can see the kindness in his eyes and the sorrow on his brow. He squeezes my hand. It's very quiet in the room. You could hear a pin drop. The teenager is hanging back by the door, not sure what to do. I can see on her face that she is overwhelmed by the hospital. She's my daughter. I just don't remember.

I nod at Carlos. He steps aside and I can see Maizey in plain view. We make eye contact. She comes forward. I can sense that she wants to touch me, so I raise my hand a little bit and she takes it into hers.

"Mom, I love you, Mom." A little tear forms in her eye and I instinctively wipe it away. I'm trying to figure out what to say when Nurse Sarah's pager goes off.

She looks at me and says "Sorry, Jenny, I've got to take this. I'll be right out in the hallway. Are you okay for a minute or two?" I shake my head. She goes out to the hallway and I hear her talking to another nurse.

Carlos and Maizey and I look at each other. I finally say: "I must look like a mess." He lets out a big sigh.

"You look good to me." Maizey agrees. Carlos looks at the half-eaten food tray and asks, "How's the food?"

"They just let me eat this morning, so not so good."

"I'm going to bring you some of my famous empanadas."

"That sounds great."

Maizey blurts out, "I'm sorry, Mom. I'm sorry for the fight we had." I wish I knew what she was talking about, but she looks like she needs me to say it's okay, so I do.

"It's okay. We'll work it out." She starts to shake a little like she's been waiting to apologize. There's a wave in my brain and I am starting to feel lightheaded.

"Carlos, can you get Nurse Sarah?" I look at Maizey. Sometimes these waves of dizziness just come over me. "I am sorry."

"Don't be sorry, Mom. You have nothing to be sorry for."

There's something deep inside of me that knows that's not true.

Carlos returns with Sarah. She asks me how I'm feeling, and I say, "Dizzy, lightheaded, and I'm starting to get pain here." I point to where the bump is on my head.

"Okay, Jenny, I'm going to draw the curtains now and get rid of that desert sun. I think it might be a good time for you to try and take a little rest."

Carlos says, "We'll go now." He kisses me on the cheek and says something in Spanish. Maizey comes over and kisses me as well. "I love you, Mom."

They both exit the room, and Sarah adjusts the pillows and the lighting.

"How's the pain now? On a scale of one to ten."

"About a three."

"That's good!"

"But I feel really tired."

"Visits can be tiring. Just shut your eyes, Jenny, and let your brain take a rest. I'll check in on you in an hour or so." She hands me the call button and says, "If you need anything beforehand, just push this and I'll be here ASAP."

"Okay," I say.

She shuts the door behind her, and I shut my eyes. I start to count down from ten to one, but I barely make it to seven. My mind goes blank.

Chapter Six

Man in the Black Car: Tuesday, January 28

I woke up early. It was still dark out. Sometimes the quiet is too much. It's never quiet in jail ever. Someone's always coughing or swearing or belching. Makes you feel like you're part of something.

I'd been in there long enough to know how to play the game and be a model citizen. Lots of guys try to pick fights with you and have something to do. They don't have a long goal in mind. I thought I'd seen it all until I met Crazy God. I'd only seen him at first across the yard, but then he was sent to our block, and when Rudi got himself transferred to solitary. I got him as a roommate.

At first, he kept to himself. We didn't talk, we circled each other in our cell, like rivals. I could always sense a predator. It takes one to know one. Kill or be killed. Crazy God was slick. He knew how to talk. And he knew how to act crazy. He wasn't, though. Some of the other inmates would make fun of him. He'd smile and bide his time. One day something would happen. Like a bleach stain on their pants or diarrhea. I knew it was him. Others suspected, but I knew it was him.

We'd been cellmates for about two years and he almost slipped up. He had stolen a fork from the kitchen. I'd seen it in his bunk. I'm not sure what he was going to do with it, so while he was out I took it and dropped it on the floor of cell block #17. What did I care who found it? It wasn't our cell block and those guys were always causing trouble. To my luck a guard found it.

Cell block #17 got punished.

Crazy God knew it was his fork. I thought he'd slipped up but it was a test. That night I found a note under my pillow in distinctive block letters. *Find the money*. Crazy God likes to play mind games. I thought I understood him. After that, we talked. Well, he talked, and I listened. I half-listened to his messed-up stories. I half-listened to his prayers. I only really listened to the part about money. He said there was money, and all I had to do was find it. We'd split it 50/50. I'd shake my head and agree.

So, when I was up for a parole hearing, it went well and I got out early. I had to stay in Cali for three years and stay out of trouble for five.

Cali was a big state, but staying out of trouble? That's gonna take work. Because the booze is what gets me every time.

So when Crazy God explained what he wanted me to do to find the money, I thought, "This is really F-ed up." So I made him write it down.

I like to keep things just in case.

He was so ecstatic about having someone to follow his plan, that he hadn't realized writing something down is a mistake. Maybe he was just getting old and his brain wasn't working right. Didn't matter to me. I have written evidence just in case.

So that's why I am sitting in a damn apartment complex parking lot in Phoenix waiting on some chick to be freaked out by the package I left at her door.

Instructions:

#1

Take the bus to San Diego

Go to the Golden Harvest Food Coop. on South St.

Ask for Lily and give her this note.

She'll give you a package, a credit card.

Trail Carlos Peña, Yuma AZ.

He'll lead you to Jenny Morales.

Once you find Jenny you are to wrap the package and address it using this lettering. Wait for her to get the package and then follow her.

She knows where it is.

Chapter Seven

Man in the Black Car: Wednesday Morning, January 29

She's not back. I spent a night in the car and then went back to the complex. Her car's not there. She must have been in the car accident the other day. Carlos is here overnight.

This job is starting to get on my nerves. At least I got this credit card, and I'm gonna use it because I ain't seen anything that looks like money. They live on a decent side of town, but they don't have a house. At least I can park in the lot of the complex. It's easier than if I had to park on the street and will be simple to break into the apartment. Phone guy should work. I got the outfit back at the hotel.

I got to get back to Yuma and get a shower, and back to Cali on Thursday to meet with the parole officer. Maybe I'll catch a break. I want to be rid of Crazy God.

He has a way of how he wants things to go. Three instructions, he said, like the holy trinity of fear. One creepy dude.

I got to call him. He's probably pacing that cell – I can see him. Nutcase.

How anyone could think he wasn't? Well, that's 'cause he's slick and he knows how to play the game.

I got that Jenny is in Memorial Hospital. It doesn't take much to get info from people if you say you're going to deliver flowers. You just want to make sure you get the right room. I'll wait to see if she's released by the time I get back on Friday.

You think they'd eat better than McDonald's. I'm going to a steakhouse tonight and have a couple of beers. I deserve it. So I gas up and head back on the highway towards Yuma. I don't like being this far away from Cali, because I'll get sent back for breaking my probation.

I want to speed through the desert and get to my hotel, but I see a speed trap ahead, so I got to slow down. I'm stuck behind a truck. I'm trying to get around the truck a few times, but I see an unmarked cruiser two cars behind me, so I poke back in. The lights go on, but he pulls over another car, so I make a break for it.

I'm slowing down past a turn-off. I think maybe I should take a short break, but then I see Carlos get out of his car, put on his sunglasses, and look toward the traffic.

Shit, this is a sign to keep going. I need some real food, a real bed, and beer. I say I need a chick too, but it's too much hassle right now. I don't want to answer any questions.

So, I'll handle Crazy God. He'll know that I've gone on to instruction #2 by the credit card. I guess Lily goes to see him. I'm not sure how that works. He keeps me in the dark, or gives me only what he thinks I should know.

I could just use a break. I got to think about what I'm gonna tell my PO about what I've been doing. I just keep thinking in six months, I'll probably be fishing and drinking beers in Mexico if there's a lot of money like Crazy God says there is. I won't give a shit about probation or him. I'll have enough cash to buy protection. I'll find me a nice girl who'll straighten me out and we'll sell shells by the seashore.

Now I'm thinking Crazy God's getting to me.

The truth is, I'm just gonna find my next con after this one and blow all my money.

You can't teach an old dog new tricks.

Instruction #2

Get a white pillowcase and buy a rattlesnake. Place it on Jenny's bed.

I ain't getting a real rattlesnake. I don't do well with things that crawl. There's enough of them in the desert. So I go to a toy store and if someone can help me find a toy rattlesnake for my ten-year-old nephew. Got one that makes a rattling sound. It's so easy to lie and people believe whatever you tell them.

Chapter Eight

Jenny: Early Thursday Morning

I wake up and it's the middle of the night. I feel disoriented. I hear the faint beeping of a monitor and I remember where I am. I start to move, and I see that my arm is in a cast. I blink my eyes shut tight, and there's a shooting pain in the right side of my head. I must have made a loud enough sound because a nurse comes by to check on me.

"Hey, Jenny."

"Hi."

"Are you experiencing any pain?"

"Yes, very sharp pain here."

"Okay, hang on, let me get your night nurse."

She leaves the room. The night nurse comes in and introduces herself as Barbara. She reminds me of my mother.

"Let's see here." She's looking at my chart. "I can give you some Tylenol with a little bit of codeine. Your chart says you've never had any issues with drugs."

I shake my head. I just want the pain to go away. Whatever the chart doesn't know won't hurt me. It was a long time ago.

"You'll probably sleep again for a while. I'm wondering if you're hungry – you haven't had anything to eat for more than sixteen hours."

"I think yes, I think I am."

"Well, the best I can do at the moment is toast."

"Tea?"

"Sure, tea and toast."

"With butter and maple syrup?"

"I don't think we have maple syrup, but we do have honey."

"That will do."

I put my head back on the pillow and Nurse Barbara comes back with toast and tea, alongside milk and sugar alongside some pills. She adjusts the bed, and I am sitting up. I eat the toast quickly. It's hard for me to drink the tea without help. Barbara holds the cup, and I let the tea quench my thirst.

Behind the cloud, there was a thought jiggling in my head. I want to pull the quilt up over my shoulders, but it's a thin hospital blanket. The drugs are starting to take effect and Barbara's face blurs into my mother's face.

Neither one of them is smiling. Both of them have wrinkled brows and concern flares out around their eyes. Nurse Barbara says, "I'm going to leave this here," as she pulls the side table away from the bed.

"Do you want the bed put down?"

"Yes," I reply slowly. I'm getting sleepy. She pushes the hair away from my head. I think she's kissed my forehead, but she's just checking the bandages.

I mumble, "Thanks, Mom." Everything's quiet. I wake up when the sun comes up through the window. Dreamless night.

I rub my eyes with my good hand. I push the nurse call button.

Nurse Sarah comes in. "Good morning."

"Hi."

"How's the pain in your head?"

"No pain."

"Excellent, Jenny! Can you tell me your name and date of birth for the records? I have to do this every so often. Hospital rules." Somehow there is something she's not saying, so I know that I have to be careful. Somehow, I feel like it's a trap.

"Jenny, Jenny Morales. My birthday is in June."

"Do you know the year?"

"1951."

"Jenny, do you know where you are right now?"

"The hospital."

"What city?"

I see something written on my blanket. It says *Phoenix*. I shut my eyes. "Let me think," I say. "Phoenix."

"Okay, thanks. I think you're cleared to have a full lunch. What would you like to eat?"

"I don't know."

"How about a tomato soup and grilled cheese sandwich? They've made a great apple pie today, so maybe that?"

"I'll order a water."

"Okay. Do you want the TV on?"

"I think so, sure."

I flip the stations between soap operas. It must be the afternoon because that's all that is on.

I settle into *Days of Our Lives*. There's a news break, and the anchor comes in with a report from Concord High School in New Hampshire. There's snow on the ground. I turn up the TV to pay attention.

"We're here just three days from the *Challenger* explosion with students at Concord to honor their teacher Christa McAuliffe, who died in the explosion."

The cameraman pans to the crowd and a man steps up to the podium. My mind is trying to work out something. The *Challenger* exploded? A teacher was killed?

It's on the fringes of my memory. I can't watch it. It's too sad, so I turn off the TV.

I start to think and remember. There are so many empty spaces. I'm not sure who to trust exactly, so I decide to keep my thoughts to myself.

Nurse Sarah brings in the food and I eat every last bit. I feel more like myself.

"Are you having any head pain, dizziness, or nausea?"

"No."

"Okay, I'm going to say we'll try again to use the bathroom instead of the bedpan."

"Okay. Sorry."

"Don't be sorry, Jenny. It's my job and I am happy to be taking care of you. Okay. So, I want you to try and drink all of the water, and then we'll get you up and on the commode. The doctor will want to check on you when he does his rounds. Let's see how you do with it. Maybe you'd like a sponge bath. I can help you with that."

I drink the water and soon enough my bladder is full. Nurse Sarah is there to guide me to the commode. It feels like my body is waking up a little bit at a time.

"No dizziness."

Sarah starts up again. "Sorry I can't wash your hair, but I can wash around your bump. Not the most attractive smell, the soap."

I've smelled it somewhere before, I think. Standard hospital issue.

"It smells better than dirt," I say.

"Well, that it does," Sarah says.

"Do you think you're up for visitors?"

I look at her blankly.

"Carlos and Maizey. Lisa?"

"Carlos has been charming the nurse's station," she giggles.

I think, *Carlos. Carlos and mud.*

"I say maybe later after I talk to the doctor."

"All right, we'll settle you in. You seem awake today. Do you want anything?"

"A newspaper."

"Okay, that I can get you." I've settled into my bed, and I notice to the right a huge bouquet of flowers. How did I not see those?

Sarah says, "They came the other day. Would you like me to move them so you can see them better?"

"Yes please."

I take a look at the bouquet. Roses, orchids, and desert succulents.

"Here's the card. It reads: Get well soon. All your friends at Phoenix Payroll."

Phoenix Payroll.

I was going to Phoenix Payroll. I must work there. It's like I'm seeing things without glasses. I know it to be true, it's just not clear. I'm thinking about everything. I can hear Sarah in the hallway. "She's very orientated today. I think her memory is coming back to her." I don't know who she's talking to, but there's a relieved sound in her voice.

I put the TV back on and Marlene and John are right where I left them in the drawing room. Soap operas move at a snail's pace. Which is exactly my brain's speed.

I hear them before I see them. My door is open so all the noises of the hospital drift in. I straighten myself in bed.

Carlos comes in first. I recognize him. It's his eyes. He looks older than in my memory, but I do know who he is. The girl Maizey still hangs back by the door. I can tell she's not sure whether she wants to come in or not. Carlos motions to her to come and she takes a couple of steps toward the bed. She's keeping her head down so I can't really see her.

"Hi."

"Jenny."

"Carlos."

Carlos continues talking with me, slowly but confidently. "Fresa," he says. That's "strawberry" in Spanish.

I reply, "You sure know how to pick them."

He laughs. "My Jenny's back."

I know this is a joke we share but I'm not sure why.

"Maizey, come see your mom," he says.

Maizey moves slowly toward the bed. I look at her and I see her. It's like a movie playing in my mind. There are small snippets of me looking at her. I realize that she was the girl in my dream from the first day.

I say "Maizey," and I extend my hand.

"Mom."

She comes over, and I pat the side of the bed and tell her to get on.

"I don't think it's okay to do that."

I say, "It's my bed, my rules." Maizey climbs up and it feels good to feel her shoulder against mine. I stifle a yelp because she's hit one of the bruises.

"You okay, Mom?"

"Couldn't be better." I run my fingers through her hair.

Carlos is looking at me and smiling.

"I thought I lost you again, Jenny."

"Nope, still here," I say, but I'm haunted by the word *again*. Had I been in a car accident before?

"Do you need anything?"

"I wouldn't mind a Coke."

"I think I saw a vending machine down the hall – I'll go and get you one. How about you, Maizey?"

"The same," she says.

He shakes his pocket. "I'll have to get some change from the nurse's station."

"Wait, I think my purse is over there." I point to a small dresser. "There's usually some change in the bottom."

Carlos brings over my purse, and Maizey shakes it around. Sure enough, quarters roll out and into her hand.

"What you got in here, Jenny? Feels like the whole bank?" Carlos laughs.

I say to Maizey, "Can you put my purse on this table? It's hard for me to reach with my arm in the cast."

She moves the purse within my reach. I'd like to see what's in it later.

"Mom," Maizey says.

"Yes, honey."

"You remember me?"

"I remember you."

"When do you think you'll be coming home?"

"I don't know, the doctor hasn't said yet."

"Do you remember what happened?" she says. "I mean, the accident."

"I was driving the car. The sun was low in the sky and the car in front of me stopped short. I thought I would be able to avoid the car because I could go into another lane, but there was a car trying to pass, so I swerved to the right and hit the back of the car in front of me and rolled over."

"Were you scared?"

"I don't think so, it happened so fast."

Carlos is back with the Cokes. "I got you a straw at the nurse's station."

Maizey and I sip our Cokes. Carlos is looking out the window.

"I like the flowers Lisa sent," he says. "They're so pretty."

"Can you call her for me?"

"Of course, we were going to call her after we saw you."

"Please tell the nurses to call Lisa and let her I love the flowers."

Nurse Sarah pokes her head in and grabs my chart off the end of the bed. Maizey goes to jump off the bed.

"Thanks, Maizey," the nurse says. "I can't have you sitting on the bed."

Maizey moves and Sarah puts the cuff on my arm.

"134/70," she says as she writes it in her chart. "Starting to come down, that's great, Jenny."

I finish my Coke and I get a sudden pain in my head. Carlos sees the distress, and Maizey pushes the call button.

Sarah's back, and I'm squeezing my eyes shut but I can hear still hear Sarah. She sounds far away. "Jenny, can you open your eyes?"

I'm trying. I open them, and there are some bright lights around her face.

"Jenny?"

I mumble and put my hand to my head.

Stay with me.

I say, "I really like Santana," and everything goes blank.

Chapter Nine

Maizey: Early Morning, Thursday

The phone rings. I look at my alarm clock. It says 7:00. It's Thursday. I pick the phone up, but it sounds like Carlos got it first.

"Hello, yes, may I speak with Carlos Peña?"

"This is Carlos."

"I'm Dr. Francis Cullen. I'm a neurologist at Phoenix Memorial. I'm calling about Jennifer Morales. Mr. Peña, are you there?"

"Yes, Doctor."

"You're listed as her contact."

I'm afraid. I gasp and Carlos can tell now that I am on the line. The doctor doesn't say anything if he notices.

"Ms. Morales had very disturbed sleep last night. She had two episodes of trying to rip off her IV. It's very common for patients with head injuries to do this. The CAT scans show she had quite a blow. She's very lucky however; it looks as if all the fluid and swelling may be only temporary. If I can get her brain to rest."

"What do you want to do?"

"I am calling to ask your permission to put her in a medically induced coma."

I gasp.

"I'm sorry, is someone else on this line?"

Carlos says, "Her daughter, who's seventeen."

"You okay, Maizey?"

"I didn't mean to," I say.

"It's okay, Doctor, say what you want, I wouldn't be as good at explaining all this as you."

"Okay, Maizey," He lowers his voice. "This is what I want to do take care of your mom. Right now, she's working her brain too hard to figure out everything."

She doesn't remember me. I think.

"Her memories are all there, they're just jumbled."

"Doctor. Will she ever remember me?"

"Maizey, the brain is an amazing organ. It never ceases to amaze me. The most important thing right now, though, for me as her doctor is to calm down the brain activity."

Carlos says, "So she'll be sedated."

"Yes, we will monitor her brain activity and the fluid. I'm going to give her twenty-four hours. We'll need to move her to a different room so she can be monitored closely. I've asked the nursing staff if anyone would like to be reassigned while she's moved to a different floor. Sarah Pennington said she would. I've found that it's comforting for the patient to have consistent care."

"Maizey, what do you think?" Carlos asks.

"I say, whatever will make my mom better."

"Okay, then, Doctor."

"Let me be clear. You are permitting me to induce a medical coma on Jennifer Morales starting at 7:30 am, January 30, and ending at 7:30 am January 31?"

"Yes," says Carlos.

"Does Jennifer have any known allergies?"

"Not that I know of."

"Since you have given me verbal consent, I will treat the patient accordingly. I'm just going to ask Nurse Donna to verify this conversation. Okay, we're set. There'll be some paperwork for you to sign later related to this request. Any questions?"

"Can I see my mom today?"

Dr. Cullen says, "I'm sorry, not today."

"You can call the nurse's station today. She'll be in ICU. She should be settled in her new room about 9 o'clock."

"Okay, I'll call back then. The nurses have our number if you think of any more questions."

"I think I'll have some better answers for you in twenty-four hours."

We both hang up the phone and go out to the kitchen. Carlos is running his fingers through his hair.

"Come here," he says, and he gives me a big bear hug. "This doctor sounds good."

"Yeah, he sounds like he knows what he is doing. So we just have to have patience and faith."

"I think what we should do is go to Yuma for the night. I need to get back and do something, and also Gregg is going to let me know about your mom's car. I miss Maria and the girls."

"What about school?"

"You can miss a day. We will come back tomorrow."

He looks in the fridge and scrunches his nose. "All healthy."

"McDonald's?"

"McDonald's."

"You get an overnight bag together. I'm going to call Maria. Do you think Jenna's mom is home now?"

"She should be."

"I'll call her first, and let her know so Jenna won't be worried if we're not here."

I throw some things in a bag and grab my toothbrush from the bathroom. I can hear Carlos speaking Spanish so I know he's talking to Maria. Carlos hangs up and says, "Jenna's mom says to have patience, and she is praying for all of us."

Prayers. Can't hurt, I think.

Carlos says, "You can get your homework for the rest of the week at the main office in about an hour."

"Okay."

"So McDonald's first. Hospital second. And high school third. Then off to Yuma we go."

We get out to Carlos's car and drive towards McDonald's. He insists on eating inside the restaurant in case any smells are left over and Maria finds out.

"I could just tell her, you know."

"But you won't?" Giving me puppy dog eyes.

Again, grown-ups are weird.

I don't want to go to the hospital, so I just stay outside in the car. Carlos comes back. I wonder which window my mom's room is in. Probably one of those with the shades closed. Carlos hops back in the car and we get to the school.

He parks in the visitor's spot. Jenna and I always laughed about who'd ever *want* to visit this place. He puts his hand on my arm.

"You want me to come in with you?"

"No, I am all set."

I go up to the front desk. Mrs. Sullivan says, "Maizey."

"Hi, Mrs. Sullivan."

"We are so sorry to hear about your mom. I spoke to your teachers; they said not to worry about your assignments."

"I don't want to fall behind."

"We'll help you, Maizey." She goes around to get a manila envelope with my name on it.

"Here you go. Take care of yourself."

"Okay." The hall bell rings. Students start to come out into the hallways. The noise is thundering. I wish Beto would walk by, but I know his schedule and he's on the other side of the building.

Damien is talking to some other kids and takes a quick double-take.

"Maizey."

"Oh hi, Damien."

"You here at school today?"

"No, just picking up my homework."

"Beto's gonna be pissed he missed you."

"I gotta go."

"Hey, Maizey."

"Yeah?"

"Sorry about your mom."

I start to shake my head.

"Oh shit, I didn't mean to make you cry. Damn, I'm not very good at it. Words."

"You're fine, Damien. You better get to class."

"Okay, Beto wants to talk to you. I know about the assignment."

"What assignment?"

"Chem class."

"He wants to ask you out."

"Really?"

"Yeah, but now he doesn't know what to do."

I'm so excited my insides could break.

"I gotta go. I'm staying overnight in Yuma."

"So he probably can't talk to you then."

"Yeah, probably not."

"Maizey I gotta go 'cause I'm going to be late for class. What should I tell Beto?"

"About what?"

"The going out."

"Give him this." I write *Yes* on a piece of paper and sign it *Maizey.*

"Okay, thanks. I'll give it to him at lunch."

"Bye!"

The bell rings and I hear Mr. Fallon's voice. "Damien, detention, today after school!" He looks back at me and shrugs his shoulders.

I get back to the car. Carlos asks, "You got everything?"

"Yup."

He looks over at me. "Okay, spill it."

"What?"

He starts whistling, and I recognize the tune: "Maizey and Beto …"

"Okay, okay. I saw Beto's best friend. He said Beto wanted to ask me out, but that he doesn't know what to do now."

"And…?"

"I gave him a note that said yes."

"Well, my little girl is growing up."

My face is red.

"Okay. Let's see if we can have Mr. Beto over for empanadas and let him do the asking himself."

"You won't embarrass me."

"I never embarrass you!"

We start the drive to Yuma. I'm looking out the window as the cacti pass us by. I like to try and find a road runner, but it doesn't happen until about halfway there. As I'm looking in the side mirror door, I see a black car three cars back. It's trying to pass a truck and keeps poking in and out.

"I thought you were asleep. Any road runners out there?"

"No, but there's a black car behind the truck that's going to come by any minute. He's been trying to get around that truck for the last five minutes."

"Let's pull over at the rest stop here and give Mr. In A Hurry plenty of room." Carlos pulls over into the rest stop and sure enough, the car flies by but starts to slow down when it notices us at the rest stop.

Freaky. "Hey, do you think that guy was following us?"

"I don't know. But let's stretch our legs for a minute." We get out of the car. Carlos waits about ten minutes.

"Time to go."

It's desert pretty much the rest of the way. No sign of the black car. No road runners. Not seeing Mom today.

We don't see the black car the rest of the way to Yuma. I feel how hot it is the minute I get out of the car. Carlos's house is cute. I always liked the way it looked from the outside. Maria has put out some potted plants, and there are so many pretty tiles. It makes you feel welcome. The way Maria and Carlos make you feel when you walk inside.

The twins were at school, so the house is quiet. Maria comes out of the back room and comes over to us. I think she's going to go straight to Carlos, but she comes to me first. She hugs me and sits me down at the table. She goes over to the oven and opens it – there's a plate of enchiladas and beans and rice.

"I kept it warm for you both."

After she settles me in, she and Carlos kiss and hug. He tried to swat her bottom and she pushed his hand away.

Maria comes back over to the table and starts talking to me. "How are you?"

"It's a shock. I don't know. I don't understand. How can my mom forget me?"

"Sometimes we protect the things we love the most to protect ourselves."

I hadn't thought of that. She continues, "Somewhere in your mom's mind, she knows she has a daughter. I know this as a mom, so I can tell you: whatever the mind might forget, the heart will not."

Carlos comes over. "You can sleep in the girls' bedroom with them if you want."

"They are so excited that you are here. They should be home in about an hour after lunch. If you want, you can go outside to the back porch where the air conditioner is on. It's not as hot as the house."

"I think I could maybe do some homework."

Carlos says, "We'll call the hospital, maybe at 2, to check in with the nurse's station. I think I'm going to take a shower and a little siesta."

Maria says something in Spanish and I can tell they want to be alone.

I take my school books out to the back porch. I work on everything except the Chem homework. I can't seem to think about anything but Beto. Was I stupid to say yes to Damien?

What if it was a setup and Beto didn't want to ask me out? I don't know, being out of school makes you wonder about everything. I don't want to think about my mother right now. I know that it's bad, but I just don't. I'm kind of mad at her for getting into the accident. I know that that is bad too, but I can't help my feelings.

Maybe I am just a teenager who wants to have a date. Maybe I just want to begin school and complain about the food at lunch or if Denise Hartwood is going to Harvard or if she made it up because people tease her for being smart. Maybe I just want to feel normal again and that means that my mom is not in a temporary coma. Is that so wrong?

I can't say anything to anyone because I don't want them to think I'm a bad person, so I'll just put it aside, I guess.

There's a rap on the back door. I can't see over the stone wall, but I recognize the voice.

"Maria, you there? It's Gregg. Maria?"

I get up and tell Gregg to wait just a second. "It's Maizey."

"Maizey, okay. You're here already!"

"Yeah. Carlos must have driven like a speed demon to get here."

I open the door and he's holding a box.

"Carlos is taking a siesta before the girls get home from school."

"Ah," Gregg says. "I got a couple of things to talk to him about. First off, can I put this box down?"

"Sure." I slide my book to the side of the round patio table and place the box down.

"I'm sorry about your mom, kiddo."

"Yeah."

"She gonna be okay?"

"I think so."

"Well if she's anything like her car, she'll be just fine." He pats my hand. "I'm going to go in and grab myself a beer from the fridge. It's so hot today."

He goes into the house and I look into the box. It's random things from Mom's car. There's a packet of papers, a shawl, some gum, a pair of turquoise earrings that I gave her for Christmas, and a half-empty tube of mascara. Then there are a few things I've never seen before.

I take the three unfamiliar items and put them on the table.

Gregg comes back to the porch.

"Got all these things out of your mom's car."

I'm surprised that the 45 didn't get swiped. I mean, anything with Santana's signature would be worth something. There's a bracelet that says *Pvt. Ambrose MIA August 1968*. There's a cap that smells like maple syrup.

Gregg says, "I don't know what your mom was doing with maple syrup in her car, but it got over everything. I think in the heat it might be the car's new air freshener."

"I've never seen these things before."

Gregg says, "They were in the car with the other stuff, so I grabbed them."

I don't really have time to think about all the stuff because Carlos and Maria's twins come running onto the porch. Gregg puts everything back in the box and the girls come over to me.

"Mom says we aren't supposed to ask you about your mom."

The older twin, Carla, says to Maggie, "But I'm going to ask anyways."

She comes over and drapes her arms around my neck.

"How's your mom?"

What do I say to a six-year-old?

"Sleeping. So I can't visit her. Lucky for me, I can visit you!"

"Well, we can't bother Mom either when she's having a siesta."

Gregg chuckles.

"Okay, girls, what do you have for an after-school snack?"

"Mom said we can have cupcakes as a special treat since you're here."

"I know where they are," I say to Gregg. "Be right back."

"Hope there is one there for me!"

Carla pouts. "They're all pink icing, so *girls only*."

"Figures."

We go out to the kitchen. Carla is on a stepstool trying to get the box from the top of the fridge. I grab it before it hits the floor.

Carlos is laughing behind me in the bedroom doorway. The girls run to him.

"Gregg's out back."

Carlos goes out back and leaves the box with the girls' sparkly pink cupcakes. Maggie asks me if I can come to their dance recital in a few weeks.

"I think so. Ballet, right?"

"Yes, we are getting our tutus tomorrow."

"Pink?"

"Pink and sparkly."

Maria opens her bedroom door and steps into the living room.

"I see the girls have shown you the cupcakes."

Maggie says, “Maizey says she’ll come to our recital. Will we have more cupcakes then?”

The door to the porch creaks open, and Carlos and Gregg come in, walking over to the dining room table. “I want cupcakes too!” Gregg says.

“Okay, Maria says we’ll get you some cupcakes, but they will have to have sprinkles.”

“Sprinkles are good, I like sprinkles!”

Carlos and Gregg pat each other on the back as guys do, and Gregg goes out the front door.

“Maizey, Gregg said your mom’s car is going to be able to be saved. That front bumper took quite a hit, as did her side door, but most things inside the engine are working.”

I want to ask him about the things in the box. But before I can, he says, “Let’s call the hospital.”

He calls the nurse’s station. They tell him that she’s resting comfortably, no change. Dr. Cullen is happy with her brainwaves. He thinks that he’s going to take her off the drugs slowly, starting around midnight. She perhaps could wake up fully by breakfast. He said not to expect any change until then.

After the phone call, Carlos thinks quietly for a minute. “I think we should just leave tomorrow after the girls leave for dance class. We’d get back to Phoenix around 11.”

“Ok, that sounds good to me.”

"I'm going to get busy now and get something at the store for dinner. How about a cookout tonight?"

"Yeah!" The girls jump up and down.

Carla says, "And then can we get a movie from the video store?"

"Yes."

"Can we get *Cinderella*?"

"Again?"

"Please, Papa, pleeease."

"Okay, *Cinderella*."

"Can we have popcorn too?"

"Yes, we can."

Carla put her arms around my neck and whispered, "I'm glad you came, Maizey. Papa never agrees to *Cinderella* without a fuss."

I giggle. "Happy to help."

"Do you want to color with me now?"

"Sure!" We take out the coloring books and I'm a little girl again.

We have burgers and salad and popcorn for the movie. Both girls climb under the blanket with me and I see the fairy godmother. I know what my wish would be. Beto, my Prince Charming.

For a moment, I forget about my mom.

Is that how it is for her?

Longer moments of not remembering me.

Maybe at the stroke of midnight, her memory will return and we'll live happily ever after.

Chapter Ten

Maizey: Friday, January 31

I wake up to Carla staring into my face. She says to Maggie, “She’s awake.”

Maggie says, “You didn’t wake her?”

“No, I’ve just been watching.”

Maggie says, “Mom said we could not wake you up. That you needed to sleep.” I rub my hair out of my eyes. Carla whispers to me: “We are having breakfast burritos this Friday before school because we have a special dance rehearsal class.”

I rub her head and say, “You like breakfast burritos.”

She rubs her stomach and licks her lips. She looks just like Carlos. I giggle.

“You look like your dad.”

“He likes breakfast burritos too,” Maggie says, “and she acts like him too.”

Carla sticks her tongue out at Maggie. Maggie ignores her.

Carla pulls me up from the bed, "Come on, come on! Mom won't make them until she sees you're awake."

I look at the clock: it's only 6:30. We go out to the kitchen and no one is around. Maria comes out of the bathroom, and says to the girls, "Shhh. It's too early. You girls didn't wake up Maizey, did you?"

Maggie looks at me with wide eyes. "I'm awake at this time anyway because of school."

"Well then, maybe you could watch some cartoons while I take a shower."

They decide on *Scooby Doo*.

Maria's out in the kitchen and I can smell eggs and chilies. We have a good breakfast and then Carlos says, "We can leave right for dance class so we'll take the two cars. I'm going to look at your mom's car at Gregg's while the girls are in dance class. Who wants to come with me?"

Carla jumps up and screams, "Me, me!"

Maggie says, "I think I'll stick with Mom."

Carlos winks and says, "You always do."

Carla says, "So it'll be just me and you, Papa."

I say, "Yup it'll be the three M's in one car and the two C's in another."

"Yeah," Carla says.

Maggie says, "I'm glad you're coming with me. I want to show you my drawings."

"Okay, we can sit together in the back if that's okay with your mom."

"Sure," she says.

I gather up my stuff and get into the car with Maria and Maggie. Carlos and Carla are already gone. We're just pulling out of the driveway and onto the main road when I see a black car at a light. It can't be. The same car.

I watch it. It takes a left turn and we're going right. There are probably a million cars just like it but it makes me think of the one on the highway.

We get to the dance studio and Carla is already inside waiting. The two are hopping around.

I watch them. Maggie is more refined and precise in her pirouette and Carla jumps with abandon.

"They are so different," I say.

Maria laughs. "Yes, they are. One is like me and one is like Carlos."

I laugh and think she's right. I wonder if Beto and I had kids, would it be like that? What would Beto Jr. be like? I'm getting ahead in my thoughts, even though we haven't gone out on a date yet.

Dance class is over and the girls line up to get their tutus. Carlos is back and he says to me, "Let's say goodbye to the girls and get on our way. I've already put your stuff in my car."

I give both girls a group hug. Maria looks me deep in the eyes. "I'm praying for you and your mom. So is my mother, so you know how that works."

"Thanks." Carlos and I jump in the car and we are on our way back to Phoenix.

"You okay there, Maizey?"

"Yeah, just nervous about my mom."

"Faith and patience."

"Yeah."

"I say we go to the hospital and then call what's his name, Bob."

"Beto, you mean?"

"Yes, of course, Beto. See if he can come over for a homework date."

I'm squirming.

"I promise I won't embarrass you. But if he's a bad dude, I'm throwing him out. I mean I will pick him up and throw him out."

The image of Carlos picking up Beto and throwing him out the door makes me laugh an uncontrollable laugh. Carlos says nothing and lets it take its course.

He says he's going to use that one again, maybe on Carla when she's older. Good to know the dad jokes still work.

"Carlos, did you know my dad?"

"No, I met your mom after. No, I didn't know him."

"Mom won't say."

"I know. Sometimes things are best left alone."

"She gets mad at me when I ask."

"I know."

"I mean what would happen to me if …"

He shakes his head. "You're like a daughter to me, so you know that. Your mom is strong and she'll get through this. You have to believe."

"Okay, but will I ever know who my father was?"

"That's up to your mom." He pulls down his shades so I can't see his eyes. I know he knows more than he lets on. Carlos and my mother have built a silent wall around my dad.

Carlos suggests we look for road runners and I know that's the end of it. There won't be any more answers.

I had almost forgotten about the things from my mom's car. I grabbed the bracelet. I take it out of my purse.

Carlos sees out of the corner of his eye. "What you got there?"

"It's something Gregg brought from Mom's car. It's a bracelet. It says *Pvt. John Ambrose MIA July 1969*. I've never seen it before."

"A lot of teenagers had those for missing-in-action soldiers from Vietnam. I was traveling with Santana and sometimes we'd see girls with those bracelets. So many guys just got lost in that jungle."

"I wonder if this guy ever made it home?"

"I don't know. I try not to think about Vietnam. I lost a couple of cousins and friends when they were drafted."

"I didn't know. We never get that far in history. We just get to World War Two mostly."

"It's a heavy time. Lucky for me I met Carlos Santana and he gave me a job."

"That's weird."

"What's weird?"

"There was a 45 signed by Carlos Santana in my mom's car."

"What?"

"Gregg said that he was surprised it wasn't swiped because it might be worth some money. Why would Mom have that in her car?"

"Maybe she was buying it for me?"

But I sense he's lying.

"What was the song?" he says.

"Soul Sacrifice."

He clears his throat. "Great song."

"Gregg said she had a bottle of maple syrup, and it broke."

"Yeah, I did smell that in her car."

"Why would Mom have maple syrup?"

Carlos is trying to hide his feelings, I can tell.

"Your mom's a mystery."

"Carlos, I'm afraid for today. What if my mom is not going to be okay."

"Maizey, we will figure it out, okay? You're not alone in this. Faith and patience."

We're quiet the rest of the way to Phoenix. I spot a road runner sprinting away into the desert.

We get to Room 304 and the door is open. Carlos looks back at me and squeezes my hand. He goes right into the room. I stay in the door. It's probably only a split second, but it feels like hours. Carlos looks back and motions for me to come in. I take a couple of steps. I can't look up because I'm afraid she won't remember me and I don't want to know if she doesn't.

"Hi, Carlos."

"Hi, Jenny."

"Carlos."

Carlos says, "Fresa."

"You know how to pick 'em."

Carlos laughs. "My Jenny's back."

This is some private joke between Carlos and my mom, something to do with their time in California. They usually both laugh, but I notice Carlos is the only one laughing today.

"Maizey, come see your mom."

I move slowly toward the bed and I finally look at her.

Mom says, "Maizey," and extends her hand. I hear myself say, "Mom."

She pats the side of the bed for me to get on. I'm not sure I should do it, seeing all the machines blinking. I hesitate, and say, "I don't think it's okay to do that."

"My bed. My rules." I climb up on the bed. I touch shoulders with her. I feel her wince and hold back a quiet *ow*.

"You okay, Mom?"

"Couldn't be better." she says, putting on a brave face. I know that face because she taught it to me.

She puts her fingers in my hair, and for a moment we are back at the apartment. She's telling me "Don't worry, baby girl, things will be good. You'll see you got your whole life ahead of you." I think of this time when JoJo stood me up for the dance and I had to call Mom to pick me up. I so want to tell her about Beto now, but not here.

Carlos interrupts my thoughts by saying, "I thought I lost you again, Jenny. Do you need anything?"

Mom says, "I wouldn't mind a Coke."

Carlos says, "I think I saw a vending machine down the hall, I'll go and grab you one. How about you, Maizey?"

"The same."

He goes to shake his pockets to see if he's got any change, but I know he doesn't, since I saw him give it to the girls when he thought no one was watching for a treat after school.

"I guess I'll get some change from the nurse's station."

Mom says, "Wait, my purse is over there. There's usually some change in the bottom."

I know there is a lot more than change at the bottom. My mom always carries cash with her. Once when I needed her checkbook, I went into her purse. There was a wad of cash on the bottom. When I asked her about it, she said that she meant to go to the bank but ran out of time. I looked a week later and the money was still there.

So I'm not surprised when I shake it and about three dollars in quarters roll out into her hand. Carlos says, "What you got in here, the whole bank?"

Mom asks me to put her purse on the table closer to her because it's hard for her to reach with her arm in the cast. Sitting on this side of the bed I've almost forgotten she has her arm in a cast.

"Mom?"

"Yes, honey."

I blurt out, "You remember me?"

"I remember you."

"When do you think you'll be coming home?"

"I don't know. The doctor hasn't said."

I need to know, so I say to her, "Do you remember what happened? I mean the accident."

"I was driving the car. The sun was low in the sky and the car in front of me stopped short. I thought I would be able to get into another lane, but a car was passing, so I had to swerve to the right and wound up hitting the car in front of me and rolled over."

"Were you scared?"

"I don't think so, it happened so fast."

Carlos comes back carrying three Cokes. "I got a straw for you from the nurse's station." We sip our Cokes and Carlos goes to the window. He notices the flowers. I guess he sees the card.

"I like the flowers Lisa sent you."

"They're so pretty, can you call her for me?"

Carlos says, "Of course, we were going to call her after we saw you today."

"Tell her the nurses brought me the flowers and let me know she called, and that they are beautiful."

I see Nurse Sarah and I go to jump off the bed. She grabs the clipboard from the end of the bed and says, "Thanks, Maizey. I can't have you sitting on the bed."

I move out of the way so that she can take Mom's blood pressure, forgetting that she can only take it with the arm closest to me because of the cast.

She pulls off the cuff and sums 134/70 and writes it in her chart.

"Starting to come down, Jenny, that's great." Sarah leaves the room.

I'm sipping my Coke and I can see my mom is almost done with hers.

She must have been thirsty. I'm about ready to take the empty Coke can from my mom when she grimaces. I jump off the bed and push the nurse call button.

Nurse Sarah comes back.

She sees my mom's face. She goes over to her. "Jenny, can you open your eyes?"

My mom doesn't respond. She's just making a horrible face – it's messed up like she's squeezing away the pain. She opens her eyes a tiny bit and puts her hand to her head.

"Yes."

"Stay with me."

Mom says, "I like Santana," and her face softens.

Nurse Sarah takes her blood pressure and it's gone low. She adjusts something and listens to her breathing.

Carlos is pale and blank.

She takes Mom's pressure again. It's 140/80.

"I'm sorry, she must have had a blood pressure spike, which caused a mini seizure," Nurse Sarah says, looking at us and seeming a little shaken. "She just had a can of Coke?"

Carlos feels guilty.

"Yes, that's all."

"Okay, I'll write that down. Might be a trigger for her at the moment."

She can see Carlos looks distraught.

"No one knows what the triggers can be. You got to know that." Her monitor is starting to be rhythmic, so Sarah says, "She's resting comfortably. You would never know that she had brain trauma talking to her. She's good at hiding her pain."

"Aren't we all?"

"I suppose so. Call in about an hour or so for an update. Well, I'm going to have to ask you to leave. I've got to watch her and make sure she's stabilized."

I kiss my mom on the cheek and think to myself, *I love you, Mom.*

Carlos squeezes her hand and we walk out of the room.

Carlos is quiet.

"It's my fault."

"No it isn't. Sarah said so." But he's as stubborn as my mom when he gets a thought in his head.

He shakes it and says something in Spanish under his breath I can't make out.

We walk in silence to the parking lot. I see the black car with the Cali license plate still there. I hope whoever owns it has a better visit than us. Carlos doesn't know what to do.

I don't know what to say either, so we just drive home in silence.

"We better call Lisa before she leaves work. Do you want me to talk to her?"

"No, I will do it." Carlos looks like the wind has been knocked out of him. He retreats to Mom's bedroom before saying, "I'm going to take a rest. It's been a long day."

"Okay, I'll call Lisa. Jenna will probably be back soon so I'll call her too."

I get Lisa on the phone. She says, "I'm so glad you called. I have been worried sick. I know they can't tell me anything. How is she?"

"Her memory is coming back. She loved the flowers you sent. She wanted me to tell you thank you."

"It was nothing." I imagine Lisa swatting away air with her free hand. "Well, it sounds like she's getting stronger."

"Yes, that she is."

"Okay, honey."

"Carlos is still with you?"

"Yes, he's taking a nap right now. We had an early start from Yuma."

"Okay, well, tell him if he needs anything call me."

"I will. Thanks, Lisa." I hang up the phone and pour myself some water.

It's so quiet. I can't stand it. It's too quiet because all I see is my mom's face.

I put my head in my hands and start to whimper, for how long I don't know. There's an urgent rapping on the door and I hear my name. I know it's Jenna. I open up the door and she's talking but stops mid-sentence. She waves her hand in front of my face.

"Maizey, you okay?"

"Yes – I mean, no."

I walk back into the apartment. Jenna shuts the door behind her.

"What's happened?"

"My mom had a seizure."

"A what?"

"A seizure, while I was sitting next to her on her bed."

Jenna is speechless. wide-mouthed.

"But, Jenna, she remembered me."

"Of course, I knew she would."

I tell Jenna what happened in the hospital room. For once she lets me finish the whole story before she says anything.

"I'm sorry, Maizey. I just – I just don't know what to say except that I'm sorry."

We sit on the couch, and I can tell Jenna's got something to tell me but she doesn't know whether she can 'cause it's something good and I'm feeling so bad.

"Fill me in on what's been going on at school."

"You sure?"

"Yes, ma'am."

Jenna starts with the usual rundown of high school drama. I'm only half listening. I can't help it, half of my brain is still in the hospital. But when I hear her say Damien's name, Jenna seems to notice I've perked up.

"Well, remember how I got detention?"

"Right."

"Well, Damien had it too on the same day. The only two in the whole school. So we wound up talking the whole time. Well, maybe *I* was doing most of the talking and *he* was doing most of the listening, but we found out we have more in common than two friends, Beto and Maizey."

"So does that mean what I think it means?"

"Yes. We're going on a date. A real date tonight, down to the movies and pizza."

"Wow, you got a Friday night date."

"That's not the best part. Beto likes you. I mean that's what Damien said. He's been trying to get your attention since after Christmas break. He's been too shy to say anything to you."

"Really?"

"Really. He wants to talk to you but he doesn't want to bother you."

"He could never bother me."

"That's what I said. Anyway, I thought you should know."

We hear Carlos coming out of the bedroom. I make the motion to Jenna to zip it.

Carlos is back to his almost old self.

"Hi, Jenna."

"Hey, Carlos."

"So what shall we do for dinner?"

"Well, I got a date tonight."

Carlos says, "Well it looks like it's just you and me, Maizey. Unless…" He turns with dramatic flair and I know what he's going to say before he even says it. "We call Mr. Beto."

I'm mortified.

"Do you think he'd come over for some of my famous empanadas?"

Jenna is so excited she's making the couch move up and down.

"Yes, and yes he would."

Carlos picks up the phone, "Should I call him? Oh here's his number."

I know he's teasing me, but I stand up and look at the blank sheet. He hands me the phone.

"I'll leave you to it. I'm going to make a list for dinner." He goes back into Mom's room, whistling "Beto and Maizey sitting in a tree."

Jenna says to call him. "I bet he's home from track practice."

"I don't know."

"*I* know. Where is his number?"

"The numbers in my notebook. The blue one."

Jenna comes back and dials the number. She puts her finger on the connecting button – once she lifts it, the call will go through.

"No, hang up."

She hangs up the phone. "Okay."

I take a deep breath. "Okay. Let's do it this time." I let her follow through, and she hands the phone to me. It rings four times and I'm almost ready to hang up when I hear: "Hello?"

It's a woman's voice.

I say in a polite tone, "May I please speak to Beto?"

"May I ask who's calling?"

"Maizey Morales."

"Hang on, he's just coming in now from practice. Beto, you got a phone call. Maizey."

"Thanks, Mom."

I hear him breathing before he says anything.

"Beto?"

"Hi, Maizey."

"Beto." I'm getting tongue-tied. Jenna is motioning widely with her hand to get on with it.

"I've been thinking about you. Chem class isn't the same."

"I know it's short notice, but do you think?" A long pause then my words tumble out. "Do you think you might want to come over tonight to do some of the homework for Mr. A's class and have empanadas?"

"I would like to see you, Maizey. I'll have to check with my mom about using her car. Be right back."

It seems like he's gone for a long while.

"Mom says I can use her car."

"What time?"

Jenna runs to Carlos. I hear him say seven.

I give him my address and tell him when to get here.

"Okay, I'll see you at seven."

"Maizey. I'm sorry about your mom."

"Thanks, Beto. See you later."

I hang up the phone.

"Now was that so bad?"

Carlos comes out of the bedroom. "I better get going to the grocery store since we are having three for dinner." He walks away, whistling his new favorite tune.

"He's so funny."

"Yeah, he's a riot."

"We both have dates tonight! Let's pick out what you should wear."

Friday Night

I could smell the empanadas. Carlos is famous for them. His secret ingredient is a special pepper from Mexico where he grew up. He says it always reminds him of home.

I'm ready early. Jenna and I have both gone with the casual look and only a tiny bit of makeup because it's supposed to be a homework date.

I get out my Chem homework papers from the brown envelope.

Mr. A sent some copy pages about the astronauts with a handwritten note.

Hope your mom is feeling better soon. If you need any help with Chemistry come see me. Mr. A.

Mr. A is a decent guy. No matter what the kids say. I wouldn't want him blown up in space. I haven't thought much about that explosion because of everything going on.

I have all the papers laid out on the coffee table and I'm sitting on the couch. Carlos comes over and looks at them. "So sad," he says. "So brave, these people. Is this your homework?"

I explain to Carlos what it was like in school when the *Challenger* exploded, and I tell him about Mr. A's assignment.

He says, "That's a good teacher right there. He's right: you'll always remember this day. Some days just stick out in history and your mind."

"Like the JFK assassination?"

"I wasn't in the United States then. I was still in Mexico, but there are things in Mexico I won't forget."

He shakes his head.

"Carlos. I'm glad you're here."

"Where would I be otherwise?"

The mood shifts to light-hearted Carlos. There's always something. A secret. A regret of something that keeps him carefree. The same feeling I get when I ask my mom about my dad. It's like grown-ups don't think we can handle the truth. I'm the same age as my mom was when she had me, so I know stuff.

The timer goes off on the stove and Carlos goes over to turn it off. He claps his hands together. "All right, all ready for Mr. Beto, can you set the table, please?"

I get up and set the table, trying to figure out which seat would be best for Beto and what view he should have to look in the apartment.

"I think I should sit here back by the stove. That way Mr. Beto can look at you. I don't think he wants to look at me, even though I am one handsome hombre."

I don't even have time to smirk because there's a rap on the door.

Carlos looks at his watch. "6:55. Good for Mr. Beto."

He motions for me to go to the door. I open it with a quick motion taking Beto by surprise. He's wearing a white polo shirt and khakis and holding some flowers and a paper bag.

"Hi, Maizey."

"Hi, Beto."

We kind of sit there for a minute, not knowing what to do.

"Thanks for coming."

"No problem."

Carlos says, "Are you going to invite him in?"

"Oh yes. Come in." Carlos strides over to him. "I'm Carlos. I'm a family friend and master empanada maker. Well, I am sure those flowers aren't for me."

"I wasn't sure, so I just got daisies."

I like daisies from this day forward. It's my favorite flower.

"My mom gave me some homemade chocolate chip cookies. She said I shouldn't come empty-handed." Carlos takes the bag and looks inside.

He pulls one out and pops it in his mouth.

"I love chocolate chip cookies. "

I laugh and I look at Beto. "Maria, Carlos's wife, doesn't allow sweets, so whenever Carlos comes over here he eats all the sweets he can."

"Maizey, stop telling my secrets!" He goes to the fridge. "Can I get you guys a drink?"

"How about some iced tea?"

"Sounds good."

"Do you want to work on the assignment first and then eat? I've got all the papers Mr. A gave me. I brought the handout from class today." We go to sit down on the couch.

We work on astronaut Judith Resnik. Our knees are touching. Beto says, "Maybe you can write it down or copy it over. My handwriting isn't as good as yours."

Time moves slowly because I'm just conscious of Beto's presence.

Carlos says, "Can you guys take a break to eat? It's almost 7:45."

"Sure." We fold our papers and put them down on the coffee table.

"You sit here, Beto, and Maizey, you can sit over here. I'm the chef so I'm closest to the kitchen." He serves us empanada and rice and beans with a slice of fruit.

No one eats until he sits down; then he says, "Go ahead."

I watch Beto's face when he takes the first bite of his spicy empanada.

Carlos gives the side eye. I know this is his test.

Beto chews slowly and says, "These are good."

He takes another bite. Carlos widens his eyes and winks at me.

He takes a bite and sits in smug satisfaction.

"So, Beto, you're taking Chemistry."

"Yes."

"What are you thinking of doing after high school?"

"Well, I'm waiting to hear back from a couple of colleges. I might get a track scholarship. At least that's what the coach says."

"You run?"

"Yes, sprint and relay."

Carlos asks, "Where are the colleges?"

"Well, Cali, Arizona, and Boston."

"Boston? You going to like the cold?"

"I don't know, but I'd like to see snow sometime other than in the mountains."

I'm thinking, *Boston – that's so far.*

"Nothing decided yet. Not for a few more weeks, anyway. My dad says go where the money is. If they're willing to pay you, then they must want you."

I'm relieved to not have to talk so I can just look at Beto. He makes my heart stop.

Beto says, "I heard you are going on the DC trip?"

"Yeah," I say. "I can't wait. I have never been to the East Coast. I signed up last week. Damien and I got the last two spots."

Carlos stays quiet.

I pick up the conversation.

"Jenna told me that she and Damien had detention together."

"Damien told me that Jenna likes to talk."

"Jenna told me Damien likes to listen."

"Maybe they'll be a good match."

"I'm going to clean up this plate if you are done," Carlos says. "Why don't you take the cookies and finish up that homework?"

We go over to the couch and I hear Carlos whistling "Evil Woman" by Santana as he rinses the dishes. I just shake my head.

I take a bite of the cookie. It is sweet and buttery in my mouth.

We are talking softly, our faces close over the books. I can feel his breath.

And I can smell the chocolate chip cookies.

I'm startled by the phone.

Carlos says, "I'll get it in your mom's bedroom."

He goes in, and I can hear him talking in English, so I know he's not talking to Maria.

He comes out of the bedroom. His face is pale.

"I'm sorry, Beto, but we have to cut the night short."

Beto doesn't know what's going on, but he can read the distress on Carlos's face.

"Sure, let me get my stuff together."

"Maizey, why don't you walk Beto to his car?"

Beto and I are a bit stunned, but we follow Carlo's directions. I get the car.

"I don't know, I'm sorry. It must be about my mom. Carlos isn't usually that bossy."

"It's okay."

I'm staring into his eyes.

"Maizey, thanks for dinner. I think we got a lot done."

"Yeah, thanks for coming."

"I was just so glad to see you. I wanted to come over but…"

"It's weird, Beto, having my mom in the hospital."

He goes to open the door to his car.

"Maizey, I wasn't going to say anything, but if everything's all right with your mom, do you think you'd go with me to the Valentine's dance?"

I nod my head.

"Good. It's the last day for tickets tomorrow. Can I hug you?"

I nod my head. I can feel his heart beating.

He says with a sigh, "I can't stop thinking about you," and kisses me on my cheek. "I got to go." He hops into his car. I watch the red lights of his car turn onto the road and disappear into the night. Beto kissed me! Well, my cheek at least.

I walk back up to the apartment in a daze.

"Nice boy. I like him." Then Carlos says in a serious tone, "That was the hospital. It was Dr. Cullen. You remember him?"

"Yes, the doctor from the other day."

"He called to give me an update. Come, let's sit on the couch." I don't like the sound of this, but I follow him over to the living room.

"Your mom woke up and he thinks she's either hallucinating or confusing time and place. She had to be medically sedated because she got quite upset and angry. She was yelling." Carlos continues, "She was yelling for you. She wanted you."

"She wanted me?"

"She was afraid. Very afraid someone had taken you."

"I want to see her now. Carlos, please let's go."

"Sorry, my little fresa, your mom has said no to any visitors."

"What, even us?"

"Even us. And since she's awake, she can say what she wants."

"She doesn't want to see us?"

"The doctor said this is quite normal, and a good sign that her memory is coming back. Her brain is healing, and patients often get angry and agitated when things are strange to them. Dr. Cullen wants to give her forty-eight hours to rest and eat, and to let her brain sort things out on its own. He stays he's seen it before – patients want to remember so hard that they tire themselves out. He says we are very lucky because we have Nurse Sarah. Sarah has agreed to do overtime and be on shift every day. Somehow she's bonded with Sarah. Sarah thinks your mom feels safe knowing someone else is there. That is lucky for us and it doesn't happen all the time. We could meet with him on Monday morning to decide on the next steps. If her tests continue to improve, he'll decide to keep her in the hospital or maybe a rehab. He says he probably wouldn't recommend her for outpatient care for at least another week. He likes to have a solid two weeks of healing before he sends patients to outpatient care."

Then Carlos looks at me. "It's good news."

I start to cry.

"Come here," he says, giving me a strong hug. "Your mom is strong, she'll be okay. She'll get out of that hospital before you know it. I'm just going to ask you if you'll come back to Yuma with me for the weekend. I know the girls will love having you."

I start to cry again.

"Maizey, it will be okay, you'll see."

"We can call every day and see how she is. What I think is, you need a break."

"Carlos, do you think Maria could help me with something?"

"I'm sure she would, what do you need?"

"I need a dress for the Valentine's dance."

"Valentine's dance?"

"Yes, Beto asked me to go with him. I wish Mom could help me."

I start to cry.

"Maria would probably love it. She talks about doing those girly things all the time. I know, I know. I want your mom back too. Beto asked you tonight?"

"Yes, the last day for tickets is tomorrow."

"Mr. Beto is a good one. I approve."

I look at him and smile. I say, "Looks like you approve, too."

"I'm going to get ready for bed and call Maria. Do you want me to say anything about the dress shopping? She might have two tagalongs, but if you don't want that I can watch the girls."

"Let's see when we get there. I'm kinda tired now. Carlos, I'm happy and sad at the same time. I want to be so happy about Beto, but I'm sad about Mom. I know she's missing out on this and I'm worried about her."

Carlos says, "Look at me. Your mom would want you to have fun and be happy. I'll talk to her about it. Beto *and* your eighteenth birthday party. Oh, you thought I forgot about that? I don't forget anything, Maizey. Now like I say to the girls, off to bed, you little peppermints."

I fall into bed and I'm almost ready to fall asleep when I remember the pencil from Chem class Beto gave me. I go to get it from my purse and the MIA bracelet falls out.

I look at it and say, "Did you make it home, Private Ambrose? I hope you did. I hope you had a nice life." I take the pencil and put it under my pillow.

I'm going to the Valentine's dance with Beto. This has to be a dream. Mom's in the hospital; that's a nightmare for sure.

Why is everything good and bad at the same time?

Chapter Eleven

Jenny: Friday Night

I wake up. It's dark. Where am I?

I look around and start to put things together. Accident. Hospital.

Someone left the TV on mute but I can see JR, so I know it's Friday night. I should be home watching this with Maizey.

My mind is still foggy but I think, *Maizey. Where's Maizey?*

I try and put the pieces together, but it's not clicking.

I call the nurse.

"Jenny, you're awake. How are you feeling?"

Better, I think.

"When can I get out of here?"

"That's up to the doctor."

"Where's Maizey?"

"Who?"

"My daughter. Where's my daughter?"

I'm starting to get agitated because I can hear all the buzzes going off.

"Where's my daughter?" This time I'm almost yelling. "I know you have her. Where is she?"

"Jenny. Your daughter is at home."

"I don't believe you. I think you're lying. I want to see him. I want to see *him*. You know who I mean. Get him now."

I am screaming because another nurse comes in. There's something about this nurse that's reassuring.

"Jenny, it's Sarah."

I look at her blankly.

"I've been taking care of you since you got here at the hospital. You have a broken arm, see? And a good blow to the head. Julie tells me you're looking for Maizey."

I take a deep breath. "Yes."

"Maizey went with Carlos."

"Carlos was here?"

"Yes, Carlos and Maizey came to see you."

"I don't want them here again. I want to get out of here and I don't want them here again."

"Jenny, you need to breathe. I need to check your blood pressure, okay?"

I let her put the cuff on my good arm.

She looks at the other nurse. "Your blood pressure is a little high. We're going to adjust some of the meds now. It might make you feel a bit groggy at first, but then you'll feel a bit better." She fumbles with the IV line. I can feel a cooling sensation in my veins.

I take a huge breath and I start to relax.

"Okay, Jenny. Now I'm going to get you some dinner. Sorry, only sandwiches at this hour. You liked grilled geese the other night."

"Grilled cheese and tomato soup."

Okay, I am starting to feel more relaxed.

Carlos has Maizey.

I shut my eyes and I see him.

I feel like he's in this room.

When I open my eyes, it's just JR on the TV.

Sarah comes in with my sandwich, and one for herself. "I was hoping you wouldn't mind but I wanted to catch the ending of *Dallas*. I thought we could eat together."

"Sure."

Some part of me is thinking I'd like to watch it too. There's something familiar about the theme music.

"I usually have Friday nights off so I watch *Dallas*. Linda Evans is my favorite."

I'm chewing on my sandwich and I see a closeup of JR. It blurs together, but I manage to say "Wasn't he on *I Dream of Jeannie*?"

"Yes, he was, Jenny. I'd almost forgotten that."

There was a time when I wished I was Jeannie with her long, blonde hair. It had seemed to me that those blonde-haired girls had all the luck. I made a wish to get out of Burlington. Now I'm looking out the window and the snow is falling. I'm cold so I take the extra quilt off my bed and watch the show in the dark. Mom says electricity is so expensive. I tell myself I won't ever be this cold again.

"You okay, Jenny?"

"Just thinking."

She says nothing, but she's waiting for an answer. I say something about being cold.

Sarah jumps up and says, "Let me get you another blanket." She tucks it around me. "Better?"

"Better."

"That *Dallas* is something else. They always leave you with a cliffhanger. You want me to keep the TV on for you? I think *Knight Rider* is coming up, or *Miami Vice.*"

"You can turn it off, if that's okay."

"Now that you've had some food, let me check your blood pressure again." She gets up and preps my arm. "120/80 is perfect. I'm going to call the doctor and see what he wants to do, but I am thinking he's going to want closer monitoring of your blood pressure, so it might mean a cuff on your arm overnight."

"Sarah – I don't want Maizey or anyone else visiting me."

"I'll tell the doctor and write it in your chart… Are you sure? The doctor's going to ask me why."

I think to myself: *It's too dangerous*. But I'm not going to say that, because I can't explain the feeling. I say, "I just want to rest by myself. My brain hurts."

"Okay. Let me talk to the doctor."

"Sarah, when I get out of here, I'd like to have you over to the house to watch *Dallas* with Maizey and me."

"I'd like that, Jenny. Let's get you better."

Sarah comes back in with news from the doctor.

"He said let's try forty-eight hours, no visitors. He wants you on a full blood pressure cuff overnight and three meals a day plus snacks. So eat and rest. He said if the light is too much in the room, we can draw the shades for you. He's going to come in and check on you tomorrow after lunch. He wants to see how you do when you've got some good solid food in you. Do you need to use the toilet before I go?"

"Yes, thanks." We take care of business and I see the shower. I say to Sarah, "Do you think I could get a shower tomorrow before the doctor comes?"

"I'll write it down in the chart."

"Sarah, thank you."

I crawl back into the bed and pull up the covers. Something is lurking on the outside of my memory. Something dangerous that I don't want to remember. I just know it's there.

I have to get my strength back. I know I'm not right yet, but maybe all I need is a couple of days and then I can get out of here.

Chapter Twelve
Man in the Black Car: Friday

I get back to Phoenix and go straight to her apartment. I like to do a trial run when I break in and see if anyone's around. After the school bus goes, the parking lot empties. So, I knock on several neighbors' doors and put notices under a few. The one thing about doing a con is, you have to look the part. Most people don't register anything. You become invisible. I get to Jenny's apartment and see the door is easy to open, so I go in and look around. I'm careful not to touch anything. Nothing, that is, except a white pillowcase I find in the closet. I take that with me. I put the bug under the kitchen table – not a place someone would look. On the way out, I notice the tape. Carlos is smarter than he looks. I just think to myself, *Game on*. I'm not worried about him. I've seen guys like him before, guys with some shady past that turn into Mr. Good Guy. Old habits die hard. I go to the florist on Main and Cactus. I get the flowers. I change the badge to look like a delivery guy. I got the number of Room 304. Maybe she'll be asleep.

I'm walking down the hall and see Carlos and Maizey coming from the other way. I duck into Room 312. No one's in there, so I just leave the flowers. I'll have to try again tomorrow. As I'm going out, I hear buzzers going off at the nurse's station. One of the nurses jumps up. Shit. What will she say? "Call Dr. Cullen, that's Morales in Room 304."

I decide to stay in the doorway of 312 during the commotion so I can hear the nurse's station from my hiding spot.

"Dr. Cullen, Jennifer Morales appears to have had a seizure. I administered a sedative. Her family visited. Yes, she seems to be making progress with memory retrieval."

"Okay, we can monitor her here on this floor. We have three empty beds. Yes."

Okay, I think it's best for me to get in the elevator before Maizey and Carlos, so I get out of the hospital. I already got a place to park and to listen at the apartment. Shit, if she's having seizures, this could take longer. Crazy God's not gonna like this. He doesn't like going off plan.

<u>Friday Night</u>

I get an earful of kid stuff. Some guy comes over to do homework. Like that's what he's thinking about. I think it's the best entertainment. Carlos knows it too. Chicks are kinda dumb in that regard, no matter how you look at it: he's looking for a bit of tail.

I guess it makes me think maybe I can get that chick who serves the drinks at the steak and brew.

I can't get distracted. I gotta stay focused. I almost blew it with the PO. I want to be done with Arizona. I feel like I'm always swallowing dirt while I am here.

Wait.

Carlos has changed his tone, and the kid is leaving. What I'd miss?

Carlos tells Maizey about Jenny not having visitors for the weekend and that we could come back Monday 'cause she might be transferred to rehab. He wants to go home to Yuma. Maizey says okay.

So that means the apartment will be free for a couple of days. Guess that means no time to rush to get instruction #2 finished.

Final instruction: #3. I got a postcard to send to Lily. It doesn't matter to me that Jenny ain't gonna see the fake rattler. Crazy God gets what he paid for, which is nothing right now.

Crazy God. Man, how'd she get hitched up with him?

Money, stay focused on the money.

Instructions #3:
White Gardenia. Twelve.
Brought to her room.

The florist only has eleven because of the last order. I can't wait. This will be my last chance to get the flowers in her room.

Crazy God talked a lot about the Last Supper. He thought about numbers and shit like that. Twelve good guys, one bad. One guy leaves supper. Maybe it's an omen now.

He's got me crazy thinking. Money starts me thinking about Mexico.

The stupid PO in Cali won't find me once I get the cash and dash across the border in Yuma. Crazy God's plan ain't perfect, and neither is mine. Jenny gotta remember by my next PO appointment Thursday or I'm letting this go. Crazy God ain't worth it. Money or no money. There are plenty of other cons to be run.

Chapter Thirteen

Jenny: Sunday Afternoon, February 2

I wake up from my afternoon nap. I'm a bit groggy, but I smell the flowers before I see them. My heart starts to race and some monitor goes off. I pull at the monitor so that it becomes dislodged. Nurse Mary comes in and says, "Okay, looks like this is what's causing the problem."

She fixes my monitor, but it is still running a bit high. I shut my eyes and will my blood pressure to go down. It does. He taught me that. Now he is doing this again to me.

Yesterday, when I woke up from a dream about California, the doctor gave me some relaxation medicine and I couldn't think clearly. I remember now. I remember almost everything.

I just don't remember what he wants with me. All I know is that he is dangerous to me and Maizey. I don't want to open my eyes because I know they will be there.

Right there as a sign. No one else would send me those particular flowers. I have to practice keeping my heart rate steady so that I can get out of here.

I look to see a huge bouquet of white gardenias. I hate that you took the meaning of the flower and used it for your purposes. Gardenias say you are lovely. They symbolize joy and purity and are a symbol of secret love. I hate that I associate anything with you. I have to keep my emotions even. I notice everything again. I think my fight-or-flight response is kicking in.

Nurse Mary comes back in. "Just have to check your vitals. Take a breath." I take a big breath, but all I can smell are those damn gardenias.

Nurse Mary sees me staring at them.

"They are so pretty; I can smell them when I walk by your room. Smells like spring to me."

"When did they come? I must have been asleep."

"They were here when I arrived at three, so I'm not sure."

"Do you think I could get some dinner? I'm a bit hungry."

"Sure." She goes and gets the menu.

I order a cheeseburger, fries, side salad, and chocolate pudding. I eat everything. I can't smell the flowers when I'm eating, so it makes it better. I'm so angry. I can feel it inside me. I want to walk around, so I ask Nurse Mary if it's okay.

"Just give me a minute."

I ask her, "Can we walk around the loop? I'm doing great. I don't feel any dizziness like yesterday." Nurse Sarah says it's a miracle because she would not have expected this quick of a recovery. She says that I would probably be moved Monday to rehab. "The doctor says it looks like there won't be any permanent damage."

I'm thinking about that when I walk by a different room and I smell gardenias.

Mary sees my face change. "The patient in there got some gardenias before you. A secret admirer, maybe. Same bouquet."

I think shit, he's sent someone twice to this hospital. I think of what was in the box. What was he getting at? I should know, but there's a small part of my brain that's blocking the memory.

We get back to the room and sit in the chair facing away from the gardenias.

I'm tired but I don't want to let it go. I look through the drawers and closet. I don't see any clothes.

I buzz Nurse Mary and ask, "Where are my clothes?"

Mary says, "I think they are at the nurse's station. We were getting things ready for your probable transfer tomorrow. I think your daughter and Carlos are going to be bringing something tomorrow if the doctor okays it."

I don't want Maizey here again. I want her safe with Carlos.

She brings me the bag and I can see my pants and underwear, but my shirt is gone. I think they probably had to get rid of it because of the broken arm.

I look at the clock; it's still light out, so I say to Mary, "Could I maybe try and go down to the gift shop? They have something down there like t-shirts and things. I'd like to try on some real clothes."

Mary frowns. "I don't know… I might have to get the doctor's approval."

She leaves for a moment before coming back and says "Dr. Cullen is encouraged by your wanting to do things for yourself. He said that he would okay a visit to the gift shop if you'd let a volunteer push you down in a wheelchair."

"Mary, I was wondering, do you think I could try on some scrubs? I don't really want to go down to the gift shop in this breezy robe."

She brings back a pair of scrubs and I put them on. It feels good to be out of the hospital robe. An elderly woman with the name tag *Christine* comes in. Mary helps me into the chair. I'm happy to be out of the room and away from the gardenias.

Christine talks the entire way about her grandkids, her late husband's service at the church, and her famous chicken pot pie. I nod my head, half listening.

I'm starting to get my senses back. I practice noticing things. I make note of the color of the shirt of the security guard. I notice the mother with a daughter carrying a Care Bear. Which one was it?

I do these mental exercises and feel myself getting sharper.

When we get to the gift shop, I use my credit card to purchase two shirts (one without sleeves), a couple of Snickers bars, two packs of Juicy Fruit gum, and a *National Enquirer*. I get pushed back to the room and thank Christine for helping me.

She goes over to the gardenias and smells them. “Lovely!”

She says to me, misty-eyed, “My late husband used to give me gardenias. You know they mean you’re lovely?”

I pretend I don’t know. “Really?” Then I get an idea as Christine is looking fondly at the flowers.

“Would you like to take them home with you?”

“Oh dear, that’s not what I meant.”

“Well, I’m probably going to get transferred tomorrow, so I won’t probably be bringing any flowers with me. Really, take them!”

I see she’s hesitant. So I say, “Besides, it’ll make my family get me some new ones. Really, take them.”

“You’re sure?”

“Yes.”

“Okay, then I can’t thank you enough. I wasn’t going to say anything, but next week would have been our anniversary and…”

"And I think your husband sent you this sign."

"Yes, I was praying for a sign."

I take her hand and say, "It looks like you got one."

As she leaves the room, I think to myself that I got one too, loud and clear.

Chapter Fourteen

Maizey: Sunday

Maria has done everything she could to spoil me. The girls have done everything to distract me. Carlos has done the rest. Gregg brought over Mom's car. It's got a new side that's a different color, but other than that it runs good. Gregg said it's probably better than good. He fixed the brakes and changed the oil.

Carlos says he said he will take it to Maaco next week. Carlos tries to give Gregg money, but he won't take it. I can hear them arguing about it. I know Gregg will get his way this time, but next time it'll be Carlos. That's the way they are. All of them. Gregg, Maria, my mom, and Carlos. They take care of each other. I don't know where that comes from, but I see it now after spending the weekend without Mom.

Since I've been in Yuma, I haven't been able to talk to Jenna about Beto. I haven't been able to finish any homework either. I'm going to be so far behind. I wonder if my mom still remembers me. I'm sitting on the girl's bed looking at the dress Maria and I picked out. It wasn't exactly the color I would have gone with, but Maria said, "You won't know until you try it on." It's a dark teal floor-length gown. I must have tried on fifteen different dresses at Macy's to finally decide on this one. Some other girls were trying on gowns, but they were too low-cut. Carlos would never let me wear one of those. Maria said she would kill me if I came back with a dress like that. So, we settled on the teal dress. It made my black hair shine. I felt like a princess. Maggie said I looked like a Disney princess. Maria thanked me for letting her take Mom's place.

I wish Mom was there. I wish she was out of the hospital. It's been a long weekend. Carlos says that if Mom is allowed to go to rehab, then maybe Jenna could come over and stay with me. He has to get back to work. I say that's fine. I think Jenna's mom will let her stay over. I'm weirded out by having to stay in the apartment by myself. I only did it once before, last year when Mom went away for her annual overnight trip.

I want to get back to class, and I want to see Beto so I will. I feel selfish saying things like that, but I can't help my feelings. I'm glad Carlos approved of Beto. That's one less battle. I'm not sure Mom is going to like it. Carlos said he talked to her about things so she'll give up. Carlos has that effect on people. I know that Carlos is like a dad to me, but I want to go back to the apartment. I'm starting to feel like a burden.

My thoughts are interrupted by the girls bouncing on the bed.

Carla says, "Come on, Maizey, you've got to see Papa." She yanks me so hard that I almost fall on the floor.

Her sister asks, "You okay, Maizey? But hurry before Papa isn't doing it anymore!"

I see Carlos in the kitchen. He's got on a tutu and he's swinging his hips around while he's stirring a pot. He looks at me like this is a normal thing and says, "I'm going to be in the show!"

"What?"

Carla can barely stand it and she blurts out, "They need some dads to be in the show, so I said my papa. My papa."

Maria says, "She signed him up and the teacher gave him a tutu."

I laugh. The girls and I really *really* laugh. Out of the corner of my eye, I see Carlos nod to Maria. I understand now what he is doing, and I love him even more.

I don't think I could ask for a better kinda-like-a-real dad.

I wonder if my real dad would ever wear a tutu.

Chapter Fifteen

Jenny: Monday Morning, February 3

I'm just finishing my breakfast when the nurse on duty comes in. I wonder where Sarah is. I wanted to say goodbye, but the nurse tells me that she had to go to the ICU because of another emergency. I think to myself, *Maybe that's better anyway*.

"Denise," I say, seeing her name on the whiteboard. "What time is Dr. Cullen coming in this morning?"

"I think he was called away to Tucson last night. Dr. Scott will be coming in fairly soon. Are you finished with these dishes?"

I look at the remains of French toast, eggs, and fruit cocktail. "Yes, thanks."

She says, "I've got to take your temp and your blood pressure." She pulls out the monitor. "Perfect," she says, "120/80, 98.6."

I look at the clock. I really want to get out of here as soon as possible, but I can't let on to my idea. “I’m ready to get showered if someone could help me.”

“Yes, I can do that.” I want to be dressed when it’s time.

She looks at the clothes I have on the bed. “I think your family is bringing you some things.”

“I heard sometimes things are stolen at rehab, so I would rather just lose these, if that’s okay.” My brain seems to be working fine.

“I’ve heard that too.” So we take care of business. I go over the list in my mind. Repeating it again: *Breakfast, Shower, Doctor*.

I’m mulling over what to say when a very young doctor comes running into the room.

“Jennifer Morales?”

“Yes.”

“I’m Dr. Scott, Dr. Cullen’s intern. Good morning.”

“Good morning.”

“I’m here to discharge you to rehab and answer any questions.”

I want to say, *How could you let a dangerous man roam the hospital*? But I say instead, “I would like to go by taxi to the rehab.”

“It was my understanding that your family was coming to pick you up?”

“I don’t want them to do that, I just want to meet them there.”

“Let me call Dr. Cullen.” He scurries off and I start to collect my things. I take one of the packs of Juicy Fruit out of my purse and put it on the window sill. I hope that Carlos will see it before the cleaners take it away. It's in God's hands, as Abuela would have said.

Dr. Scott says, "He's encouraged that you're wanting to do something by yourself. You've made incredible progress, so yes, you can go in a taxi. It's no different from a private vehicle. I have the discharge papers here. The rehab will go over what the next steps are for you. Medically, you're cleared from our care. Just keep that arm dry and follow up with us in a month."

I sign everything and say, "Can I go now?"

Volunteer Christine is back with the wheelchair. "Hello, Jenny."

"I guess you're my ride."

"Indeed," she laughs. I wave at Dr. Scott.

One hurdle down.

Christine is her usual chatty self. I am on edge because I am almost there and I *don't* want to see Carlos or Maizey. I'm sure they are driving back from Yuma.

I don't want to see whoever delivered the gardenias either. I feel like he's close, like someone's watching me. I wonder if I'm being paranoid. It's a head injury, but I think – I felt that beforehand.

Christine gets to the doors and we sit outside. The warm desert air feels good on my face. There's a small breeze. Christine says, "It looks like your taxi is just pulling up."

She goes over to the driver and says something to him. I can see her pass something to him. I assume it's the address of the rehab.

"Be well, Jenny. Thank you again for the flowers."

"You're welcome," I say, and she helps me back into the taxi.

He taps his mileage thing and says, "Where to?"

"Anywhere out of here."

He laughs, "Well, you got twenty dollars to take you where you want to go."

I'm watching another taxi pull up behind me, the one that knows to take me to rehab. The driver looks confused. I say, "Let's go. I'd like to go to the bus station by Main Street."

"You got it," he says, and we pull out. The driver in the taxi behind me is opening the door for another patient. I'm thinking luck is on my side.

We get to the bus station and the bank is next door.

I try to give him money, but he says, "The nice lady Christine paid for your cab. Yes, she said she was happy to help."

I say, "Thanks." He lets me out of the taxi.

I watch him drive away. I hope Christine doesn't get in trouble. But I can't think of that now. I go to the bank and withdraw four hundred and twenty-five dollars.

Another clue for Carlos, if he's following.

I go to the bus station and buy a ticket.

I take a seat in the back.
I'm on my way. This has to stop.

Chapter Sixteen

Maizey: Monday

Carlos says we should start out early, after the girls have gone to school. He says that the doctor said Mom could be released at eleven to go to rehab. We'd be able to take her home first to get some clothes, and then she could settle in at the rehab hospital for a week, maybe be let go even sooner if her tests come back good. Dr. Cullen said that she had made great progress in the two days she was left alone. Carlos made a joke about my mom knowing her own mind, and it figures that would work. I'm not sure the doctor laughed, but Carlos did.

We leave Yuma and we are heading east; the sun is in my eyes. I should have gotten some sunglasses. Carlos swears in Spanish. He decides to pull over at a McDonald's.

"Hey, well, you know I love me an Egg McMuffin," Carlos says.

We go thru the drive-thru and get Egg McMuffins and juice. I have to admit that it does taste pretty good. He sees me smile and says, "See, I told you."

We get back on the road, and we're in the quiet part of the highway through the desert.

"Time to start looking for those road runners," he says, and he makes the sound from the cartoon. He's full of himself this morning. I think he's just relaxed that Mom is coming home and we can try to get back to a more normal life.

I'm thinking about school. I'm thinking about Beto.

I haven't talked to him or Jenna since the night before. I wonder how Jenna's date went. She's probably bursting to tell me.

I squint my eyes and I see a roadrunner running in the opposite direction.

It's so quick, but Carlos catches it too.

"He says he got places to be, that road runner."

"How do you know it's a he?"

"Right. Never thought of it before, but you could be right. Wherever the bird is going, it's in a hurry. Let's hope Wile E. Coyote isn't around."

"He never catches the road runner," I say.

"Let's hope not, the girls would *not* like that."

We settle into the ride and I see Phoenix. The traffic gets heavier. Greyhound buses and RVs are leaving, and cars coming into the city for work.

We have to stop at the apartment to get some clothes. Carlos goes first. He makes a face, mumbling something about the tape.

I look around and everything looks the same. Nothing is different.

I go into my mom's bedroom, and I get the feeling someone's been in there. I try to shake it as I grab some clothes for my mom.

Something is not right. I look at her bed and realize it's made, and that there's a different case on one of the pillows. It doesn't match exactly.

I call to Carlos. He comes to the door. "Hey, did you change the pillowcase?"

"No."

"I think someone's been in here."

"Stand back by the door." He goes to the bed and hits it; it makes a noise. He flips it open and a snake pops out. I scream. Carlos shuts the door. He picks up the snake and says it's fake.

"It sure did give you a fright."

"Who would put a snake in your mom's bed?" he asks.

"I don't know, but that's creepy. Maybe we should call the police."

"Later," Carlos says. "We have to get your mom to rehab first."

We drive to the hospital in silence. I'm really creeped out by snakes. I have vague memories of a man with snakes who used to shake them around. He scared me then and he scares me now. I'm never quite sure if it was something I saw on TV or if it was something real.

We get to the hospital and park in the lot.

We both notice the black car from the day before. I think it must be someone who works here. Carlos wonders out loud if the car had been moved since the last time. I tell him it must have because we are on another level.

I look at the clock, and it says 11:30.

"I bet Mom will be ready when we get here."

We get in the elevator and go to Room 304.

It's empty, and the cleaner is there getting the bed ready for the next patient.

Carlos says hola to the cleaner. The cleaner is about to throw something in the trash before Carlos interrupts her.

"What's that?" he asks. He picks it up. Juicy Fruit gum.

The cleaner says that she can't keep it, hospital policy. Carlos says he'll take it since he knows who left it behind.

He takes the pack of gum and sees it hasn't been opened. He sighs.

"What was that about?"

He says nothing, but I know that it's not nothing because he starts to walk very quickly to the nurses' station.

"Hello, we are here to pick up Jenny Morales. Room 304. We are a few minutes behind."

A nurse we don't recognize says, "Let me see. It looks like Ms. Morales checked herself out after speaking with Dr. Cullen's resident Dr. Scott at 10:30 am. We called your house in Yuma, but no one was there."

Carlos is trying not to get mad because he knows it's not this nurse's or the resident's fault. "We were driving here."

"Okay, let me page Dr. Scott. Why don't you take a seat in the lounge."

Same chairs. Same vending machine.

Dr. Scott is young. He's what I imagined is who my mom wants me to meet.

He has his stethoscope dangling lopsided around his neck and he's carrying a chart when he gets to the lounge.

He shakes hands with Carlos.

"The patient, Ms. Morales, told me that she would prefer to take a taxi to rehab. I asked her if she was sure. She said she was."

"So you just let her go?"

"I confirmed with Dr. Cullen it was okay that she ride in a taxi to rehab. He said yes, and that I should call you and tell you that you could meet her there. There was no answer at the number you provided."

"We were on our way. It takes two hours."

The young doctor clears his throat and says, "I'm sorry I couldn't have reached you sooner." He scribbles the address of the rehab on a piece of paper and gives it back to Carlos.

His beeper goes off. He says, "I'm sure Dr. Cullen will want to speak to you later this afternoon. He was called away for an emergency in Tucson."

Carlos and I walk out of the hospital. I can't understand what is happening. I don't know but I've got a bad feeling.

"Don't you worry, Maizey, we'll find your mom."

"I don't understand what's happening. Why would she do that when she knew we were coming to get her?"

"Only your mom knows." He slides on his sunglasses to hide his eyes. I get the feeling Carlos knows more than he's saying.

He opens the pack of Juicy Fruit gum and offers me a piece. I say, "No thanks."

He chews the gum and there is something again vaguely familiar about the scent.

I shut my eyes and I see a snake being rattled at me and I can smell the Juicy Fruit on his breath.

I gasp.

"You all right, Maizey?"

"Yeah."

"You'd tell me if you weren't. No secrets." I shake my head and he says, "Let's go see your mom."

As I stare out the side window, I think, *We all have secrets*.

What are Carlos and my mom hiding?

Part Two

Chapter Seventeen

Carlos: August 1969

Carlos had been in California since 1965: hanging out in the grimy streets of East L.A., washing cars and hustling at night as a dishwasher at a club on 39th Street. He'd gotten his mother out of Chihuahua before the rebels took the village, and got her settled into a nice apartment over the laundry where she picked up work as a seamstress.

Back in May, he'd been closing up the kitchen when a man in a hat he didn't recognize came into the back. Latino, like him. He'd heard him play the bass and sing the first set before he'd gone off to the kitchen. Carlos and the guy in the hat struck up a conversation about Mexican food. Carlos was always bragging he could make the best empanadas anywhere. He mentioned the part of Mexico he'd come from. The singer in the hat introduced himself as Carlos Santana. He said he'd heard about the kidnappings and the village burnings from his cousins.

Santana asked, “Carlos, who’d you come with to L.A.?”

He responded, “My mom.”

“That’s it?”

“That’s it,” Carlos said.

He didn’t want to get into the rest of it with this stranger – no matter what. He wouldn’t be fooled again like he was down in Nogales. Someone pretending to be your friend, and before you know it you wake up with a knife to your throat and all your money gone. He was always trying to protect his mom, but that day back in Nogales, she proved herself to be stronger than he could ever imagine.

She’d hidden some cash in her bra and one of the guys tried to find something in her belongings. She’d put her rosary beads in there too. When the dude tried to get to her, the rosary beads tumbled out and his mom started praying right there for his soul.

He gave up the quest, as if his mom had pushed some Catholic button and he was worried about his soul. Instead, he smacked Carlos with the butt of his gun and gave him a quick kick before letting them go.

Carlos’s mother finished her rosary and wiped the blood off Carlos’s face.

He asked her, “How’d you know to do that, Ma?”

She'd taken his face in both hands and said, "How'd you think I survived all these years? I've seen those types many times. I learned the hard way."

Carlos's heart broke a bit thinking about what the hard way meant. All those years of threats and intimidation, guns and dust. His heart was completely smashed when he thought of Isabella. His mother knew what he was thinking.

"Your sister was too beautiful for this world and she wanted to believe in good. We have to believe in the good too. God, I pray she didn't suffer."

Carlos said, "Me too," but he'd heard otherwise. He'd never share that story with his mother.

The rebels had taken Isabella. He tried to get her back but the guy kicked him in the head and he stumbled. They grabbed her around the waist and dragged her away screaming. Screaming for Carlos, and then the screaming stopped.

The only thing he found was her scarf tied to a pole. There was nothing. He'd known the rebels were brutal. He knew these men had no souls, only black hearts, which was what he'd come to call them. He knew they'd as soon leave his Isabella out for the vultures or bring her along to their camp for the rest of the soldiers to gang rape her. He couldn't put his mind around either scene. No one got out of Mexico in 1965 without a story untold.

He never forgot or forgave himself for not being able to protect Isabella.

Carlos Santana said Carlos should put his money where his mouth was, and invited him to his house to make empanadas the next weekend. When Carlos got there, he realized this guy was a somebody – or he was going to be a somebody, if he kept his head above the drugs floating around.

Despite the drugs that were everywhere in 1960s Cali, Santana had attracted the attention of some big shot execs and the band was starting to get bigger gigs than the small club on 39th Street. Santana offered him a job as roadie and empanadas chef for double the pay he'd make as a dishwasher /car washer.

So that's how Carlos Peña wound up here in Bethel, New York, at the Woodstock music festival. He felt like the luckiest man alive.

He'd never seen anything like it – so many naked and half-naked white kids covered in mud. He'd spent a half day trying to get to the festival by bus, but when Santana realized his crew could not get in, he'd gotten a helicopter and flew Carlos and his buddies onto the stage. Flying over the road, it was immense. Someone said fifty thousand people in fields in the rain. Carlos thought he preferred to be in the helicopter looking down, but he would soon know what fifty thousand drugged-up free-loving kids looked like up close.

The crowds were dirty and primal. Carlos was certainly not modest, but there was no privacy for any acts. Sex in all its forms, shitting and sleeping in the mud. He thought then about the drugs. He'd tried a few on the road when he didn't have to worry about taking care of his mom, but they only intensified his memories of Mexico and Isabella. Santana seemed to play better on them. He was so intense with his music, but he didn't have the hallucinations and the nightmares it brought Carlos.

He spent most of the first day with the crew but one by one they'd found hippie girls who'd hook up with them and they were off to slosh in the mud with them.

He'd gone round the stage and seen the signs, *Acid: $1.00*. He'd seen the communal cooking pots and the blankets sprawled on the mud-soaked field. He even heard the moans of a girl bright-eyed giving birth. He thought about what a way that was to come into the world – and he heard about a guy run over by a tractor in his sleeping bag – what a way to go out.

There was a drug-induced buzz in the crowd. He could feel it. The chants about Vietnam and the anti-war songs. What did these kids know about war? Maybe that was the point – they could screw each other, light up, and blow their minds, but they wouldn't have their heads blown off by a grenade or wind up face-first in the mud unless they did it to themselves.

He thought, *I'm not that much older than these kids yet I feel like a dad.* He'd paid for some food for some of the rowdy skinny hippies that looked like they'd be carried out on the stretcher. He had a job to do for Santana. He had to set up the equipment.

Carlos Santana said they'd be going on earlier than expected. He could tell by looking into Santana's eyes that he was as high as a kite. He'd told Carlos that he figured the drugs would have worn off by the 4 pm showtime, but now it was only 1 pm.

So Santana was going to have to do whatever he did in front of this massive messed-up crowd. The amps almost blew out, but Carlos was able to keep them going, so when Santana played "Soul Sacrifice," the crowd exploded. Drugs or no drugs, it was like the earth opened up and swallowed Bethel, New York.

He was just winding up the cords of the amps when he heard a sound. He could tell it was a distressed sound and it triggered him. He stood frozen trying to figure out where it was coming from. It sounded like the last quiet sounds he had heard from Isabella before she was dragged off. He stubbed out his cigarette and popped a piece of Juicy Fruit in his mouth and went around the back of the stage. All he could see was mud, puddles, and tie-dye.

There was a small area under the stage that looked reasonably dry. That's where the sound was coming from. He'd come upon a skanky, skinny white guy who was obviously high as a kite.

He was trying to stand up, but he could not. Carlos went to walk away when he realized that there was another person in the crawl space pinned against the muddy ground. He heard the sound again and realized that it was a girl and that she was crying out.

He stood transfixed when the skanky guy moved. The girl was Isabella. He couldn't decide what to do, slam the skanky guy or grab Isabella. The skinny dude walked away as Carlos stood frozen in time.

He went over to Isabella, and when she looked up at him he realized it wasn't her at all. It was someone else. She looked like a scared fragile bird.

Carlos had seen that look of terror before; this time he could do something about it.

He went over to the girl and took off his shirt. He paced around her near-naked body. She looked at the shirt and said, "I like Santana."

He looked into her glassy eyes and asked her name. She said her name was Jenny. He asked if she had some friends at the concert. She shook her head no. Carlos reached into his pocket and unwrapped a piece of Juicy Fruit gum.

"You gotta get out of here. Take my hand."

She took the gum and then looked deep into his eyes and somehow she knew she was safe. Carlos brought her backstage and got her some water. It started to rain again, and all he could think about was getting out of the mud. He was grateful this concert was almost over. Saturday night.

It took Jenny quite a while to say anything. She just kept chewing the Juicy Fruit and rocking. Carlos felt that this girl who looked exactly like Isabella was his redemption for what had happened in Mexico. He was going to take care of her no matter what. Get her out of the mud and drugs. Get her back to her family. Maybe if he did that, someone else would do it for Isabella. He wasn't sure he believed in God, but he took it as a sign.

Maybe Isabella was okay after all.

Jenny had nothing to look back at. She'd left Rutland and she wasn't going back. Johnny was gone, and she wasn't going to end up like her mom.

She got on the train and headed for Albany. She figured if she could get to New York City, she could get a job and start again. She knew how to smile and open doors; at least that was what people told her.

She got to Albany and was ready to hitch a train to New York when she saw a few tie-dyed girls chatting by the water cooler.

They called to her, "Hey, you got a light?" She shook her head no.

"You coming to the festival?"

Jenny said she wasn't planning on it.

One of the girls, who introduced herself as Star, said, "You'll miss out on the biggest music festival of our life. Biggest anti-Vietnam rally ever."

Just the mention of Vietnam made her stiffen and wince.

Star noted the reaction and said, "Where are you going, then?"

"New York City."

"By yourself?"

"Meeting someone there," Jenny lied. Even she could tell it wasn't convincing enough to be believed.

"Come with us to Woodstock."

Jenny looked the girls over and decided that maybe they weren't the most reliable. She went to walk away, but Star trailed after her.

"Come on. What've you got to lose? And, you'll be able to tell everyone that you were at Woodstock. It's all over the news. They are saying maybe twenty thousand people. Don't you want to be part of history, man? They'll have lots of guys and some drugs and some music. If you don't mind me saying, it looks like you could use a little bit of each right now."

"I got to go now and get my ticket." But when she looked down, her suitcase was gone and so were Star and her friends.

Now she had only a few dollars left and not enough for the train. The station was crowded. She sat down against the wall and put her head in her hands. A tall Black guy with a huge afro sat down next to her. He had a sign that read, *Woodstock or Bust*. He said, “I saw what happened, man. Do you want a smoke?”

“Sure.”

She took a long drag of the cigarette and almost choked. The guy said nothing.

“I have seen that girl Star hustling people all morning. She’s a con, man.”

Jenny looked at him and said, “Think I’ll ever see my stuff again?”

“Probablyyy not. She’ll sell it for acid or food or whatever she needs to do to get herself to Woodstock. I’m going to Woodstock. They say the best way is to try and hitch a ride. The roads are clogged up, but I think I’ll make it. I want to see Hendrix. You by yourself?”

“Yeah for the moment,” Jenny said.

“You wanna come with me? I won’t con ya ’cause I know you got nothing.”

Jenny laughed, “Whatever the hell else am I going to do?”

“Besides, a girl will get a ride in a car before a guy,” he said.

Everyone’s got an angle, she thought.

“Brian.”

“I’m Sarah.”

Jenny was learning, you could be anyone you wanted to be.

They stood up and walked out onto the road. Lots of campers and cars going south. It didn’t take long for Brian and "Sarah" with the long black hair to get into a camper van going south. They put the sign in the back of the van and started towards Bethel New York.

Brian and Sarah sat in the back of the van. There were two guys and two girls in the front. One of the girls was wearing a crop shirt and bell bottoms and a flower crown, hanging all over the passenger in the front seat named Mike. He was smoking a joint and running his fingers through the girl's hair. Every once in a while he'd yell back at Brian and Sarah. He said it was cool with him that they were together, being from different races.

Brian said, "Yeah man, got lucky I guess. Hey man, I really wanna see Hendrix. You got anything by him on those tracks?"

"Nah, been sold out for months."

"Yeah, Hendrix, he's cool."

"What do you know about Santana?"

"Heard some Latinos out of East L.A. do some heavy bass."

All of a sudden, the guy driving the car said "Shit," and the camper lunged to a stop. He got out of the van and there was steam coming out of the front.

He came back to the front and said, "Well, that's it. Ain't going nowhere."

The camper van just stopped in the middle of the traffic.

"How far do you think we are?"

"I don't know."

Another guy came over and asked for a light. "Hey man," he said, "that's a bummer. Guess you're going to have to walk."

"How far, ya think?"

"Five miles, maybe."

Brian and "Sarah" hopped out.

"End of the ride, man."

Brian said thanks and tossed him a fiver. "For your trouble." The guy folded it and put it in the back pocket of his jeans.

"Sarah, come on, let's get going. If you take my hand, no one gonna bother you. They'll think we're together. You got me closer than I thought I'd get, so let's stick together for a bit more."

"Okay," said "Sarah."

She hadn't done any pills, but in the camper van the smell of smoke was so strong she thought she might be high.

The guy was right: it was about five miles and the fastest way was walking. There was traffic backed up and cars abandoned all along the way. Hippies just wandering this long country road.

And every once in a while, the sky would open up and get everyone soaked. You could tell by the people's reactions what drugs they were on. How they responded to the rain. Some danced around in puddles, others swore and got angry, and others like Brian and "Sarah" just pushed forward through the crowds.

Brian was determined to get there to see Hendrix. "Sarah" was going because she had nowhere else to be.

She thought of Johnny. MIA. She was MIA. In the mud and rain, same as him. She was in a drug-infested jungle of hippies. They were peaceful, but unpredictable. One minute it was all cool, and the next minute peace and love were replaced by violence. It was the up and down of the drugs. No one was on the same high at the same time.

"Sarah" and Brian reached the gates finally. Brain said to her, "Hey man, it's been real. Look after yourself." He pointed to a group of hippie girls who were making flower crowns and stirring pots of something.

"That looks like a good place to start for you. Me, I got to find me my homies. I know they're supposed to be here. Ghetto boys. You don't want to be with us, man."

"Okay, thanks, I guess."

He gave her five dollars and said, "Take care." He walked away into the crowd, just another guy.

Jenny took his advice. She made quick work of being friends with the girls serving up the food. People shared everything. Pots, pans, blankets.

The gross part was going to the bathroom all over. Jenny was used to cow country, but this was something else. Ah, that smell! Maybe it was the rain, or that the porta potties were all stuffed up.

The first night she was there she made friends with a girl named Moondancer, whose real name was Linda White from Cleveland, Ohio. Linda said, “You gotta give yourself a new name, Sarah.”

Friday night’s bands sang songs about Vietnam. She found herself getting into the concert. By Saturday she decided to use two of the dollars to buy her and Moondancer some acid.

Moondancer said, “The high is great, the coming down is a bummer.”

“Sarah” smiled and took a tab. She let it dissolve under her tongue.

At first, nothing happened, then everything went wild. *Everything* was intense.

The colors and the smells made her want to puke, and the *sounds,* especially the *sounds*. She and Moondancer were drawn closer to the stage; well, as close as they could get. The band was wild, and Santana was up next. People were mumbling about Santana – they had some following, but not as much as some of the other bands. Moondancer and “Sarah” were able to get closer to the stage. Sarah heard the chopper above them, and Woodstock was far away. She saw Johnny jumping from a helicopter into the jungle. She saw Johnny being ambushed in the jungle and held at gunpoint. Someone lit off some firecrackers. Moondancer laughed, and Jenny, horrified, ran away farther into the crowd, away from Moondancer, her voice sounding warbled and distant. No one had told

Jenny how the drug would meld her mind. The only thing that Jenny could think of was to get herself small. She trusted no one. She had to hide. Maybe Johnny would find her. She wasn't sure.

She settled in on a log. She blocked out everything. Her heartbeat came back. Time moved at a different pace. When "Soul Sacrifice" came on, the instrumental music soothed her. She felt more relaxed, and she came down a little bit. It was getting closer to the end of the afternoon, and she wanted to find something to eat. She remembered she still had a couple of dollars left, so she walked toward a group of hippies with kids. The mom asked her if she wanted something to eat. Jenny said sure. "Do you think you could watch the kids while I go for a pee?" asked the mom.

"Sure," she said. So Jenny rocked the baby and played peekaboo while their mom went off somewhere.

She wasn't sure how long she sat on the blanket with them, but by the time she came back, Santana was wrapping up and saying their goodbyes. The girl thanked her, and Jenny realized she had to keep moving. She wanted to try and get away from the crowd. She remembered in Rutland that usually under the bleachers there was a small space, so maybe it would be the same with the stage. She thought if she could only have rest for a few minutes to herself, she'd figure out how to handle the down.

Jenny was right about one thing. There was a space under the stage. She was wrong about something else.

Someone had been watching her. Someone had been eyeing her long black hair and pretty figure. Someone had followed her.

Jenny was about to sit down when she felt a hot breath on the back of her neck.

"Come on, Momma, show me what you got."

Jenny was shocked, and tried to push him away, but he got her around the waist.

He started fondling her up and down and grunting.

Jenny tried again to push him away, but he was stronger than her and he tugged on her long black hair.

She couldn't see his face because he was behind her.

He shoved her into the small area below the stage.

Jenny knew what was coming. She tried to scream but nothing came out of her mouth. She bit his arm and he said, "That's all you got, sweetheart?"

Jenny froze. Jenny thought she should try and run, but he had her pinned well.

He just kept grunting. Jenny's mind went blank. She went somewhere else.

The next thing she remembered was the tie-dye guy pulling up his dirty jeans and another guy putting his shirt over her. He gave her a stick of Juicy Fruit gum and he had the deepest brown eyes. There was something about his eyes that made her feel safe. He pulled her out of the mud and got her a drink of water.

Chapter Eighteen

August 1969

Carlos's mother sat at the small round kitchen table in her apartment over the seamstress shop. She liked the quiet of the morning before all the cars started. She had just finished the first decade of prayers on her well-worn rosary beads. She had felt that God was personally looking out for her after the episode near Nogales. Most of her prayers had been answered. She knew in her heart that Isabella was an angel and was watching over her brother Carlos.

If anyone needed watching over, it was Carlos. He'd always been the silly one making his sister laugh, with not a care in the world. He was able to talk his way in and out of trouble at school. Even the priests had to laugh at his confession of big sins, but that was long ago and now she lived in America.

She didn't think she'd ever get back to Mexico, but it didn't matter. She had Mexico all around her. The other thing about Carlos was that he was the most kindhearted soul, almost to a fault. Saint Francis was certainly the best choice for his confirmation name, because he was always attracted to the strays. The strays that needed help. He would give the shirt off his back.

She got up and lit her candles. She had one for Carlos, one for Isabella, and one for all the girls who needed protection from violence. She had thought that in coming to America, the American girls would be safer than the Mexican girls, but that turned out wasn't the case. They just had different predators.

She sucked in her breath and thought about how many girls had come through that kitchen in the last four years. Some had heard of it and some had not. She didn't pass judgment on them, because if she did she would have to pass judgment on herself and Isabella. Though she was right in the city, she was only a bus ride away from the farms outside of L.A. where most of the girls worked. Well, most of them, because she knew some had been recruited to work downtown at night. She could see it in their eyes, the blankness so young.

She got up and got mad at Mexico, at men, at cartels, at drugs. Her husband had betrayed his family and sold himself to the devil. Carlos's mom was abandoned in his village with two children. She took in a big sigh; she should have listened to her mother. Her mother had told her La Lechuza, the strange owl, had perched itself in the tree outside their house and watched her and Jose come back from the dance. She didn't want to listen to her mother's old ways and said that she could make up her own mind. Her mother and La Lechuza had been right. Jose brought bad news and death with him.

Carlos's mom had become fairly superstitious after her husband left. Warding off most birds and lighting candles. She knew it was a sin that she confessed every week to Father John. She could not and would not pray for his soul. He could rot in hell forever as far as she was concerned.

She opened the cupboards to make her morning coffee and heard a sound outside on the fire escape. She grabbed a kitchen knife from the counter and held her breath.

The doorknob jingled and rattled. It sounded like a key was being put in the lock, so she didn't scream quite yet.

A few seconds later, the door swung open and there was Carlos with his dirty duffel bag, and behind him a dark-haired girl. When she looked quickly at the girl, she saw Carlos, *and* she saw Isabella. Yet they both knew it wasn't her…and yet it *was*.

She dropped the knife and grabbed Carlos by the shoulders. Carlos relaxed when he got his mother's immense hug. The girl stood half in and half out of the door, not sure what to do. Carlos's mother said, "Come in, come in," waving the girl in to sit.

She pulled out a chair for the girl. She noticed she was wearing one of Carlos Santana's shirts. The one she'd washed a million times.

She said to Carlos in Spanish, "Are you hungry? I could make you some breakfast."

Carlos said, looking at the clock, "Doesn't the shop open soon?"

"They can wait."

"No, Momma. I can take care of this. You go downstairs, and when you come up for lunch we can talk. It's been a long journey back from Woodstock."

Carlos then turned to Jenny, and said in English, "Jenny, this is my mom. The one I have been telling you about. She takes care of our community and all the girls here, so everyone calls her 'Abuela.' She will take care of you too. She doesn't speak much English, but she wants you to know you are welcome here."

Jenny looked down at her hands and said, "*Muchas gracias*."

Abuela smiled. She said to Carlos, "You feed her and put her to bed in my bed. I just washed the sheets today. You'll make your empanadas for me at lunch?"

"Yes, Momma," and he gave her a little kiss on the cheek.

His mother grabbed her bag and walked out the door. Carlos counted the tinny creaks of the fire escape stairs and the sound of the shop door slamming. When they first got to California, Carlos insisted that she slam the door. Somehow, this made him feel she was safe behind it. It took a very long while for Carlos not to worry about his mother. She was stubborn, but she still slammed the door. Carlos smirked thinking about it.

He looked at Jenny and rubbed his hands together. "First we'll have some breakfast and then you can take a shower and a nap in a real bed."

He opened the cupboards and fridge. His mom always had extra food, extra everything for situations like this. He decided on beans and rice and eggs with chiles.

Jenny had picked at her food like a bird on the way back from Woodstock. He was happy to see her eat all the food on her plate.

Jenny had noticed the Jesus picture on the wall and shut her eyes down at her plate. Carlos couldn't tell what she was thinking, but she finally said, "Do you think your mother will dislike me because of what happened?"

Carlos said, taking her hands, "She's seen much worse, Jenny. She's helped a lot of girls. She'll help you. Just be patient with her English. If you go to church with her, she'll love you forever."

Jenny half smiled. She did see three candles lit on the windowsill.

Carlos went over. "See, this one is for me. I think she has this lit twenty-four hours a day."

He had a way about him, this Carlos. Jenny was just happy to be somewhere warm, dry, and safe. She hadn't felt like that in a long time. Not since Johnny had gone to Vietnam. She hadn't realized how tired she felt until she had a full belly.

Carlos had found a towel and cotton shift. It was a little big, but it would do for pajamas. He had placed them on a twin bed with a beautiful quilt. Jenny just wanted to look at all the squares and colors.

"My mom makes these quilts with the extra fabric from downstairs. Anything they don't want, she turns into something like a gown or a quilt or anything. She's quite a seamstress."

Jenny thanked Carlos and folded the towel and the shift and brought them into the shower. She undressed and looked at herself in the mirror. She looked wild and tired.

She certainly didn't look like the photo she'd given Johnny to bring with him to Vietnam. Her, all smiles and black hair that shone after being brushed a hundred times.

She hadn't inspected her body since Woodstock. Sure, she'd taken a shower in the motel, but she would not look at herself. It was too much to take in. Jenny hadn't realized how acid worked. She hadn't ever taken anything except some Boone's Farm wine and some drags off her best friend's Marlboro for a lark.

At Woodstock, she'd done acid and smoked something. She thought it was pot but maybe it was hash or something with something in it. The hippies had way more experience with drugs than she did, so they weren't exactly worried about what was going into their bodies.

She turned on the shower and took the soap, a lightly scented lemon bar. The face cloth would take away the remaining dirt. She washed between her legs for the first time and saw the small bruises. There was a bit of dried blood too. She didn't have to worry that Johnny would take her back in this state. He was gone. It didn't seem like the rest of the world would care either. It seemed to her that in 1968, Free Love was the way.

She didn't feel free, though; she felt trapped. So much had happened.

She didn't want to be a bad houseguest, so she hurried with her task of showering and washing her hair. She watched the last bits of mud from Woodstock go down the drain. She put on the brightly colored shift and wrapped her hair in the towel and pulled back the sheets. Everything smelled clean, even her.

Carlos had been on the phone with the manager of Santana when his mother came back for lunch. He'd been arranging the next phase of the tour with him. He was in charge of the equipment. Santana wasn't upset with him for leaving Woodstock early; in fact, he was grateful – it was a mess for the performers to get their stuff out of Bethel after Hendrix played.

Carlos had wanted to see more acts, but once he'd found Jenny, he took it as a sign from Isabella to get the hell out of there. So he went backstage and talked to the man himself. Santana was relaxing and coming down from his high, so he was particularly chilled out. Carlos admired him and his musical talent. Carlos explained he wanted to take the equipment out of there because he'd seen some stuff getting damaged.

"Hey man, thanks."

He told him he'd found a girl wandering under the stage who looked pretty bad and he wanted to get her out of Woodstock too. Santana said, "Whatever you want man. Just leave me my guitar, you can take the rest."

He called the manager. "Get Carlos and Mike and gather up the stuff; get them out of here before the next big act. The crowd will probably go wild. Hey Carlos, are you sure you don't want to stay?"

Carlos said, "I've seen enough. You can tell me all about it back in L.A."

"Sure, man."

At least, that's how Carlos remembers it. After Woodstock, Santana was going on a world tour, and Carlos went too.

Abuela made the coffee and set two cups down in front of them. Carlos told her the whole story from beginning to end. She looked at him and said, "You did the right thing bringing that girl here. Do you know if she has any family?"

"She wouldn't tell me – all I know is that she comes from Vermont. That's all she'd say."

"Did she say she wanted to go home to Vermont?"

"No, she didn't say. She looks Hispanic," Carlos said.

"She's not, that I can tell."

"Not everyone is as smart as you, Momma. Maybe she wants a fresh start."

"Maybe." Then she looked at him very sternly. "Carlos Francis Peña."

"Yes, Momma."

"Don't you get this girl in any more trouble."

"I won't, Momma. I was thinking that we'd get her a Mexican-sounding name and a new ID, and maybe she'd be able to work out on the farm for the strawberry season."

"Carlos, it's almost September, the strawberries are long gone."

"Okay, so maybe we can get her something else on the farm. I think the guy I know is still there. She could pick up a little Spanish, or you could teach her some. Maybe she could learn to sew while I'm gone."

"Carlos, you planning on marrying this girl?"

"No, Momma. She's like a sis…" He stopped abruptly.

"Then why, Carlos?"

"You know why, Momma." They stared at each other both with sadness and longing in their eyes.

Carlos broke the silence. "I know it's not Isabella, but maybe God will finally forgive me if I help this girl."

"You're not the one God has to forgive."

Carlos and his mother held hands and cried. They held hands and cried about what they both thought they had done or hadn't done for Isabella. Isabella's candle was still lit.

It didn't take long for Jenny and Abuela to get into a routine after Carlos left to go on the world tour with Santana. Abuela would wake up, make breakfast, and give Jenny a lesson in naming objects in the kitchen in Spanish. She would have Jenny write them down in a notebook and say them three times. She felt Jenny must have been a smart girl in Vermont. She would go to work downstairs until lunchtime and do the Spanish lesson all over again. In the evenings, she would bring up some extra sewing – some easy items – and cloth, and show Jenny how to do basic repairs, and how to add things like sequins and rhinestones on denim. It was all the fashion right now, so she could teach Jenny how to make some good money. She also worked on starting a quilt for Jenny. This was something she would have done with Isabella.

For Jenny's part, she was still disoriented from the experience at Woodstock. Every day she woke up under the quilt and her body ached. She would get up and eat, and then as soon as Carlos's mother went downstairs, she went back to bed. She knew she couldn't hide under the quilt forever, but right now she just felt so tired.

Carlos's mom was the kindest person Jenny had ever met. She was patient too.

She didn't speak much English, but she communicated her care for Jenny in a way she had never experienced before.

So Jenny got up every day and ate the rice and beans and cheese that Carlos's mother served. At night, they would watch sitcoms and Jenny would give Abuela English lessons. She'd been moved to a smaller room that she thought must have been Carlos's when they first came here.

She'd been with Abuela for about a month when she decided to take Abuela to church one Sunday. Jenny had sewn a pretty shift and had decided she needed to get out of the apartment. She was feeling closed in.

Jenny and Abuela went to Santa Maria for the 8 am mass. It was in Spanish, but Jenny found it easy to follow along because her family had gone to the French mass at St Pierre's in Burlington before moving to Rutland. It wasn't exact, but it was close enough. Jenny had forgotten about the incense: *lots* of incense. Abuela and Jenny were sitting right up front when the priest came swinging by with the incense.

Jenny assumed that her stomach was queasy this morning because of nerves. She knew that church was important to Abuela, so it was in great horror that Jenny could feel her stomach lurch. She couldn't stand it. She knew if she didn't get out of the church she'd throw up right there, and that would be worse.

Jenny stood up and put her hand over her mouth and ran out of the church. She barely made it to the sidewalk when she threw up behind the bush. She felt weak and clammy. She felt another wave of nausea come over her but this one passed and she sat there shaking.

Her breathing returned to normal and she looked to see Abuela holding out a cotton hanky. Jenny took it and wiped her face. Abuela put her hand on Jenny's head to check for her temp, and said to her, "Come on, love, let's get you home."

Jenny thought that was the nicest thing anyone had said to her in the past seven months.

They walked home in silence. Abuela would sneak a glance at her every once in a while, but Jenny focused on walking a straight line and picking out the landmarks she knew. She could make it back to the apartment without throwing up again.

As soon as Abuela opened the door, Jenny ran into the bathroom and threw up. Abuela gave her some tea and dry toast and told her to go to bed.

Jenny slept most of the day and woke up to soup and bread. This seemed to settle her stomach. Abuela seemed to know something that Jenny did not, but it wasn't until a week later when she took her to her doctor that it was confirmed that Jenny was pregnant.

Abuela could see how young Jenny actually was when she got the news. She was not prepared to take care of a baby; she could barely take care of herself. Abuela couldn't think of Jenny getting rid of the baby. She didn't believe in that, and she was afraid that Jenny would be hurt more. She knew there would be talk that Carlos was the dad, but it didn't matter, because *she* knew the truth.

She told Jenny that she could stay with her as long as she wanted and she would help her take care of the baby, but she would have to get some type of work. She asked her if she minded physical work – she had some migrant workers as friends who worked up at a farm. There were other girls her age, and she could get out of the apartment. It was hard work, but Abuela knew she had to strengthen this girl somehow.

So Jenny agreed. She had little choice in the matter.

Abuela and Jenny made their way to the small farm outside of town. It took two buses, but it was good to get some fresh air. Jenny was already tired, and she hadn't even reached the fields. She wondered if she would make it a full day, and she was worried about what would happen when Abuela left. Her Spanish wasn't that good, and her hands were too soft. She'd picked apples a couple of times as a kid, but this was an entirely different experience.

Abuela was greeted by two men with baskets. There was a long field of small green plants. Everything looked dirty again. She'd been living in a dream world in the apartment with Abuela. Abuela had brought a large basket filled with Mexican loaves of bread and ham. She gave some to the men and spoke to them at length in Spanish. Every once in a while, they would look over at Jenny, sizing her up.

Jenny didn't smile or move; she just waited for directions. The first man came over to her and extended his hand. He quickly introduced himself to her in English.

"Hello, I'm Juan." He took her hand and turned it over. Soft. His hands were calloused and hard. He walked back to Abuela.

He kept shaking his head.

Abuela looked discouraged. He took another look at Jenny, and then back at Abuela. He took the bread and then walked away.

Abuela turned to Jenny, and quietly said, "Let's go."

They walked silently away. Jenny thought to herself, dejected, *I'm not getting this job.*

She walked by some of the other workers, and they looked up at her. She could see that some of them were even younger than her.

They were all tanned and worn. She hadn't thought much about how fruits and vegetables got to her plate. Back in Vermont, there was a farm nearby, but it was nothing like this.

She felt relieved that she wouldn't be out in the fields, but she realized that she might have to get something. Do *something*. Abuela was right, she had to make her way. She wasn't going back to Vermont, but where was she going?

Jenny and Abuela got back on the bus. At the first stop, there was a sign in English for Harmony Farms. She looked out the window and saw someone with blonde hair sitting behind a farm stand, away from the sun. The bus slowed to a stop at this juncture. Some people got on, some got off, and there was more of a mix of English and Spanish than at the previous farm. Jenny heard the girl in front of her talking about Harmony Farms.

She tapped her on the shoulder. When the girl turned around, she asked, "Is Harmony Farms close by?"

"It's just up the road there."

"Oh," Jenny said. "I'm looking for work. I just got into town."

"Well, see that girl there? That's Lily – she'd know if anyone would. Jobs are tough right now around here, but I overheard them talking to Lily and another girl, Rose. They are always looking for help at the farm."

"Thanks," Jenny said to the girl.

Jenny and Abuela got home, and Jenny set to work cleaning the house.

Abuela thought to herself that maybe that type of job would suit Jenny better, or maybe she'd get something else. Her sewing was good, but not great. Her stitches weren't straight enough for paid work.

She had heard Jenny speaking with the girl on the bus. Maybe she'd find something on her own. Abuela felt especially protective of Jenny. She wasn't sure *why* she and Carlos had decided to do this. But she was in it now. She would find something for Jenny to do.

Abuela treated Jenny like all the rest of the Mexican girls who came through her door. But Jenny wasn't Mexican. She was American, and she could speak English. Jenny thought about that for a bit. She wasn't sure what difference that would make, but she thought she might be able to get something using her English.

Jenny had been thinking about Vermont too. There wasn't any reason for her to go back there. Johnny was gone, and if she got back to town, she'd just be the slut who let him get away. Once she decided that she wanted to keep the baby, she decided that "Jenny La Chance" was gone. She would take the ID that Carlos got her, and she would become "Jenny Morales."

She could make a fresh start. She was an adult now with a baby on the way, and she'd have to look out for both of them.

Chapter Nineteen

October 1969

Jenny was starting to show when she got on the bus by herself one day about a week later. She practiced taking the bus out of East L.A. towards the farms. She didn't like the grimy part of L.A. and didn't feel safe there either. She liked being on the bus because she could watch things outside the window.

Abuela encouraged her to get out of the house. She'd gotten her a few jobs cleaning shops in the early morning. She didn't want her out after dark. Jenny knew she was being overprotective of her. She just could not figure out why.

The bus slowed down and reached the place for Harmony Farms. She could see the girl Rose sitting behind a huge basket of tomatoes. Jenny impulsively decided to get out and buy some tomatoes and corn. She had a few dollars with her that she earned from cleaning, so she could purchase the produce. Jenny hopped on the bus and walked towards the farm stand.

"Hola," Rose said, smiling at Jenny as she made her way over to the produce.

"How much for a pound of tomatoes and three ears of corn?" Jenny said.

"You speak English?" said Rose.

"Yes, I speak English."

"Sorry, I just thought – never mind. That'll be two dollars."

As Jenny was paying for the produce, the bus pulled away silently. Jenny didn't see it because she had her back toward the bus, but Rose did. She said, "Looks like your bus is leaving." Jenny turned to see the bus back down on the highway.

"Shit."

"Don't worry, another one will be coming in an hour or so. Hey, what's your name? My name is Rose."

"I'm Jenny."

"Well, Jenny, seems like you're stuck here. Hey, you can keep me company."

"Okay, Rose."

"I hope you don't take this the wrong way, since it's kind of a personal question. Are you having a baby?"

"Yes, I'm just starting to show."

"Well, then you better get under this awning. It's going to start to get hot, and it takes forever for the ambulance to get out here if you faint."

"I'm not going to faint."

"Well, let's make sure of it."

Rose waved her under the covering. "Here, sit down on the stool. You can have my hat too." Rose went and got two crates, placing one on top of another before sitting down next to Jenny.

"Jenny, are you thirsty? I got some lemonade here. I can run up to the farm and get more if we run out, but I think it'll last us until your bus comes."

Jenny took a swig of lemonade. "That's good."

"Are you hungry? I have some sandwiches here. Avocado tomato cheese on whole wheat, or peanut butter and jelly. These are on me, don't worry about the money. I usually try and sell them to the workers down the road. I got plenty for everyone. I mean there's more up at the farm."

"Okay, then thanks, I'll take a PB&J." Jenny chewed her sandwich slowly. She hadn't had a PB&J sandwich in months. The taste was so familiar it brought tears to her eyes.

Rose saw. Rose saw everything. "You okay there, Jenny?"

"Yeah, just been going through a lot lately."

"Are you eating okay? I mean, with the baby and everything. I can grab some food for you up at the farm if you need it."

"No, I'm good."

Rose gave her an inquisitive look. "I've been looking at you funny because I thought I'd seen you before. Have you been to the farm?"

"No, I haven't been to the farm."

"I'm good with names, but faces not as much."

Jenny thought about asking Rose about a job. As if Rose could read her mind, she said, "The farm is looking for someone to watch the stand here two times a week. It doesn't pay much, but you can get free produce."

"Two days a week?"

"Yeah, you stay here and greet the buses. Do you know Spanish?"

"A little."

"Then you can sell sandwiches to the workers, and produce to whoever stops. You think you'd be okay with that?"

"Maybe."

"Well, like I said it'd be any two days you'd want. I've got other things to do up at the farm, so you'd be giving me a break. We could help each other. Well, think about it. I'm here every day except Tuesday. Tuesday the stand's closed."

"Ok," Jenny said.

Rose kept pushing. "If you come here to work at the stand, you can have all the PB&J sandwiches for free and free produce."

Everyone's got an angle, thought Jenny. What was Rose's?

"Here comes your bus. I put another PB&J in your bag for your bus ride. Maybe I'll see you soon, Jenny."

"Maybe."

Jenny hopped on the bus and sat in the back as the bus pulled away.

She opened the bag and there was a wrapped PB&J sandwich with a stamp of a gardenia on it and the words in block letters: *Harmony Farms*.

Rose wasn't surprised when she saw Jenny get off the bus the next Monday. She was curious because she looked well cared for. Her hair was brushed and she had a new shift. She even had her hat. Jenny approached the farm stand and Rose said, "Welcome back, Jenny. I hope you are here to work – not that I wouldn't like to sell some more of these tomatoes." She picked one up to squeeze it.

Perfect, she said to herself.

Jenny looked at this odd girl. The other day she felt she was overly friendly, but that didn't make her a bad person. She'd seen enough contradictions in her life. First in Vermont and then at Woodstock. Jenny knew she had to get a better gut feeling and instinct of her own to trust. Right now, she was relying heavily on Abuela.

Jenny said to Rose, "I thought maybe I'd try it out today and see if I like it. If the offer is still there."

Rose jumped up from her seat and said, "Of course it is. Come on and sit down here."

She looked at her watch. "Some of the workers are coming on the next bus, so you can see how I sell the sandwiches and where I put the money."

Jenny said, "Okay."

It wasn't long before the bus pulled up and five farm workers got off: three men and two girls. She recognized one of them from the other day. The first man was smoking a cigarette as he approached the stand.

Rose had put out the sandwiches and explained that the colored ribbons designated the type of sandwich. There were three today, she said, "Ham, tomato and cheese, and PB&J." The man pointed to the ham and put up three fingers. Rose smiled and gave them to him. She took his money, but Jenny noticed she didn't give back the proper change. Rose did this with the other four people as well. Jenny wasn't sure what to make of it, but didn't say anything to Rose until after they were gone.

"How much are the sandwiches again?"

"Two dollars for ham and a dollar for the others."

"You overcharged them."

"I know," Rose said.

"That's… not right. I don't think I can work here."

"Hang on, Jenny. Let me show you what I do with the extra money."

She had a coffee can under the table. "There all the extra money goes. So at the end of the day when they come off their shift, they can buy any produce they want."

Rose continued, "You thought I was stealing from them, didn't you?"

"…Yeah."

Rose said, "Stealing isn't allowed here at Harmony Farms."

"I don't understand why you do this."

"Well you see, there's one guy up at the farm who likes to take any money the workers come with. So Juan and I came up with this system. All the produce gets sold at the end of the day and the workers get fed."

"I'm sorry I thought –"

Rose waved her hand away.

"I hadn't explained the system to you. They each have to have a dollar to pay the man, the rest goes in the jar. So if five people get off the bus, give them five ones back. If they don't have enough to buy everyone a sandwich, just give them one sandwich and a dollar per person. Got it? Some days they don't have the money, and some days they overpay. It's how it works."

Jenny nodded. "Do you get other customers?"

"Yes, we have regulars who stop, and sometimes a random person like you who gets off the bus to stretch their legs. We have a good spot here."

Jenny looked around. Rose was right; it certainly was a beautiful location, and an ideal spot for a farm stand at the crossroads of two bus stops.

"You get to know the people who come on certain days," Rose said. "People are predictable." Jenny wasn't sure about that but she nodded anyways.

The morning flew by. Only one car stopped and bought some tomatoes. Jenny gave them a big smile and told them to have a nice day. Rose liked to talk. She liked to chatter, because if you listened to her she wasn't saying anything. Jenny had become more sensitive to conversation because of spending six weeks or so as a non-Spanish speaker in a heavily Spanish-speaking community.

Jenny asked if there was a place to use the bathroom. Being pregnant, she couldn't hold it for long.

"Of course, it's just a short walk up to the farm from here. Here's the sign you put out if you have to leave the stand for any reason." It was a handwritten sign that said *Be back in 5 minutes*. Honor system.

Jenny and Rose started a good walk up the small hill away from the stand.

Once they reached the crest, Jenny looked back and could see a beautiful vista. It seemed like the horizon met the hills. It was incredible. Rose saw her expression. “It’s beautiful here. Imagine walking up to this every morning,” she said.

Jenny was pondering this idea when they came to a small cabin. “Here, this is the closest cabin. I’m sure Daisy won’t mind.” Jenny thought of flower children. Maybe it was just a coincidence. The cabin was sparse, the beds were made. There were two bunk beds and a table in front of the window. The bathroom was small and had only a toilet.

Rose said, “This used to be a kid’s camp so these cabins are basic: less to clean.” She winked.

So far Jenny hadn’t seen anyone other than Rose at Harmony Farms. Jenny’s first impression was that something was not right here. There was a dinner bell being rung. Jenny recognized the sound right away because Mrs. Clinton had one back in Vermont, and she would ring it every night to get all her seven kids to dinner. Jenny waited to see what Rose would say.

She said, “Well, you think you might like to try being down at the stand by yourself? I got some things to do at the farm.”

“I could try it, I guess.”

“Great. So I will meet you down at the stand in about an hour or so with some lemonade. If you need to use the bathroom again, just come up here.”

“Okay,” Jenny said, and she was about to ask something about if there were any other people here when the bell rang again. Rose said, “I’ll see you in an hour.”

Rose walked up the hill and Jenny walked down. She turned around once to see Rose watching her, and when she got caught looking she broke into a big wave. *Weird*, thought Jenny. She was happy to be by herself for a while. She hadn't had much time other than sleeping, bus rides, and being with Carlos's mom to think about anything. Jenny put on her hat and sat on the stool. She counted the cars that went by: five. That was it, and the bus she and Abuela used came but didn't stop. It seemed like this place would give her the space to think. It was beautiful out here. She was thinking, it was sort of like Vermont, but not really. The air was clean, and Jenny, for being thrown into the situation, realized fresh air would be good for the baby.

She was having a baby. Having a *baby*. She wasn't sure what that would mean exactly, and maybe she'd give it up for adoption later, but right now she had nothing. So she might as well have a baby. Jenny didn't focus on her life in Vermont other than Johnny. She was so conflicted. An hour passed, and as promised Rose appeared with lemonade and two sandwiches.

"Here," she said, "I hope you like tomato, avocado, and cheese. I also brought you a sugar cookie." The cookie was shaped like a gardenia with purple sprinkles. Rose said, "I bet I know what you are thinking. It's too pretty to eat."

Jenny nodded because that was exactly what she was thinking. The rest of the afternoon was spent listening to Rose's chattering. Over the past month, Jenny had learned how to zone out in front of people, mostly because they were speaking Spanish too fast for her to keep up. Jenny wondered how someone could talk all day and say absolutely nothing.

Rose looked at her watch. "The farm workers will be heading home on the next bus. It's the last bus of the day, so let me show you how to handle the produce." The bus stopped and the same people came off this time, with three women coming to the stand. They pointed to what they wanted and held up their fingers. Rose put whatever they wanted in a paper bag with the block letters *Harmony Farms* printed on the outside. The woman looked grateful and nodded to Rose. One of the girls said in Spanish to Jenny, "Weren't you with Abuela last week?"

Jenny understood the word Abuela but not the rest. "I speak only a little Spanish," she said apologetically. The girl said in surprised broken English, "No Mexican."

The bus driver Stan came over and Rose gave him three sugar cookies in a brown paper bag she'd been saving for his kids. He said, "Thanks, they look forward to them every week. "

Rose turned around and gestured. "This is Jenny. She'll be on your bus."

Stan replied, "Hi, Jenny," and waved her to the bus, "Okay then, we got to go. I got to get this bus back into the lot before they lock it up for the night. Get your things and hop aboard."

Rose said, "That's it. That's the day. Maybe I'll see you again."

"Thanks, maybe," Jenny replied.

"Come on," said Stan.

Rose pushed Jenny toward the bus. She had grabbed a bag of produce and was looking out the window when she saw Rose holding up her hat. "Shit," she thought. "Well, I'll have to go back to get the hat." Jenny opened the bag and there was PB&J wrapped neatly with block letters: *Harmony Farms*.

The bus was quiet, as she could tell the workers were tired and there was something about Juan from the other farm that made them stay in their seats. Jenny got off the bus before them and she watched as the bus pulled away. The girl who had recognized her gave her a small wave from the window. Jenny waved back and walked towards Abuela's apartment in East L.A.

She wondered about the people in Vermont; if they were missing her, or even cared. Johnny's family had made pretty clear their feelings, so she stopped thinking about them. She couldn't focus on the past, just the future.

Chapter Twenty

November 1969

She went to the doctor's office a second time with Abuela. This time the doctor gave her written instructions that were both in English and Spanish. The doctor examined her but didn't focus too much on how she got pregnant. The pamphlet said to eat healthily, and get plenty of rest. Jenny could just start seeing the bump in her belly, and she wondered about what was going on in there. It wasn't until the first day she felt something move inside her that she realized she wasn't alone. There was a small peach-sized creature that was dependent on her. Jenny was overwhelmed with emotion. She'd only had herself, so when the nun at the clinic handed her a pamphlet on adoption,

Jenny's heart sank. What would she do? But that was many months away.

Carlos had sent three postcards to his mom from Europe. He seemed to like Paris the best. He left with the thought that he felt he fit in there. Jenny had been going to the farm stand for about a month. She never saw anyone except for Rose and the cabin that she used for the bathroom. She started to think that maybe there wasn't anyone else at the farm except her.

It was in November, near Thanksgiving, when that changed. Rose came down to the stand with another girl. Her name was Lily. She looked to be slightly older than Rose.

"Jenny, this is Lily. She's the one who's really in charge of the farm stand."

"Hello, Jenny!"

"I've got some things to do up at the farm. With Thanksgiving next week, people are going to be looking for some pies from us."

"You make pies at the farm? I'd like one," said Jenny.

"Let me see what I can do," Lily responded.

Jenny watched Rose walk away, and Lily watched Jenny watch Rose.

Lily said to Jenny, "how are you feeling?"

"I feel pretty good. The doctor says I'm due in late May."

"Well, you got a while to go then! Can I see your hands?" Jenny put them out, and Lily looked them over and squeezed them. "Good, no swelling."

Lily continued, "I came down from the farm because I want to thank you for keeping such clear records. How did you know how to do all the accounting?"

"I took a business class in high school."

"Ah, well that's great, because I could use some more help with some numbers. I'm not good at them, but I can see that you are."

"Thank you."

"Well, would you think of coming on Tuesday? To help me up at the lodge with some bookkeeping?"

"I'm not a bookkeeper."

"I know, but maybe you could just clean up the books and transfer the numbers. The sheets are quite messy and I need someone who can write things neatly in the ledgers."

Jenny didn't say anything. She wondered why she needed anyone to write things neatly. She'd seen the perfect printing of Harmony Hall. Jenny had thought it was a print, but she looked closer and realized each one was individually printed.

Lily said, "Of course, I'll pay you."

"In money or produce?"

"Real money. Twenty-five dollars day."

Jenny thought that one extra day a week would not be too much. With a hundred dollars a month, she'd be able to have close to a thousand dollars saved for the baby.

"Okay, Lily, I'll do it."

"Great," said Lily. She pointed towards the road. "I can see the next bus coming, so I'll leave you with it. I've got things to do up at the farm. Can I meet you here at 9:15? That way, you can take the same bus. Don't worry about lunch. We have plenty of soup and sandwiches to share." Lily walked away just as the bus came into view.

No one got off or on, so she just waved to the bus driver. This gave Jenny time to think things through. It was almost Thanksgiving. The weather was feeling a little chilly. Carlos would be coming back to East L.A. in about six weeks. Right after Christmas. What would 1970 hold for her?

Over the past few weeks, she'd been coming out of her fog and realizing what's happened in a few short months. She was beginning to feel restless. Abuela was so protective of her. Maybe she was right to do so, especially after the episode on the bus where two white guys started harassing another girl, calling her a dirty Mexican and telling her she didn't belong.

They were about to pull the girl's hair when the bus lurched and they fell to the floor. It was pretty obvious the driver had slammed the brakes on to make them tumble. He'd seen everything in his mirror. This just made one of the guys madder. The doors opened, and the girl bolted from the bus. It probably wasn't even her stop. The boy closest to her pushed himself up using the seat back closest to Jenny. She could smell his sour breath on her neck. He was smelling her hair. "Here's a sweet-smelling one," he said in English. He grabbed Jenny's hair and pulled it back. Abuela stood up, and said *Bambino*, and pointed to Jenny's belly.

"Sit down, you old Mexican hag," he pushed Jenny's head forward. "Who wants that Mexican trash anyway?" the other guy said, and spit on Jenny. The bus stopped and they got off. Abuela handed her a hanky and wiped the guy's spit off her face. Jenny took Abuela's hand, and they walked back to the apartment in silence.

Abuela didn't have to understand English to know that those guys on the bus wanted to hurt the girls. She hadn't pulled out the knives, but she would have stabbed him right in the neck if she had to come to that. She had to keep reminding herself she wasn't in Mexico. *They were just punks*, she had decided as she saw them get off the bus. What she didn't expect was when she got home and saw Isabella's candle that she would fall apart. She missed Carlos at this time. He was the only one who could understand. Abuela told Jenny that she needed to lie down. She was tired, and she needed to be alone. She went into her room and shut the door.

She had no pictures of Isabella to look at. All she had was her memory in her heart. She remembered when her husband had spit on her when he found out she was pregnant with Isabella. He had accused her of cheating on him because he didn't remember. He didn't remember because he was in a drunken stupor, and he had raped his wife.

Abuela kept this detail to herself because Carlos had been just a baby at the time and he had looked up to his father until the day he vanished. Abuela shut her eyes and dreamed about a time before all the violence when she rocked her baby girl to sleep in her arms.

Jenny had her own thoughts about the two punks on the bus. She knew she wasn't Mexican, but they didn't. She had seen the look in Abuela's eyes; the first time she had met her it only lasted a split second before Abuela realized it was Carlos at the door. It was terror. Jenny realized for the first time that the world didn't revolve around her. Bad things had happened to Abuela and Carlos. Maybe even worse than what happened to her at Woodstock. Jenny started to think.

Johnny had always told her she thought too much. Jenny would have to ask Carlos about the candles. There were four candles now. One for Carlos, one for her baby, and two others burning away. She didn't know who the other two were for. Jenny was certain that the candles held the key to why Abuela was overprotective of her.

She had all these thoughts running through her mind as she nibbled on a PB&J sandwich from the farm.

Chapter Twenty-One

Winter to Spring, 1969–1970

There was no real winter in California. This was a strange realization to Jenny. It did get a little cold, but no drafty windows or howling winds. There were no snowdrifts or frozen toes. Jenny started to get sentimental about Vermont around Christmas.

She longed for a real Christmas tree and pancakes with real maple syrup on Christmas morning.

Abuela had done her best to make Christmas beautiful, and the church had some pretty decorations, but she was feeling homesick. Jenny knew though, in her heart, that she was homesick for a place that didn't exist. Jenny La Chance's life in Vermont was far from ideal. Her chance at the American dream came to a crashing halt when Johnny was lost in the jungles of Vietnam.

Jenny's mom had only taken a brief interest in Jenny's affairs, since she had a new boyfriend and spent most nights at the biker bar outside of town. No matter what Jenny had tried to do, like joining the right clubs at school or trying out for the cheer squad, she couldn't shake her mother's behavior and the ridicule it provided for the popular girls.

Jenny had taken up bowling and was actually quite good at it. She had met Johnny there one night. He told her that he liked her right away.

Jenny was skeptical because she had seen this happen before; a really popular guy would make moves on one of the outcasts for fun. Soon though, Jenny sensed that Johnny wasn't like that at all. If she needed any more proof, a week later she overheard Dorothy Chase telling Marion Madison who did Jenny think she was, turning down Johnny Ambrose, and what could Johnny see in her? She let herself relax a little.

When Johnny asked her to the Valentine's Dance, it became the biggest scandal to hit Rutland High School. Jenny initially said no since she didn't have a proper dress. Her only friend Debby had mentioned it to her older sister Allison, who was home from New York City. If everyone's got one fairy godmother, then Allison was Jenny's. She invited the two of them to NYC the next weekend, where they went out dress shopping. Jenny couldn't believe how kind she was to her. She thanked Allison profusely, but when she asked her why Allison would buy her a dress, she turned to her with a sly grin on her face.

"The Chase family thinks too much of themselves, that's why." Dorothy Chase had acted to Jenny like Dorothy's older sister had acted to Allison. So she showed them. When Jenny and Johnny were named king and queen of the dance, it sealed her fate with the popular girls. What jealousy they had for Jenny and Johnny's relationship seemed to fuse them together.

Johnny wanted to be his own man. But more importantly, he wanted to be Jenny's man. Johnny was a year ahead of Jenny, so when he gave her his high school ring at his graduation party, it made it official. Jenny La Chance would someday be Jenny Ambrose. Jenny could sense, though, that his mother would do everything in her power to keep that from happening. She didn't say it directly to Jenny, but she almost always forgot to invite her to any family parties. Johnny knew what his mother was doing, so he would bypass her and give Jenny a nod in advance. It was like a game to them.

Jenny and Johnny were typical teens, with just one exception. Jenny refused to go any further than second base with Johnny. He wanted to, and deep down Jenny knew she really wanted to too, but she was so consumed by what could happen and how Johnny's mother would use it against her that she blocked any possibility of even crossing that line. Jenny wanted a real ring from Johnny. Jenny wasn't aware of it at the time, but Johnny was working on just that (asking around, looking for rings) and planning a proposal on the day when he got that letter to report to duty in Vietnam.

Jenny had been opposed to the war, but Johnny's family had a long-standing military background, so when Johnny got the letter, there was no turning back. It seemed to delight Mrs. Ambrose that Jenny and Johnny would be separated – maybe he'd forget about her while he was away in the war. Johnny wanted to give Jenny a ring, but his best friend convinced him it was better to wait until he came back. Why he listened to that friend, Jenny never did know, but despite it all, she had his high school ring, and his word.

All through her senior year, she wore the ring around her neck, close to her heart.

The letters came only once in a while, and sometimes she questioned if her mother threw them away. She had been cleaning up after a night of her mom's drinking when she found a letter torn in two in the trash. Jenny was furious, but when she went to confront her mom, she was nothing but scornful.

"Don't be fooled, he is just using you! Mark. My. Words. That family doesn't want *anything* to do with people like us."

Jenny was crying by now. "I'm not like you!"

Her mother laughed. "Not yet you're not, but you got plenty of time."

Jenny was counting the days down until high school graduation, her eighteenth birthday, and when Johnny would be home for good. She had in her mind that 1970 was going to be the start of a new year, and a new decade. She'd have a new name and a new life – but it wasn't Jenny Ambrose having Johnny's baby and living in New England. It was Jenny Morales, having a hippie's baby, in East L.A.

January turned into February without any real differences except that Jenny was getting bigger and bigger by the day. She was hungry *all* the time. Abuela made extra food for her, and Jenny ate it all. She couldn't talk things out with her because of the difference in language. Carlos had only been home once for a few days, and Jenny barely got a chance to talk to him. He patronized her like how she imagined a big brother would do. He told her to relax. "We'll figure it out." He wasn't exactly thrilled with them up at the farm, but he could understand her need to get out of East L.A.

He had asked her if she'd seen the guy who lived there.

"Only once, from behind."

She'd been up to the lodge with Lily. She'd finished transferring the figures from the green book to the black book's ledger when she heard the bell ring.

Lily got up quickly. "I hadn't realized it was this late!" Jenny saw some other girls, a few who she had never seen before, coming out of a side door of the lodge. They walked single file down a garden path to a grove blocked by several large bushes.

Jenny shook her head. She looked over her shoulder to see a man in a golden robe walking towards the bushes. Jenny knew so little about the people living there, despite having worked at Harmony Farms for almost five months.

Abuela could sense Jenny's restlessness. She wished she spoke better English because she wanted to know what Jenny planned to do about the baby. Jenny would have to make some decisions soon. She wasn't fooling herself by thinking that this girl was Isabella, but in her heart, she had a fantasy that she would adopt the baby and make it her own. Jenny could go back to school and start a new life. That's what she prayed for when she lit the candle for the baby. It was selfish of her, but she thought that maybe God would have a little bit of mercy for her soul after all that she'd been through.

She couldn't mention it to Carlos; she felt he wouldn't probably go along with that plan. But she often wondered if Jenny had any family, or if she wanted to go home. A baby changed things. She worried about the influence of the farm girls. She had overheard a conversation on the bus about the guy who ran the farm. He wasn't exactly abusive to the girls, but from what she could figure out, he seemed totally crazy. He did weird things with snakes and drugs. It was all rumors because none got past the farm stand's gate.

Carlos couldn't get comfortable being back in East L.A. It seemed grimy and small after being on the road with Santana. He took a break from being a roadie and went back to the club. He worried about his mother. He worried about Jenny. He worried about the baby. He had a lot of time to think on the road, and he wondered if he had done the right thing by bringing her back to California with him. What did he know about her? Nothing. Just that she had gotten herself into a bind at Woodstock and she was a twin to Isabella.

He worried that his mother was getting too attached and that Jenny might split. He'd seen how hard it was for her at church. No one would speak or could speak to her. People still gossiped that Carlos was the dad. Abuela said to just let them talk.

He didn't think that was healthy for any of them, but he was a "good boy," and he listened to his mother. He didn't want to break her heart any further; he still felt it was his fault Isabella had started to go off on her own. She said she wanted to find a way to get them out of Mexico and not tell their mother. Carlos had listened to her, and now she was dead. He didn't want to give his mother any more pain. All of these thoughts also came to him when he thought of Jenny; but what did Jenny think of them? He knew she was curious, but he would just keep putting her off until the baby comes.

Santana was bugging him to go back on tour by mid-April. So he did. He knew that Jenny would have the baby before he came back, but the money was too good not to take the job. He'd also been seeing a girl named Maria, and he wanted to get her something special – but everything special cost money. The day came when he needed to say goodbye to Jenny, but she was at the farm stand; he took the bus up to find her. He was alone on the bus ride up, so he struck up a conversation with the driver (who could speak both English and Spanish). The bus driver introduced himself as Stan. Stan talked about the weather at first, but eventually, Carlos got him talking about the farm.

"Juan's in on it. He watches out for the guy at the farm who takes all their money."

Carlos was a little confused. "How can that be?"

Stan had a quick laugh. "How can it *not* be? But Juan made some sort of deal with the farm stand to hold their money until Juan can get it so *he* can't grab it. It happens on Tuesdays."

"The guy at the farm hasn't figured it out?"

"Not yet."

"What about Harmony Farms?" Carlos continued, hesitantly.

"What about it?"

"What do you know?"

"I don't know much, only rumor. The girls there don't leave, and they don't take the bus. I only get little snippets from the farm workers. There's one guy who lives there with all those girls, maybe twenty girls. I've never seen him, but I heard he's shown up at some county meetings. Other than that, he keeps to himself. He's got the neighbors creeped out, you know, after all that Charlie Manson stuff," Stan said.

"What do you think?"

"I think he's doing something up there. I don't know how illegal it is, but it is definitely secretive."

"Has anyone been up there to look around?"

"No one gets by Lily. She's in charge of the farm stand, but there's another girl who is nice and works on Tuesday. She's having a baby. I don't know her story, but she doesn't seem like the others."

"Why's that?"

"Well, first of all, she doesn't dress like them, and her name is not a flower."

"They all got flower names?" Carlos asked.

"Yeah, real flower children, I guess. I do three loops a day, so you'd have about forty-five minutes if you want to get off. You seem like you could talk your way into any place. You tour with Santana?"

"Yeah man, I'm going out again soon."

Stan whistled. "Well, man, I wish you luck. Think of me doing my bus loops every day. If you could get me an autograph that'd be great."

As they reached the ridge, Carlos could see Jenny sitting at the farm stand with a big straw hat. Stan asked him, "You want to stop?"

Carlos said, "Sure do."

Jenny's face dropped when she saw Carlos step off the bus. He strode over to the farm stand in his typical swagger.

"Hi there."

"Hi there."

The bus pulled away. Carlos said, "Guess I'm buying produce." He started to look at the tomatoes. He looked at Jenny. Her hair was pulled back in a ponytail, and she looked rested. The air seemed to do her good. Her baby bump was more like a hump now.

"How are you feeling?"

"Pregnant."

"I mean, how is the sun and everything? You got enough water?"

"I think so, but I don't want to have to pee, so I try and limit it."

"That's not good for you."

"Well, it's gotta be good enough."

"Jenny, are you mad at me?"

"No, I'm just cranky today. My back hurts." Carlos thought she was going to say something else but she stopped herself.

"Are you here by yourself?"

"Only for a little while. Rose will come down, and I will go up and have lunch at the lodge and use the bathroom." Jenny paused for a moment. "You going away again, Carlos?"

"I gotta make some more money."

"I know your mom has been saying extra prayers over your candle."

"Well then, I'll have loads of money the next time you see me. Jenny, we never really talked about it… but what are you going to do when the baby comes?"

"I don't know, Carlos. I don't know. You and your mom have been great to me, but I don't think I can stay too long in East L.A. It's too dangerous for me. I don't speak Spanish. The Mexicans aren't sure of me because I don't speak Spanish, and the white people think I'm Mexican trying to be American. I don't know how long I can stay here either."

"Why is that?"

"I don't know. I just got a feeling about this place. The girls are nice and all, but the guy is definitely on something."

"Maybe they're all on something. You don't think they'd hurt you?"

"No, I don't think so. They just sell produce and baked stuff. They help the migrant workers from the big boss ripping them off. I think they might be okay."

She paused again and seemed to be thinking. "I don't know, but sometimes I get ideas that the neighbors don't like them."

Carlos looked at Jenny; she looked parched. "You feel okay?"

"I feel a little dizzy."

Carlos said, "Here, eat these strawberries."

Jenny hesitated, but she wasn't feeling too great and so quickly ate some of the fruit. She definitely felt a little better. Carlos smiled and said, "Here's a piece of gum. Chew on this until I get back."

"Where are you going?"

"To get you something to drink."

"You can't go up there."

"Who says?" he responded. Carlos had strode away before Jenny could say anything else. The gum seemed to help. Carlos and Juicy Fruit always seemed to solve all her problems.

Carlos made it to the top of the ridge before he saw anyone. He saw three girls, all dressed the same, sitting around a table spreading seeds from a distance. It looked like that to him. He waved to them and they jumped up, knocking over the tray.

Two of the girls started to pick up the seeds from the ground. The one in the middle who commanded the situation came toward Carlos.

"Who are you?" she demanded.

"Well, good afternoon to you too."

"I asked you, who *are* you? And what are you doing on this property? It's private. Did you not see the sign?"

"Yes, I saw the sign."

"Who are you?"

"I'm looking for the man of the house."

"What?"

"You heard me!" This startled the girl. She wasn't sure what to say, but before she could figure out what to do, Carlos had opened the back gate beyond the lodge.

The girl rang a huge bell and three more girls appeared, all dressed the same.

Again, another girl said to him, "Who are you?"

He ignored her question.

"Why are you here?" she asked again.

"Men's business. Where is the man of the house?"

Carlos heard one of the girls yell out "Someone get the Gardener!"

Carlos walked down a garden path filled with flowers that opened to a small clearing. When he went through, he could not believe what he saw. It was like something out of a movie. There was this dude with a golden cape, sitting on some silk pillows, being attended by three girls. One caressed his feet, one fed him strawberries, and one rubbed his shoulders. He opened his eyes when he heard the bell.

Carlos glared at him and locked eyes. The golden cape man's eyes were foggy, and he was definitely on something. Carlos thought maybe acid, but he wasn't sure. The bells rang three more times. Three girls who were sitting with the man stood up and took their places behind him. Carlos counted maybe fifteen girls, all the same. They started to hum, and when they got to a fevered pitch the man stood up and faced Carlos.

Carlos said, "Hello."

"Who are you, and why are you on my property?"

"Well, I came up here to find you to ask for some water for the pregnant girl sitting down in the sun by herself at the farm stand."

The man motioned to one of the girls. "Rose, Rose, is that true? Does she need water?"

Carlos was starting to get angry. "Of course, she needs water, rest, and to be able to go to the bathroom when she needs to! She is growing a baby, or weren't you aware of that?"

"No need to get snippy with me, sir. Lily and Rose will take care of her."

"How can I be sure of that?" Carlos steeled his eyes on the man.

"I guess you can't."

Carlos was ready to punch the man. He was getting on his nerves. So much for trusting this guy. All of a sudden, the man started to laugh.

"I have fifteen girls here who can take care of girl things. Daisy, can you run down right now and relieve Jenny so she can go to the bathroom? And bring her some water."

Carlos said, "The baby's going to be coming soon. She needs to be set up at St. Maria hospital if she's here when she goes into labor." He scribbled the address on a piece of paper. "Call a taxi and tell Juan. He'll know what to do."

"Who are you again?"

"Carlos. I am Carlos."

"Carlos, we'll have Rose ask Jenny what she wants."

Carlos was gritting his teeth. "Just get her to the hospital."

The man strode confidently around his other girls. He knew this bothered Carlos. Stroking their hair, and squeezing their shoulders. Carlos wanted to take this guy out, but he could not do it. The girls, whether they were on something or not, gazed at him with adoring eyes.

"I suggest, Mr. Carlos, that our conversation is over."

Carlos put the paper on the silk pillows and turned to walk away. He walked down to the farm stand. Meanwhile, the Gardener took the paper and put it in the small round basket next to the pillows that housed the snake. The snake bared his fangs and swallowed the paper whole.

It was the first time the man had given thought to Jenny's baby, but now it began to consume his thoughts. He'd have to see if it was a little girl first. If it was a little boy, that was simple, but if the gods were talking to him now, there would be a little girl born. He swatted all the girls away and took a hit of the hookah. He was going to be a real father.

Carlos was red hot. He wasn't sure why he held back. Maybe it was because he knew instinctively that the flower children would stand up for the creep on the silks.

He passed by the table where the girls had been earlier. He saw some of the seeds mixed in with some dried herbs, so he pocketed a bunch. Better to know what exactly they were growing. He found Jenny standing in the doorway of one of the cabins. She looked a bit better, not so pale; but he could tell the pregnancy was taking its toll.

"Hey."

"Hey."

She opened the screen door and motioned him to come in. She waddled over to a chair and sat down. Carlos looked around the room. It was pretty empty. Just beds and a desk. Nothing fancy, like what he had seen with the creep who runs this place.

"Are you feeling better?"

"Yeah, Daisy and Rose came down and got me a peanut butter sandwich and some lemonade. They told me to come up here and lie down for a bit."

He went to go fluff the pillow, but Jenny waved him away. “If I lie down, I’ll never be able to get back up on my own.”

“You like it here?” he asked.

“It’s okay. The girls are good to me.”

“They live in this cabin?” Carlos asked.

“Yeah, I think so. Well, at least Daisy and Jasmine. I’m not sure about Lily and Rose, where they live.”

“Why do they all have flower names?”

“I think it has something to do with the Gardener. Or the gardenias. They don’t say things in front of me, but a couple of times I’ve overheard them.”

Carlos was suspicious. “What are they planting?”

“I’m not sure. I only see vegetables and fruits and baked goods, like brownies or small cakes. That’s what I sell.”

“Jenny, I got a weird vibe here.”

Jenny laughed, “It must be all the clean air. I mean nothing says ‘weird vibe’ more than the grimy streets of East L.A.”

“Okay, you got me there. I got to go back on the road with Santana. It’s a short trip this time, like two months. I want to buy something for Maria.”

Jenny smirked.

Carlos said, “You’ll probably have the baby by the time I get back. Promise me you’ll take yourself to St. Maria’s. Maria said she’d go with you. I mean, she can speak English and Spanish.”

Jenny looked away. Carlos said, "No one's gonna take your baby. Unless you want them to." Jenny's eyes were welled up.

"It doesn't matter how this baby comes to be. It'll be loved right and I give you my promise right now. I'll do whatever's best for you and the baby."

"Why is that, Carlos? Why is that? Why are you and your mother so good to me?"

Carlos pulled her into a bear hug and took her face into his hands, so she was looking directly into his dark brown eyes. "That's between God and me."

Jenny tensed, and then relaxed. Whatever deal Carlos had made, at least it was with God and not the Devil. It took Jenny a couple of minutes to regulate her breathing, and then she let out a small yelp. Carlos jumped. Jenny patted the bunk. "Sit."

She placed his hand on her belly and Carlos could feel a real foot moving around. He looked panic-stricken. Jenny laughed. "This happens a lot, it's okay. Yeah, it's okay. I think it's the baby saying 'I'm going to come out kicking.'" Carlos looked at her with wide eyes. He'd never really been this close to a new life. Women were amazing, he thought.

Chapter Twenty-Two

Carlos: May 1970

A few days later, Carlos was on a bus heading north. He'd given the seeds and the herbs to his friend who had a friend who had a friend who could figure out just *what* that stuff was. He'd also had a good couple of dates with Maria before he left. Maybe God was finally forgiving him for his role in Isabella's abduction and murder. Because when he looked into Maria's eyes, he could see the future. He could imagine himself as a father. He just had to make enough money to get out of East L.A.

Maria had mentioned going back to Mexico or Arizona. He'd known she'd been born on purpose in Yuma so that she'd be American. She was lucky – she'd gotten some of her family into the States because of it. Mexico was still too dangerous for Carlos or his mother, but maybe if Maria went to Yuma, he'd follow and he'd get his mother to come as well.

One of the guys on the bus jolted him and tried to pass him a joint, but Carlos shrugged him off. The guy laughed. "More for me." Carlos didn't touch any drugs after Isabella. He liked his tequila alright, but no drugs. No money in the pocket of the cartels. All he could think of was that at the next gig, he'd be able to use the pay phone after the show and call Maria.

That was hours away, so Carlos shut his eyes and drifted off to the sound of wheels on the bus going round and round. He had a fitful nap, and had a dream about his mother whispering in his ear, "All is forgiven," and kissing his forehead.

The bus hit a pothole and the tire blew, jolting him awake. Carlos looked out the window just in time to see a large owl sitting on the telephone line. It gave him the creeps, maybe because he was just waking up, and it stared directly at him before taking off into the clouds. The large bird reminded him of his childhood stories. Carlos hadn't thought about La Lechuza since he was a little boy. He had made fun of the superstitious old ladies in the village when they talked about the owl being a harbinger of bad luck. He'd have to tell his mom about the flat tire and the owl when he got back to East L.A.

He made the sign of the cross and went out to help the guys fix the flat. The dream and the owl were drowned out by complaints of being stuck. Carlos got to work on the tire with the driver's help. He couldn't trust any of his fellow roadies to do much of anything other than smoke up whatever. He wasn't going to end up staying in a ditch.

Santana played extra long. He said it was worth it, 'cause these were the true fans. He liked being out on stage. It took Carlos several hours to break down the stage set. By then it was too late to call Maria, but he'd check in with his mother. He always called her when he'd get to the next place. It was close to midnight. It was too late now, he'd just wait 'til the morning.

They were staying overnight before moving on to the next show in the morning. Santana had messed up the schedule, but what did he care – it was just another night in a hotel, and he got paid regardless. He was moving his stuff into one of the motel rooms when he saw a sheriff coming towards him with the hotel manager. This was never a good thing. They could just pull a guy off and it would make his job harder, but he was in charge of the roadies, so he put on his best face and walked directly toward the officer.

The hotel manager said, "This is the guy I was telling you about, he'd be able to help you." The officer looked at Carlos.

"I'm looking for Carlos Peña."

Carlos's face went pale.

"You know him?"

Carlos said, "Yeah, what's this about? Is he in some sort of trouble?"

"No, nothing like that. I got some news for him."

Carlos figured he might as well get this over with. He saw the handcuffs and the gun.

"I'm Carlos Peña."

"I'm Officer Schmidt," the man said, and he extended his hand. He said, "Why don't we take a seat over there in those chairs."

Carlos was baffled by this but he said, "Okay."

Once they were sitting down, the officer said, "I've been given your name as next of kin for Mrs. Gabriella Peña."

Carlos's stomach squeezed. He knew what was to come next, but he couldn't stop it.

"Yes, she's my mother."

"I'm sorry to inform you, but there was a fire at your mother's apartment building. Your mother made it out of the apartment, but I'm sorry to say she didn't survive. The smoke got her."

Carlos didn't move. He froze. His mind went blank, yet at the same time it was racing. It took the officer a good three or four minutes to shake him back into reality. Carlos stared expressionless at the officer when he asked him if he wanted a ride back to L.A.

One of the roadies, who was high as a kite, came over and slapped him on the back, and said "Sorry, man."

Carlos didn't even feel the guy's hand or the officer who guided him to the cruiser. This couldn't be right, his mother was safe in the apartment over the seamstress shop. The cop must be mistaken.

He’d get it straightened out when he got to L.A. He'd kiss his mother on the cheek and make his empanadas for her. They’d talk about Jenny and the baby, and she’d show him the new quilt she was working on. He’d finally introduce her to Maria.

His mother would know whether Maria was the one. He thought she was, but he wanted to make sure she thought so. He’d do all these things when he got back to East L.A.

What he wouldn’t do was break down. What he would not do is fall apart in the police cruiser, *that* he knew for sure. He couldn’t show his vulnerability. The police could be wrong.

Carlos crumbled and then straightened up.

“Can you give me a ride back to East L.A?”

“Yes, of course, I was hoping you’d say that – I need you to identify the body. There was a young pregnant woman,” he searched for his notes, “Jenny Morales, but she wasn’t there at the time.”

“Give me a few minutes,” he said to the officer.

Carlos spoke with Santana, who said, “Sorry, man,” and said he would pay him even if he didn’t stay with the tour. Carlos walked back slowly to the police cruiser. This wasn’t how he imagined riding in a police car. He couldn’t believe his mother was gone.

Chapter Twenty-Three

Jenny: May 1970

There had been a group of tourists in a small van who stopped at the stand, so Jenny missed her regular bus. Luckily, Stan came around an hour later and Jenny was able to get back to L.A.

Jenny sat up front – it took longer for her to walk now. It was strange how her sense of balance was off, and how she couldn't see her feet. Stan smiled when she got on the bus and asked her where she was going; it was the last run of the night, and he offered to make an unofficial stop for her.

When she told him the address, he grimaced.

"You got family in that area?"

"Kinda," she replied.

"Well, something is going on down there. I think it may be a fire. I'm not sure how big, but they won't let the buses pass 27th Street. Here I am saying I'm going to help you, but I think you might just have to walk an extra block."

Stan continued, “Things burn in East L.A. all the time. Most of the time it’s just punks messing around, but I don’t know, this one sounds more serious. Be careful.”

Jenny started feeling uneasy. “Thanks, I will.”

He dropped her off at 27th Street. Jenny tried to walk quickly towards the apartment. It was almost dark, and she didn’t want to be out on the streets. But as she started to get closer, she started to notice there was a smell of smoke, and crowds around the shop. She couldn’t believe her eyes when she saw the building blackened. Everyone was agitated and shaking their heads, speaking Spanish too fast for her to understand. She got closer and was horrified when she realized that the apartment was gone, as was the shop underneath.

She scanned the crowd. Where was Abuela? She couldn’t find her. Someone pushed her from behind and she almost toppled down. She didn’t know what to do or where to go.

She decided that the church would be the place that Abuela would be; she’d go there. She walked slowly through the crowds. Still, she saw no one she knew.

Our Lady of Guadalupe Church was lit up, and when she opened the door she saw everyone. Everyone, that was, except Abuela. They were all gathered together praying a rosary. Mrs. Gonzales noticed Jenny. She got up and came to Jenny, and said shakenly, “Carlos, you know Carlos.”

"Sí," Jenny replied.

"Where is he?"

"Northern California," she said, vaguely pointing in what she hoped was the right direction.

"You call."

"Where is Abuela?"

"Dead. Dead in the fire."

Jenny put her head in her hands and began to sob.

"You come," Mrs. Gonzales said.

She took her to the priest, who brought Jenny to his office. Jenny was in shock.

"We need to find Carlos. He just started back with Santana. I think they are up in Northern California, maybe Sacramento. He works as a roadie, setting up and breaking down the equipment."

"Do you have a number for him?"

"No, it was on the refrigerator in the apartment. Father, is she gone? I don't understand what happened?"

"They don't know yet, but we have to get Carlos back here as soon as we can. I'll call the police. You stay here in the church for the night. I can get you set up in the rectory guest room. There's some food in the kitchen there too. You'll be okay for a little while."

"Yes, father. Gracias." He put his hand on her head and gave her a blessing. "For your little one."

Jenny had lost everything in the fire, all her clothes and the money she had stashed away. Most importantly, she had lost her sense of security. Jenny didn't trust staying at the church, because she overheard the priest on the phone talking to the adoption agency about Jenny and her baby. Jenny decided she needed to go back to the farm. She was sure they'd let her stay there. She left a note for Carlos, and went back to Harmony Farms the very next morning before he got back.

Carlos got the note and put it in his pocket. He had had enough. He couldn't protect her. He hadn't protected his mother or Isabella. He hated East L.A.

He wasn't going to bury his mother in a grimy L.A. cemetery. He didn't want to, and he didn't have the cash, even though Santana paid him extra and gave him a week off. Carlos made the un-Catholic choice of cremating his mother. Father at Our Lady of Guadalupe wasn't happy with him.

Carlos believed that his mother would have wanted to be back with her family in Mexico. Her hometown too, before the incident with his father. Lucky for him, Maria's family lived near that area too, on the other side of Yuma. Carlos had a big ask for Maria. Could she keep his mother's ashes? When he asked, Maria said she'd keep his mother safe until he came back from the tour, but she was going back to Yuma. She felt it was getting too dangerous in East L.A. He needed to send word to Jenny. Maybe after she had the baby, if she still wanted to, she could come to Yuma. He was still worried about her and the baby, even though she hadn't even waited to see him before leaving for Harmony Farms.

Going back on the road he could relax, knowing his mother was with Maria, and not in some concrete hole outside of Lady of Guadalupe Church.

Carlos didn't have time to go to the farm himself so he asked Stan the bus driver to help him. Stan said that he would. He gave him a note with Maria's address in Yuma.

He had another favor to ask of Stan. He talked with Stan quickly at the bus stop, handing him the address and a pack of Juicy Fruit. "I can't help her right now, but I'm worried about that *guy* up there. Give her this, and tell her that if she needs help or anything, to get Juicy Fruit gum. It'll be our signal."

"I'll do it. Is she your girlfriend?"

"No, just a friend."

"She looks like she could be your cousin, maybe even your sister."

"Yeah."

"You're gonna get me that Santana record?"

"Oh sorry, I forgot with all that's going on."

"It's nothing."

"But yeah, I'm gonna get it for you as soon as I get out of this place."

"I'm sorry about your mother. She was a nice woman; a real abuela to all those girls. She did so much for so many."

"Thanks."

"You take care of yourself."

"I'll be in touch for maybe a couple of months, okay."

"Sure. I'll still be doing this loop." He waved and pulled the door shut.

He threw the notes and gum in his sideboard and looked in the rearview mirror.

He just saw the back of Carlos's head walking away as he pulled away from the curb into the East L.A. traffic.

Carlos had lost everything. It led him to trouble. It led to him breaking the promises he made to himself. He started to get into fights and into drugs. Santana gave him a few chances, but one night he'd screwed up the wiring and the speakers blew. Santana told him he could have his job back if he got his head back on straight. Maria said she wouldn't put up with any drugs, and that maybe it was best for them to split up. She could arrange to have his mother buried in Mexico. She'd give him another chance if he came back clean.

Carlos figured without a job or direction, he'd turn to quick money. If he could just get back on his feet, he could get Maria back. Desperate and needing cash, he took up an opportunity to be a drug mule for a cartel. But the day he was supposed to meet the guy, his car broke down on the side of the road. Carlos had to walk in the desert toward Yuma. He had some time to think about Maria while he was walking toward Arizona. He'd been walking and not paying attention when a huge crow came up and started to caw at him. He started to swear at the crow, but it wouldn't let up. It seemed like no matter what he did, this crow followed him. He stopped for a moment to take a drink from his Coke, and the crow suddenly swooped down to grab a rattlesnake that was hiding in the brush. Carlos watched the crow fly off with the snake.

Not a moment later, a beat-up pickup came to a stop. A guy in the cab said to him, "Hey, that your car back there?"

"Yeah, not sure why it just stopped."

"My name is Gregg, I got a shop in Yuma. I could tow it there and give it a look over."

"Sure, man. Can I get a ride to town?"

"It's a helluva of a long walk, hop in."

Carlos got in the cab. He noticed Gregg had a bobblehead crow instead of a Hawaiian dancer on his dash. Gregg saw him looking at it. "I know, pretty strange, but no hula dancer's gonna save you in the desert like a crow can."

He told Carlos that he believed crows were protectors, if you paid attention to their noise. He'd heard a few stories from guys on the reservation that a crow had shown up just at the right time to save their life.

Carlos told him about the crow and rattlesnake.

Gregg banged his steering wheel. “See, that is what is meant to be, man. You got someone looking out for you. I always think of those crows as big sisters, always nagging. Ya know? I got three. You got any sisters?”

Carlos just said, “I did once.”

Gregg sensed he’d gone too far, so he backed off.

Carlos and Gregg made small talk the rest of the way to Yuma.

He decided right then that he’d die in the desert if he went back. He didn’t even go back to East L.A. for his stuff.

Everything he needed was in Yuma. He couldn’t believe what a fool he had been. Whatever it took, he’d win Maria back. If Jenny needed Carlos, she’d have to come to him.

His big sister was nagging him to get on with his life. He whispered to the desert wind, *Muchas gracias, Isabella.*

Chapter Twenty-Four

1970

Jenny arrived at the farm stand and found Lily there. Lily looked up, surprised to see her, as it was a day she wasn't supposed to come.

"Are you okay?" Lily asked her as she walked up to the stand.

Jenny hobbled over and said, "Not really."

"What's going on?"

Jenny explained about the fire. She hadn't mentioned much about where she lived, so she kept it to a minimum. Lily had been there the day Carlos came so rudely up to the farm, so she had figured she'd been staying with him.

Lily had to find a place for her because she could tell the baby would be coming soon. It looked to her that she'd dropped. Not that she had experience in that, but she could see it in her baby bump. "Of course, you can stay here," Lily said.

"Come on, let's get you settled in. I think there's an extra bunk in the cabin with Daisy." Lily didn't mention that she secretly had hoped Jenny would stay. For she had seen the gleam in his eye when Carlos had mentioned the baby and getting her to the hospital.

Jenny followed behind Lily until she got to the cabin. She was tired. "You rest now. It'll be good for the baby." Jenny didn't argue. She pulled the covers up and lay on her back. She had trouble sleeping now, but the baby settled in and she was able to sleep soundly.

When Jenny awoke, it was pitch black. She hadn't been at the farm the night before. She looked at the other beds. Daisy and Jasmine were sleeping, and the light from the moon crept in through the window. She looked at the bedside table and saw two sandwiches wrapped in the familiar brown paper and a pitcher of water with a glass. She was thirsty, so she drank two full glasses before she opened the sandwiches. Who knew you could survive on peanut butter and jelly? All that water made her have to get up to use the bathroom, she hoisted herself up from the bed and went into the small bathroom.

There was a mirror over the sink, and Jenny could barely recognize herself, so she splashed water on her face hoping to improve the image. Still, a tired bloated face stared back at her. She wondered if she'd ever feel normal again.

It was only a year ago she was so filled with hope. She was going to be Mrs. John Ambrose, and start a new life with Johnny outside of Rutland. The reflection asked what she was thinking, keeping this new life in her for so long. Maybe Abuela had been right to suggest adoption, but she'd already lost so much. It was a bit selfish for her to think she could take care of a baby, but Jenny thought if her drunken mother could do it, then she could do it better. She'd give this little life a real chance to be someone.

She was clumsy getting back into bed and woke up Daisy. Daisy said, "You okay?"

"Yeah, thanks." Jenny laid back down and started to think of all she'd been through in the past year. A large tear appeared in her eye and spilled down over her cheek. Things had to get better. They just had to.

In the morning, there was a bell. Daisy and Jasmine woke up and made their beds. They changed their dresses and pulled their hair back. Daisy said, "Come, Jenny, you need to get up or you'll miss breakfast." Jenny lumbered up. Her back hurt, but she didn't mention it. She wasn't really hungry either. She followed Jasmine up the hill to the lodge. When she got there, she saw a long table with fruits and bread, and another table with juices and tea.

There was a farmer's table in the middle of the room with several chairs on each side and what looked like a throne at one end. It reminded her of the tables in a medieval castle. Jasmine said, "We've made a seat for you down this end. You can go and get what you want, and stand at this seat here. We have to wait for him to come and do the blessing before we eat."

Jenny said, "Okay." She had only seen him from behind, but she'd have to follow the rules – she had nowhere else to go. There was a swish of golden fabric, and he arrived. Jenny watched the faces of the other girls and got a creeped-out feeling.

The girls started to hum. They sounded like bees. Bees buzzing around a hive.

Jenny looked down and waited.

He opened his mouth and gibberish came out. No one else seemed to notice but her. He pulled a large snake from a small basket and raised it over his head. All the girls had their eyes closed and were swaying and humming so they could not see what he was doing. Jenny pretended to have her eyes closed, but as she peeked through her drooping eyelids, he was smirking. He put the snake away and rang the bell. The girls all opened their eyes. He said he'd gotten a message about a new life, a life coming into our midst.

The hairs on the back of Jenny's neck rose as he strode towards her. He stood behind her and put his hands on her shoulders. Jenny felt an electric charge go through her body. She wanted to get up and run as far as she could from this situation. She hadn't seen this side of the farm. Hadn't she listened to Juan? Something was not right here, and she'd gotten herself in the middle of it. She wasn't listening to what he was saying because she was so distracted by his touch. He was giving her a new name. Venus.

Jenny thought of her science class with Mr. Bigelow. The Venus flytrap was kind of a flower? Right now she felt more like a fly than a flytrap. As soon as he took his hands off her, her body relaxed. He picked out three of the girls and they gathered some food and followed him out of the lodge. The rest of the girls ate in silence.

That was how Jenny became Venus.

Harmony Farms wasn't what Jenny had imagined. She had thought all the girls were happy. Instead, she found they were all competing for his attention and favor. She wasn't sure what drugs they were on, but they were all on something, willingly or not. She didn't have too much time to ponder the situation at the farm, because her baby had other plans. Perhaps it was the stress of the fire or life in general, but after a week she started having back pains. Jenny had no idea that it was the beginning of labor until her water broke.

She had been standing up separating seeds and pods when a giant gush of water flew out from under her. Daisy had been next to her and heard her groan. She gasped and said, "Jenny, it's time."

Jenny said, "Yeah, I think you're right. My water just broke." Jenny wanted to go to the hospital.

Daisy said, “Let me get Lily.” Lily came and said that she would be much more comfortable up in the garden room. Jenny kept protesting. “I want to go to the hospital.”

Lily ignored her pleas and said to her, “Venus, come with me, you'll be more comfortable in the garden room. It’s been prepared for you.”

“My name is Jenny!” she screamed.

“Here you are, Venus.” Lily called Jasmine and Ivy to help Venus walk to the garden room. It wasn’t easy for her because the contractions would make her body shudder in pain.

Ivy whispered in Jenny’s ear, “Don’t worry, Jenny, I’m here. I delivered a baby once before.”

Jenny whispered back, “I want to go to the hospital.”

Ivy said, “That’s not his plan.” Jenny/Venus stumbled along, worried about the “plan.” Ivy was true to her word. She took control of the situation once Jenny started with the real hard contractions.

He had come to watch Venus give birth but got bored when it took too long and Jenny’s screams disturbed his peace. He exited the garden room with a swish of his golden cape, followed by Lily. Lily told Ivy to send Jasmine once the baby had arrived and was cleaned up.

Ivy nodded and then whispered to Jenny, “Let it all out, Jenny, that’ll keep him away. What an ass he is.”

“Ivy, thank you.”

"Okay, now I'm going to say you got maybe three good pushes, and you'll have yourself a brand-new baby. So are you with me, big breath push?"

Did Jenny feel her inside moving?

This was happening. The pain came and went, but there was this overwhelming feeling of wanting to let go. Ivy had been right. It took two more pushes and Ivy delivered the baby. She cut the cord and said to Jenny, "You got yourself a brand-new baby girl."

The baby's cry startled all of them. Ivy said, "You got to get rid of the placenta now, just one more push." She did, and now Jenny was free from the trapping of internal birth.

She asked to see the baby. The baby took her hand and Jenny's heart melted. She could never give this child away. Ivy said, "She's beautiful. Look at that hair sticking up." Jenny laughed because it reminded her of a cornstalk.

She thought, *My little Maizey.*

"Maizey. That's what I'll name her."

Ivy said, "I think that suits her. If it's okay, I'll just wash her up quickly and weigh and measure her. Then we'll see if she is hungry. Jenny, you'll be ready to breastfeed." Jenny hadn't been thinking about that, but all she could think of was having the baby close to her. She felt safe with Ivy. When Maizey came back she was washed and swaddled; she was even cuter than before.

Maizey took to breastfeeding, and Jenny took to holding her. Ivy said she weighed seven pounds eight ounces and was nineteen inches. Time moved slowly, but he eventually came into the garden room. He came over to Jenny, and kissed her on the head. He did the same thing to Maizey. "A little bud. How beautiful," he said. "Venus and her baby in my garden."

Jenny was weak from delivering the baby but she said, "I want to go to the hospital."

He said, "There is no need for that. Ivy is here. Did she not take good care of you? She can help you and the baby. I think that you should stay in the garden room. I'll have Rose gather your things from the cabin. We will get you strong and get the baby ready for a naming ceremony."

"I've already named her."

He looked past her and said, "It's only the name I give her that's important."

Jenny had always heard about a mother's instinct. Her mother, of course, didn't have it, but Carlos's mother did. She knew that there was danger for her and the baby at the farm. She just would have to figure out how to get away. She had no money. She'd just had the baby. She had gotten this far; she'd figure it out.

Jenny and Ivy became fast friends. Jenny learned that Ivy had been at the farm for two seasons, which Jenny figured was about a year and a half. Ivy told her that she had stumbled upon the farm when she was hiking with some friends. They had run out of money, and Lily had offered her a place to stay in exchange for work at the farm and a little money. Ivy said she was tired of her friends and the drugs they were doing, so she decided to split off from them.

She had thought maybe she'd stay a couple of months and then make her way back down to Southern California and complete her nursing degree. Ivy had started working as a candy striper and moved her way up to nursing assistant. All of these dreams Ivy had were sidetracked about a month after she'd been here. She'd been watching the other girls. She'd been sure that they were being drugged. Some of them willingly, and others may be unaware.

Ivy had decided that she would leave the farm, but Lily and the Gardener had other plans. Ivy, whose real name was Cathy Mullins, underwent the naming ceremony. She had been brought to the silks like Jenny had remembered, but Cathy had been given a goblet of wine laced with some kind of drug hallucinogenic, which Ivy had guessed had been grown on the farm.

She experienced some brainwashing, fact-finding about her life, and a terrifying snake bite. Ivy showed her the mark on her forearm. All the girls had them. It was a branding. She was given a new name and a role at the farm. Since she had worked at the hospital, she was given the task of making sure the girls had health care and proper birth control.

Jenny looked at her. Ivy squinted back and whispered: "You know that all the girls here have to give one night to him a month."

Jenny was shocked. "Even you?"

"Even me," she said flatly.

"Why do you stay?" asked Jenny.

"I have nowhere else to go, and he's got files on all of us that he says he'll release to the police if we leave. I haven't been able to figure out how to get out of this place. Besides you, I'm the only one with a clear head. I convinced him that I should be drug-free so I can take care of the others, so the only time I drink from the goblet is on my one night."

Ivy continued, "You're safe for a while because of the baby and your body healing. He won't expect anything from you."

"Is he crazy?"

"I think he's schizophrenic or delusional or he's taken so many drugs himself that his brain is mush. I don't know exactly."

"He's dangerous."

"He is, but Lily really pulls all the strings around here. Be careful around her. I'm going to ask Lily if we can be bunkmates so I can help you with the baby. That way I can make sure they don't do anything to drug you or hurt the baby. She's so cute."

"Thanks," Jenny said. "Why are you helping me?"

"Well, I think you're our best chance at escaping here."

"How's that?"

"I don't know yet, but something will come to us."

"I think you're right. We can get out of here. But we have to plan it smart because all eyes are on me and Maizey."

Jenny avoided her duty as Venus for six months. That was how long Ivy could make up medical conditions (beyond breastfeeding) that he would believe were true. Maizey had started eating solid food, and Lily noticed.

One afternoon, Lily came for her and told Ivy she'd be watching the baby overnight. Jenny had no choice but to go with her. Lily told her that she was to complete her naming ceremony with the Gardener *tonight*.

She led her back to the garden room, where she was told to take a bath and wear a wispy white gown. Jenny looked for an escape but there was none.

She instead looked for evidence and looked for anything. She'd never been in this part of the farm. She was supposed to be meditating, but instead she was sleuthing.

She looked in the trash, but nothing. Where would Nancy Drew look?

She noticed a large portrait of the Gardener on the wall. The frame was embellished with gold, but it was slightly off-kilter. Behind it, there was a safe. She thought that was where all the secrets were kept. How would she ever get into the safe without knowing the combination? She heard a commotion outside the door and ran to sit cross-legged on the silks.

Lily peered in. "Good, you are preparing for his arrival." She brought in some grapes and a large goblet. "He will arrive shortly. You must be ready. Venus, this is an exciting night for you. You will finally be a full member of the sisterhood."

Jenny just nodded. Since giving birth to Maizey, Jenny's attitude toward life had changed. She was now responsible for this baby. She had never felt so much love for anyone, even Johnny. It made her protective. Her friendship with Ivy made her smarter. Jenny had always been prone to being impulsive, especially since she had always been cleaning up her mother's messes; now, she saw the advantage of patience and trying to get a plan.

She'd do whatever she had to do to get her and Maizey out of this place, even if it meant being on the silks with the Gardener. She had a flashback to Woodstock and thought it couldn't be any worse than that, but Jenny was wrong.

Lily came back and brought a small, round basket with a cover that she placed near Jenny. She then came back with two golden goblets and a carafe of wine. She placed them on a small table.

She rang a gong and the Gardener appeared. He was wearing his golden robe and silk pants. His chest was bare, and Jenny could see that he was pudgy.

Lily slipped out of the side door and the Gardener said in a loud voice, "Can you hear me?"

Jenny heard a crackle and said, "Yes."

"Let's begin then."

The Gardener added something to one of them and then poured the wine. He mumbled something Jenny couldn't hear, but he gave her the goblet. He instructed her to drink it. Jenny drank the liquid – it had a bitter aftertaste. The Gardener kept mumbling gibberish and then began to caress Jenny's arms and shoulders.

He whispered into her ears, but her head was starting to explode and she couldn't feel his caress. She knew that she had been given something powerful. Maybe she'd not make it through this night, maybe this was worse than Woodstock. She'd overestimated her ability to control the situation.

The Gardener opened the small basket and took out a snake. Jenny knew in her rational mind that it wasn't a dangerous snake, but when he pushed it close to her ear she could hear its heartbeat. It was terrifying. Then the questioning began. He asked her about her past, her family, everything. Carlos. His mother. Every time he felt she was holding out a detail he'd bring the snake close to her ear again.

Jenny tried to run, but her legs wouldn't move. The only thing that moved at the moment was her tongue, and it revealed all her secrets. When the Gardener was satisfied, he let the snake bite Jenny on the arm. Jenny didn't feel it but there was now a mark on her forearm, two fang marks.

The Gardener took two drops of the blood and put it in the empty goblet. He added the powder and wine before he drank it.

He said, "You can turn off the recording now." A woman's voice came back and said, "I got it all. Glory to the Gardener."

The Gardener raised his goblet and said, "Glory to the Gardener," and drank it down in one swig. He laid his hand on Jenny's belly. There was nowhere for Jenny to go, even though her mind was gone. So she looked past the Gardener's pudgy body and continued to examine the portrait on the wall. She knew there was something she wanted to remember about it.

Jenny must have had a blackout at some point, because when she opened her eyes, he was gone. Maybe it was good that she couldn't remember exactly what happened to her. She knew she had been raped more than once by the Gardener. She saw flowering bruises on the inside of her thighs and there were remnants of his bodily fluids there too. Her head and her arm hurt.

She pulled her arm around and she saw the snake bite. This terrified her. Her mind wasn't exactly clear, but she thought something sinister was going on here. She wanted to take shower. Lily appeared with a freshly ironed tunic and a plate of muffins and tea. She congratulated Venus and said that she could take a shower and change into the tunic.

Ivy had said Maizey was crying for her and that she should go to her cabin. Venus nodded. She noticed the portrait was moved back into place. Her brain registered it. *There's something in that safe I need.* She felt sore and scared, but she had Maizey to worry about so she showered as much as she could to get the stench of him off her, and then ran to the bunkhouse, where Ivy was rocking Maizey to sleep.

Ivy was relieved to see her, and took Maizey into her arms. Both mother and daughter sighed and relaxed.

It took Ivy and Venus six weeks to come up with a plan. They both were concerned because Maizey was starting to toddle and Lily had mentioned that she was planning a bigger ceremony for Maizey around New Year. The Gardener had gotten in his mind about time and the New Year baby.

There had also been an incident where one of the girls, Violet, went missing and was found wandering in the neighbor's land. It brought the sheriff's department up to the farm, but Lily had been ready for them, and they walked away satisfied that it was just a misunderstanding.

Ivy said they needed a miracle, but they just needed to be in the right place at the right time. Venus knew from her time doing accounting work for the farm, that things were put into the safe at a certain time each day. Lily was the one who opened and shut the safe as far as she could see. The Gardener was crazy, but Lily was smart.

Ivy and Venus came up with a two-part plan. First, to collect as many documents as they could. Second, to get out of there as quickly as they could. They would need help and perfect timing. A miracle. Venus could not believe how patient she'd become. She knew that she and Ivy had one solid chance to get away, so she wasn't going to blow it on an impulsive move. They had a backpack packed and they could move at a moment's notice.

Jenny had told Ivy that Carlos would help them once they got out of the farm. She'd spoken to Stan, and he'd given her the note after the baby was born. Jenny had wanted to say more, but Lily was always watching.

Jenny and Ivy caught a break about the week before Christmas. There had been a flu going around, and Lily herself was sick. She sent Venus down to the farm stand by herself while Ivy took care of business in the office.

Ivy had watched Lily; she knew most of the time people kept things simple as far as safe combinations. She also wondered how the Gardener could remember the numbers. Ivy had never been close to the portrait, but when she got right up to it, she could see three numbers painted on the snake's back. She tried them, and it opened the safe. Inside was a tape recording, a ledger of seeds, and quite a bit of cash.

Tomorrow would be the day. She would make sure Lily was given something to make her sleep, and they could empty the safe and finally get off the farm.

Ivy told Venus what she had discovered. The girls planned out what they would say and what they would do. Venus would talk to Stan on his first ride by the farm stand and then they would hop on the second bus to freedom.

The next day the plan went off without a hitch. Jenny, Maizey, and Cathy didn't even look back as the bus chugged down Route 93. Stan asked where they wanted to go.

Cathy spoke up: "FBI office."

"I'll call you a cab from the bus station."

Jenny said, "I want to go to Yuma."

Stan looked at her closely. "You're sure?"

"Yes, I'm sure."

Jenny and Cathy were happy to call each other by their real first names. Cathy encouraged Jenny to come with her to the FBI, but Jenny said she couldn't because she had a fake name and her daughter wasn't registered.

Cathy and Jenny decided that Jenny would take their tapes and half the money. The rest would go with Cathy to the FBI. They were certain that once this all came out, Lily and the Gardener would be arrested. They were also certain that they wouldn't let things go either. Cathy wondered out loud about the witness protection program.

Jenny wasn't convinced.

Cathy and Jenny parted ways. They hugged each other goodbye, and wondered if they would ever see each other again. Maizey gave her a sloppy kiss and a wave goodbye. Cathy walked toward the FBI office. Jenny walked towards the bus stop. She could see Cathy walking up the stairs and the door closing behind her.

Her bus arrived, and she put Maizey on the seat next to her. South to Yuma they would go. It hadn't been that long that Carlos would have forgotten them.

Meanwhile, Lily woke with a start. She felt a rough push, and opened her eyes to see three FBI agents with guns drawn. It took her a moment to realize what was happening. Lily hadn't prepared for this exact scenario, but as she looked into the barrel of the gun, she thought to herself, "This was good while it lasted, but I'm not going to take the heat for this."

The FBI agents pulled her up and slapped the cuffs on her; she barely had time to breathe – but she wasn't one to give anything away.

She asked if she could go to the bathroom. The agents shrugged; they had no reason not to allow it.

Once inside the bathroom, she found a silent button that awakened all the girls, and they had been programmed to destroy incriminating items that implicated her. No one could say that Lily did not have a strong sense of self-preservation.

An FBI agent rapped on the door. Lily flushed the toilet and emerged with a Cheshire cat smile and thought she might just get out of this mess unscathed. As she was handcuffed, she thought to herself, *It was good while it lasted.*

Carlos had just gotten home from work. He and Maria had only been married three months, so they were still living at her mother's house. The phone rang and Maria answered it. She handed the phone to Carlos. He couldn't understand the quizzical look on her face. He was thinking it was Gregg from the shop.

He took the phone. "Hello?" He nearly fell to his knees when he heard a baby being shushed on the other end.

"Maizey, shush now," Jenny said into the receiver. "It's me, Jenny. We're at the bus station in Yuma on 12th Street."

"I'll be there in twenty minutes. Stay put."

"Okay, Carlos."

He hung up the receiver and hugged Maria. "Jenny's coming with the baby."

Maria knew what this meant to him and his late mother.

“Go collect her and I’ll talk to my mother,” she said.

That was how Jenny and Maizey came to live in Arizona.

Part Three

Chapter Twenty-Five

Monday, February 3, 1986

It wasn't supposed to go down like this. It wasn't supposed to involve Maizey until she was eighteen, Carlos thinks to himself. He has three problems right now. One is getting to Jenny; the others are to explain to Maizey what's going on, and to find a gas station with a phone.

Maizey looks scared sitting in the front seat of the car, rubbing her hand and twisting the turquoise ring Jenny gave her for her fourteenth birthday.

"Hey, you okay?"

"No, I'm… It is okay. No, I'm okay. Where is my mom, Carlos? Shouldn't we call the police?"

"I'm sure the rehab hospital has probably already done that, but we got to find her first."

"Before the police?"

"Yes, before the police." He flicks his fingers through his hair and says, "There are things about your mom you don't know."

Maizey gives Carlos a cold stare. She starts to say something but instead turns away.

Carlos says, "I don't know what this accident did to your mom's memory of things, but it looks like she's got things out of whack. Your mom likes to run usually away from things, but this time she's running *to* something."

Maizey feels defensive of Jenny, and angrily replies, "Who let her run, Carlos?"

Carlos feels those words like a dagger in his heart. He let his sister Isabella run, and now he's let Jenny do the same.

Looking at Maizey in the seat next to him, he thinks, *Maria was right – we should have told her years ago*. But his plan with Jenny is just two years away. When Maizey turns eighteen, no one will be able take her away. They both have done a good job sheltering Maizey and deflecting questions about her mom's past and who her real father is.

Maizey stares at Carlos and says, "Are you going to tell me now, Carlos?"

He has to tell her something. He's just not sure Jenny would be able to tell her anything. It is now on Carlos's shoulders. He needs to think it over more, and he needs to talk to Maria. She was the one who convinced Jenny to write Maizey a letter to open on her eighteenth birthday, and she was the one who told Jenny that Maizey deserves the truth about who she is. Maria could calm Carlos down, and tell him what he should say to Maizey. He doesn't want to do this. He doesn't want to hurt Maizey, but the truth is the truth and she deserves the answers.

Carlos sees a gas station, and he pulls in to get gas and use the phone. He asks Maizey to get a couple bottles of Coke and some chips. Maizey says she's going to use to the bathroom, while he gets gas and calls Maria on the pay phone.

Maria answers on the first ring. She tells him the rehab hospital called and Jenny didn't show up. They contacted the police, and everyone is looking for Jenny.

Carlos says, "She left the pack of Juicy Fruit. I think we both know where she's headed."

"I think so too. I'll ask Mrs. Gomez to watch the girls after school and I'll drive over there."

"We got to find her before the police. I got Maizey in the car with me. She's angry. She wants to know."

Maria coos to Carlos, "You knew this day would come. You can do it."

"I don't want to be the one to break her heart."

"Carlos, stop it. She's a beautiful young woman. She's not a child anymore. She deserves the truth."

"How much do I say?"

"Just enough. Don't go into too much. It will be a lot for her."

The operator interrupts, "Deposit of fifty cents for the next three minutes."

"The pay phone numbers have been scratched out, so you can't call me back. I don't have any more change. Maizey's coming now. *Te amo*." Click. Dial tone.

Everything's moving so fast. Carlos is driving fast and talking fast. He is saying things about Mom that I don't like. I snap at him, and even behind his sunglasses, I can see he's hurt by my words. I'm sick of it now. I feel like everyone else knows what is going on but me.

I feel trapped in the car not knowing where we are going. Carlos says to me, "Your mom likes to run away from things, but now she's running to something."

I feel mean inside, so I say, "Who let her run Carlos?" I stare hard at him and say, "Are you going to tell me now, Carlos?"

He doesn't answer, but instead pulls into the gas station and hands some money to me. "Get us some Cokes and chips. I'm going to use the pay phone."

I grab the money from him and go to the restroom first. It's dirty and gross. The sink is cracked, and the faucet makes a loud clunking noise. I wash my face and look in the mirror. I'm mostly angry. I'm angry at the world. I want to wipe it away with the paper towel, but the angry face is still there. I think I would cry if I wasn't so angry.

I get Cokes, chips, and a Snickers bar for myself. Maybe I'm getting my period, so maybe I'll calm down if I eat the Snickers bar. I can see Carlos hanging up the pay phone and walking back to the car.

"Maria says hi."

I just hand him his Coke and bag of chips. He doesn't even make a joke about the Snickers bar. The doors slam and we pull out of the gas station.

I say, "Where are we going?"

He says, "San Diego."

"San Diego?"

"Well not exactly, just outside – closer to Arizona."

"Why are we going there? "

"To get your mom."

I scream at him, "Why is my mom going to San Diego and what is going on? Carlos, stop treating me like a baby. Tell me! I know you and mom have lots of secrets. I know there's something not right about something. You guys never thought I knew something wasn't right? Why don't I have any family? Why aren't there any baby pictures of me? It makes me super mad sometimes, because you and Mom don't say anything. I want to know. I have a right to know."

Carlos lets out a long, exasperated sigh. "That's what Maria told me. "

"Finally, someone with sense. Maria."

Carlos says, "We have a few hours to get where we are going, so I'm going to tell you some, okay? Not everything, because there's so much, and you'll have more questions than I can answer, okay?"

"Okay. I guess."

Carlos looked at me hard, really hard. "Some of it isn't good, Maizey. Most of it isn't."

I'm putting in a brave face, but inside I'm scared shitless.

He continues, "We still have to get your mom and get her back into rehab. Whatever her brain is doing is mixed up, so we have to go slow with her. I promise you right now that I will make sure you know everything, but we still have to take care of your mom. "

"Okay, just start talking. I love Mom and I want her to get better too."

Carlos says, "Can you give me the Coke?" He takes a large swig and starts talking. His eyes are straight on the road so he doesn't have to look at me.

"I met your mom at Woodstock. I was there helping Carlos Santana's band. It was a crazy place. Lots of music, drugs, and free love. I was starting to pack things up and went down to the underside of the bleachers. I saw a hippie leaving, and heard some crying. It was your mom, Maizey. She looked just like my sister Isabella. I thought it was her at first in my mind, but I knew she died in Mexico. I wanted to help your mom, she was so distraught. I had seen enough of Woodstock, so I asked your mom if she wanted to come with me to California and stay with my mom. Your mom said she had nowhere else to go because she couldn't go back home. So we left, and that's how we got to East L.A."

Carlos is talking and I'm trying to think about what he's not saying.

I'm thinking about the Woodstock video we watched in history class. I'm thinking my mom was there. She barely lets me do anything. I'm thinking about why my mom would be distraught, and would just go with a stranger from New York to Cali. Carlos had a sister? I want to ask questions, but I'm afraid he'll stop talking, so I start listening.

Carlos gives me the side eye to check on how I'm doing. I open my mouth, but then close it. I so want to say something, to jut in, but I'm scared he'll stop talking – this might be my only chance to hear about what my mom and Carlos have been hiding all these years.

Carlos asks, "You okay?"

"No, not really, Carlos, but…"

He interrupts me. "Maizey, it wasn't supposed to be like this. Your mom and I had a plan that when you turned eighteen, we'd tell you the truth."

I glared at Carlos, still feeling a bit mean inside. "Does everyone but me know this truth?"

"No, only me, your mom and Maria and …"

"And who, Carlos?"

"Some dangerous people."

I laugh an awkward laugh. "Right," I say.

"Maizey. Have I ever lied to you before?"

"Well, apparently all the time."

Ouch, I could see Carlos flinch; I didn't care.

"I know you're mad, Maizey. I'd be mad too, but we got a couple of hours in this car together – why don't we just listen to the radio for a while."

"Sure, whatever." I go to open my Snickers bar and say, "But I want the whole truth before we get where we're going."

He says okay and turns on the radio.

I just want to go to the Valentine's dance with Beto. I'm tired too. I decide to shut my eyes and let the desert roll by. Wherever we're going, I have to trust Carlos to know where my mom is. I wonder why they would not tell me until I'm eighteen – is Carlos serious about dangerous people and my mother was at Woodstock? I don't want to think of any of it right now. I wish I could talk to Jenna, and I wish I was putting my head on Beto's shoulder instead of the hard metal door frame of Carlos's car.

The cab driver drops me off at the bus station. He has to open the door because my arm is in a sling. He says, "You okay?"

"Yeah, I'm okay, but I've got to figure out where to get a ticket."

He points in the direction of the glass door. He says, "I drop a lot of people off here for the buses going west towards L.A. and San Diego. Sometimes I even pick people up, here's my card." He hands me a business card. "For when you get back in town if you need a ride."

"Thanks," I say. He gets in his cab and takes off toward Phoenix.

I grab my bag with my good hand. My head feels wrong. I start to walk to the door, but a man comes up behind me and says, "Let me get that for you." He opens the door and smiles at me.

"Thanks."

He says, "You look like you've had a hard time." He points to the bump on my head.

"Yeah, car accident."

"That's why you're taking the bus?"

"Yeah. Do you know where the ticket booth is?"

He says, "Follow me, I'm going to get a bus ticket too."

I follow him up to the counter and he makes a dramatic gesture. "Ladies first."

I say to the ticket agent, "I'd like to buy a bus ticket to San Diego. Well, La Plaza, California."

He says, "You'll have to go to San Diego and ask them once you get there how to get to La Plaza. One way or round trip?"

"One way."

"You're in luck, the next bus is leaving in twenty minutes. It just started to board over at platform 3."

I pay for the ticket and start to walk toward the bus. The guy who opened the door for me is walking toward the platform.

He looks back at me and says, "You going to California?" I nod yes.

"Yeah, me too."

"San Diego?"

We hop on the bus and he says, "Let's hope this bus isn't too long of a ride."

He takes a seat on the way back. I stick to the second seat behind the driver.

Everyone's on the bus, and I'm glad to be sitting down because I'm really tired. It's not a full bus at all. I look over to the seat across the aisle and I swear I see Abuela.

She smiles at me and I shut my eyes.

The bus lurches forward and heads toward California.

I blow with the wind and last night the winds changed.

I'm sitting down getting ready to enjoy my steak bomb and watch Jessica Fletcher when there's a rap at the door.

I try to ignore it 'cause I don't hear anyone say a thing. The rap gets louder, and then I hear:

"Harold, it's your PO. Open up."

I lower my voice. "How do I know?"

He says to look through the peephole. I see his badge, and I think, *Shit*. He's got me on a parole violation. I open the door because I don't want to make it worse. I open the door and he's there with some chick who'd be hot, but she's got an FBI vest on.

"Can we come in?"

"Do I have a choice?"

He looks at me and says, "You always have a choice. Now, Harry, listen, you've got lots of choices right now."

The FBI agent closes the door behind her. She identifies herself as Special Agent Mullins.

My PO starts in, "I got you on a parole violation, right? Okay, Harry. Whatever happens next is up to you. I'm going to read your rights, and you can let me know if you want an attorney. We can settle this downtown, or you can voluntarily answer some questions and assist in Special Agent Mullins's investigation."

I know how this goes. If I lawyer up, they'll be after me. I'll get no peace, so I decide to cooperate. They start with good cop, bad cop. I see where it's going. I agree to all their terms, and even sign the papers. They give me a recorder and a tracker. All I gotta do is do what I was doing for Crazy God, except now it's for the Feds.

I only look out for numero uno. They don't call me Houdini for nothing. Soon as this is over, I'm getting the hell out of this country. I never want to see an FBI or friggin' PO again. If you can't fight 'em, join 'em. By the time they're gone, the steak bomb is cold and Jessica's solved the case.

In the morning I head back to the hospital to see what Jenny's up to.

I start walking toward the entrance, when I see Jenny being pushed into a wheelchair and start to get into a cab. I think, *WTF is going on*? I reach the entrance just as the old lady turns to go inside. Another cab pulls up, and the driver looks confused.

I say, "Hey man."

He says, "I get all the way over here, and there ain't no one to pick up!"

"What do you mean?"

"I get a call to pick up some chick and bring her to rehab. They said she'd be out here."

"That cab at the light, I think he's got your fare."

"Shit, you're right. Son of a bitch, he's stolen my fare."

"Look, I'm here early to visit my sick aunt. How about we go after that cab? I'll pay the fare."

"What's the deal?"

"I don't know, just help out another working slob."

"All right, pal, we better get going or we lose 'em."

It takes about ten minutes to get to the bus station.

He says, "Maybe he didn't steal my fare. Chick was supposed to be going to rehab."

I say, "Okay. Hey, I gotta get some cash at the bank, so I'll just hop out." I hand him a tenner.

"Thanks, man, call me if you need a ride back to the hospital."

"For sure, but you better get back before someone does steal your fare."

"You know it." I watch him drive away.

She doesn't look right. She's got her arm in a sling, and she's trying to open the door. I come up behind her and say, "Let me get that for you." I open the door. She says thanks.

"You look like you had a hard time." I point to the goose egg on her head.

"Yeah, car accident."

"That's why you're taking the bus?"

"Do you know where the ticket counter is?"

I say, "Follow me, I'm going to get a bus ticket too." I make a big show of saying, "Ladies first."

She's buying a ticket to San Diego. I overhear that she wants to go to La Plaza. There's nothing in that small shithole town, but I'm almost done with this whole God damn mess.

She's talking to the bus agent. I slip the tracker into the side pocket of her bag. I gotta keep my eye on her until she's not my problem anymore. I get a ticket for the same bus.

I say, "You're going to California?"

She replies, "Yeah, me too."

"San Diego?"

"Yeah." We walk over to platform three. She takes the second seat behind the driver. I go all the way to the back. I say, "Let's hope this bus isn't too long of a ride," as I pass by her.

I settle into my seat. The bus isn't full, so I can watch her from a distance. She seems pretty knocked up, like she shouldn't be on the bus but still in the hospital, but I'm no doctor.

The bus pulls out of the terminal.

The driver announces that we'll stop in Yuma for a half-hour break, and to pick up more passengers. I can use the pay phone there and call my PO to tell him what I know.

I guess now I can just enjoy the beautiful desert.

I start thinking about Jessica Fletcher; maybe I got it wrong. If the Feds aren't after me, maybe I should try my luck up in New England.

The bus stops at Yuma and I walk by her. She's asleep. I use the pay phone and my PO says he'll meet me at the bus station in San Diego.

I grab some chips, a Coke, and a cold-cut sandwich from the rest stop.

I walk by her and she's still asleep. Someone's in my seat, so I move closer to her, two seats behind.

The bus heads towards San Diego. Just a couple of hours and I'll be done.

Carlos pulls over at the rest stop. I see a bus going towards Phoenix parked by the gas pumps. There are a few people getting out to stretch their legs. Carlos says to me, "Maizey, if you've got to use the restroom, you better get ahead of those bus people."

I say okay.

He says, "We're not gonna stop until we get to San Diego. If you want anything else to eat, you'd better grab it."

I rush off to the bathroom, and get in right before a huge line of grandmas.

I walk past the cooler case and see the cold-cut sandwiches. I can't think of eating those, so I just get two bags of peanut M&Ms and two waters.

Carlos has the car facing the highway ready to go when I get out to the lot. I hop inside and open the pack of M&Ms. Carlos dodges the traffic and we're now on a long stretch of road.

He turns to me. "Your mom, well, she never wanted to hurt you, she just wanted to protect you. You gotta know that. Everything she did was to protect you."

"I still don't understand what I'm being protected from," I spit back at him.

"The Gardener."

"Stop with the bullshit, Carlos. The guy who cuts the grass?"

"No, this one is in jail."

I'm confused, but am getting mad again because I feel like Carlos is talking in circles. I give him a super hard stare.

"Okay, Maizey. I get it you're pissed. I'm doing the best I can. So let me just start again, okay?"

"Okay, as long as it's the truth and makes it so I can understand it. Not guess at it. I got so many questions."

"Okay, so let me go back to the beginning again. Your mom came to East L.A. with me. She stayed with my mom." He crosses himself. "My mom didn't speak great English, and I had to go back on tour with Santana. Your mom looked Mexican enough, so I knew a guy who could get her a fake ID. She didn't want to go back East – she made that pretty clear to me."

I look at him, bunching my eyebrows. "Back East?"

"Yeah, I think Vermont or New Hampshire." He starts talking quickly. "I don't know what happened back there, except that she refused to talk about going back. She said there was nothing there for her. She said she was eighteen and no one would be looking for her."

"And you believed her?"

"Why wouldn't I? She barely spoke to me from Woodstock to L.A. I didn't question it, because I wanted to make things right for her."

"That's just plain weird, Carlos. You find a stranger and take her across the country, get her a fake ID, and then what?"

"It was only supposed to be a temporary thing for all of us. Me, my mother, and your mom. I thought maybe she'd want to go back after she got over her shock, but that's not what happened."

I start to get agitated again. I scream at him, "Well, what happened?"

Carlos looks at me and looks away. He won't look at me.

His voice shaking, he says, "She found out she was pregnant with you."

"Stop the car."

"I can't, Maizey."

"I can't stay in this car. I'll jump out." I start to open the door. I can feel the breeze across my legs.

"Shit, Maizey, shut the door. Okay, I'll pull over." I see a switchback sign.

I say nothing. My mind is racing. Carlos is my dad, all these years. They have been lying to me. I can't stand the look on his face. I feel so lied to. I can't believe him.

Carlos pulls off to the side of the road. I get out of the car. I start to pace.

I'm so enraged. I shout at him, "I hate you. I hate my mom. I can't believe anything you say. I thought you and my mom were like brother and sister but you …"

"No, Maizey, it's not like that." He goes to grab me.

I shout at him, "Take your hands off me."

"Maizey, please let me finish."

This time he grabs me and forces me into one of his bear hugs. I struggle and I am holding my breath. When I let out my breath, the tears come. I'm heaving sobs. A mess.

Carlos picks up my face and says, "Maizey. I'm not your dad."

I let go. I shake my head. "No no no."

"I'm not your dad."

I'm still shaking my head.

"I'm not your dad."

I can't take much more. I say, "Who's my dad?"

"I don't know. That's the truth."

I start to pace again. I'm thinking that I just want to go back to before the *Challenger* exploded. My head on Beto's shoulder. I'm crying again.

Carlos is looking anxious. He's running his fingers through his hair, and tugging at his clothes.

"Maizey," he says, "we gotta get going. Please get back in the car."

I look around at the scrub brush. There is nowhere for me to run, so I hop back in the car. Carlos is speeding. My head is spinning.

I can see the sign saying *Welcome to California*. It won't be much longer.

"Maizey, I'm sorry. I'm really not good at this."

I don't answer. I just look away. He tries to put his hand on my hand, but I yank it away. I give him the side eye and notice he's wiping his face. He adjusts his sunglasses so I can't tell he's crying.

Neither of us says anything. I'm just trying to put the pieces together. Who is the Gardener? What makes him so dangerous that Carlos and my mom had to protect me? Who am I?

I start to cry, and think, *Will Beto still like me if I'm not who I say I am?* Will I ever get to go to the Valentine's Dance?

There's a voice far away calling to me. I must have been asleep, because everything feels foggy. I open my eyes and see the driver; he's shaking my good arm and saying, "Miss, you got to get off the bus. Do you need a doctor?"

I pull myself up quickly and the wooziness hits me. I say, "Just give me a minute. We're in California?"

"Yes, San Diego bus station."

I pull myself out of the seat and I can feel all the pain. Whatever painkillers they gave me must be wearing off. I scowl, and the driver sees, and says, "Are you sure you don't want me to call a doctor?"

"No thanks."

"Someone meeting you here?"

"No, I got to get a cab to La Plaza."

"Well, the cabs are over there. Doesn't look too busy. Let me help you out of the bus." He grabs my bag and strides toward the cab station.

The man who opened the door for me is talking to another man. I am getting paranoid, because I think they are looking at me. I can see him shake hands and take an envelope with the other man and head to the bus station.

I follow the bus driver over to the cab station. One of the cabbies says, "Where are you going, miss?"

"La Plaza Cemetery."

"Okay, you got cash?"

"Yeah."

"We can settle up when we get there. Let me get your bag."

I see him take my bag and put it in the trunk.

"Hey, I want my bag in the seat with me."

He says, "Sorry, miss," and he goes back and puts it in the side door.

I rifle around in the bag. Nothing missing. I say, "You know where it is?"

"I'll call it in." I hear him over the microphone. "You want the east gate?"

"I don't know?"

"Maybe the east gate. It's the closest to the road."

I think for a minute. "Yes, the east gate."

"All set. It should take us about twenty minutes."

He pulls out of the bus station, and a cab behind us pulls out too.

He watches me in the rearview mirror. I can see my face. He says, "Me and Joe been sitting there all morning with nothing to do but eat tacos, and the bus comes and we both got fares."

"That's good."

"You got a broken arm there."

"Yeah, a car accident."

"Oww. That's gotta hurt. You been to the hospital?"

"Got out this morning."

I've got to act normal. The pain in my head is getting worse.

I say to him, "It's been a long day. I'm just going to shut my eyes."

"Okay, I'll let you know when we get to the east gate."

"Miss, we're here."

I open my eyes, and I see the other taxi cruise by us. My driver gives him a toot and a wave. The cab turns into the cemetery. It's bigger than I remember.

"Do you know where you want to go?"

"It's been a while. Just drive towards those maple trees."

He points towards some trees, confused. "Those are maples?"

"Yeah, Japanese maples."

"Well, you learn something every day. I thought maple trees only grow in Canada or Vermont."

The mention of Vermont makes my head pound.

"You sure you're okay, miss?"

"Yeah, I'm meeting someone here."

He looks ahead to the left and says, "I see a guy over there."

I look too. It's Carlos. He's leaning on his car with Maria.

I can see Maizey sitting in the car with her back to them. I say, "There are the people I'm meeting."

Carlos sees the cab and waves his hand. The driver pulls up to him. Carlos pokes his head in the car and says, "Hi, Jenny."

"Hi, Carlos."

The driver says, "Let's help you out," but Carlos interrupts him and says, "I got it from here." He grabs the bag and gives the guy twenty dollars.

I step out of the car.

Carlos says, "You doing okay?"

"I'm not sure. Maizey with you?"

"She's in the car."

"Okay. Let's get this done."

He brings me over to the Japanese maple. It was only a sapling sixteen years ago. There's a cement park bench that's engraved *PVT John Ambrose – RIP. Love, Jenny.*

"You okay? Maria brought a shovel. It's in the car."

<u>Maizey</u>

"Carlos?"

"Yeah, Maizey?"

"Is my mom going to be alright?"

"I don't know, Maizey. This time I don't know."

I want to hear more, but I don't want to hear more. I want to know who the Gardener is and I want to know why he is dangerous. I want to know, but my head is exploding. I want to run – but I can't. I just can't. I try to think of something else, like something I did with my mom that was fun. I want to think about anything else except the car accident and whatever this is, Carlos and my mom's secrets. Secrets.

The first thing that pops into my head is the time we made a blanket fort, ate popcorn, and read Nancy Drew. The batteries ran out in the flashlight. It was really funny. Well, at least at the time, it was super funny. I was about eight.

I try and think of another time we had fun together. Anything. Nothing comes to me. Why can't I think of one time in my life with her that was fun? I'm struggling, and I hit the side window with my hand. Carlos notices but says nothing.

He says after a couple of minutes, "I know I said I wasn't going to stop, but I was thinking that I'd like to get a coffee and a burger at McDonald's. I going to just go through the drive-thru. You want anything?"

I start to say no, but I change my mind and say, "Sure. That sounds good."

We are both eating our burgers and I say, "Carlos, what if Mom… you know what if."

"I don't know, Maizey. This time I don't know. Only the doctors can say."

"Carlos, I can't remember anything fun I did with my mom."

"Ever?"

"Ever."

"Maizey, I..."

"Carlos, I'm so confused inside. I'm mad. I'm sad. I'm scared. I am anxious. I'm tired of all of this."

"Maizey, me too."

"Carlos, I don't want to hear any more about it. I don't want to know who the Gardener is until we get my mom back to the doctor. I just don't."

"Okay," he whispers and the tension runs from his face and I guess he's secretly relieved.

"We can talk about that whenever you want, but right now we got to get your mom."

"Okay," I sip on the coffee. It's starting to wake me up.

"We're almost there. Maria should be there. Your mom, I don't know."

He pulls off the ramp and takes a right at the lights. He says, "Here we are."

"A cemetery?"

"I haven't been here for a long while. Where are those trees?" he's mumbling to himself.

I look out and see some real trees, not desert trees.

I point towards them. "You mean those?"

"Yeah, those Japanese maples."

We get a little closer and I can see Maria in the other car, but no one else is here except for a couple over at another grave. We pull up behind Maria.

Carlos gets out of the car and speaks to her through the window, she gets out, and they have a long embrace. He turns to me, but it's Maria who comes over.

"Hi, Maizey."

"Hi, Maria."

"You want to get out of that car and come over and sit with me while we wait for your mom to show up?" Her eyes are soft and kind.

"Okay." I get out of the car and Maria grabs my hand and gives it a squeeze.

I go sit in the car with my back facing the maple trees. Maria scrunches down and gets close to me. She says, "You'll be okay, Maizey. You'll be okay. Be gentle with yourself."

I must look doe-eyed, because she takes my face in her hand and stares deep into my heart. She starts to say something, but changes her mind. She says "I love you, come here," and hugs me. I hug her, and dissolve again into tears. There is so much pent-up emotion; I can't stand it.

We wait for about half an hour. I decide to get up and stretch my legs. I walk back and forth behind the cars. I can see the couple still at the grave but they look down when they see me look their way.

Carlos suddenly looks up. “I think I see a cab coming. Let’s pray it’s your mother.”

The cab starts to slow down, and when it gets close, Maria says, “Stay here with me – if this is your mom, let Carlos help her first.”

“Okay.”

Carlos goes over to the cab and says something in the window. He goes around the side of the cab and opens the door. I see my mom – she’s got her sling on and some weird outfit. She doesn’t look good. She shouldn’t be out of the hospital.

Carlos takes her by the hand and heads her to the maple trees. There must be a bench or something there because she sits down.

He starts to walk back to the car and grabs a shovel.

I look away from my mom and I see the couple moving closer to us.

Carlos can’t see because his back is turned and Maria is watching Carlos.

My mom doesn’t see them because her eyes are shut.

Chapter Twenty-Six

Monday

Carlos has three thoughts at the same time: *Jenny looks bad and she needs to be in a hospital; I broke Maizey's heart;* and *Thank God for Maria*. He starts walking back to the bench with the shovel. It should only take a few minutes to dig up the box, and then he can secretly drop it off at the FBI office. There should be enough stuff in the box to keep the Gardener in jail forever, and maybe even get that other one too.

He gets to the bench and sees Jenny closer up. She looks so pale, almost white. He coos to her, "Jenny, are you okay?"

She opens her eyes a crack and says, "It's gotta end here."

"I'll bring the box to the FBI. I'll take care of it. Maizey, she's safe. Maizey's with Maria over by the car. She's safe."

"You haven't given her the letter yet?"

"No, not yet."

"You will though, she needs to know." Jenny puts her hand to her head.

Carlos says again to her, "You okay?"

She says, "I'm okay," but he knows she's lying.

"Get the box," Jenny says in a hoarse voice.

Carlos has his back to the cars and Jenny has her eyes closed; they don't notice the man and the woman walking towards Maria and Maizey.

Carlos makes two scoops with the shovel and hits something metal. He bends down to loosen the box from under the cement bench. He is so engrossed in what he's doing that he doesn't notice the man walking toward him and Jenny.

Jenny opens her eyes and sees the man coming forward. She starts to get up from the bench. She moves too quickly, and puts her good hand up to her head and loses her footing at the same time. Carlos tries to buffer her fall, but she tips to the right and bangs her arm and then her head on the cement bench.

Carlos drops the box and twists around to see the man and Jenny on the ground. He looks at the man, and says, "Call 911." He goes around and lays Jenny on her back.

As he's doing this, he sees the gun holstered at the man's waist and he realizes he's some sort of cop. The man says nothing, but has put the box to the side.

Out of nowhere, a woman comes running over to Carlos and Jenny. She has a gun holstered as well; she says to Carlos, “Don’t move her.”

She identifies herself as Special Agent Mullins with the FBI.

Jenny’s eyes are fluttering, and Special Agent Mullins says, “I have some medical training, let me check her breathing.”

Carlos steps back, and Agent Mullins gets close to Jenny. She says in a really quiet voice, “Jenny, Jenny, you’ve got to open your eyes. I know you can.”

Jenny’s eyes keep fluttering but they won’t open. Agent Mullins says, “Jenny, it’s me. Ivy. Come on, Jenny. Maizey needs you.”

Jenny’s eyes open a crack. “That’s it, Jenny. It’s me, Ivy. Open your eyes. We got away. Remember, we got away. Maizey’s safe. Come on, Jenny, open your eyes and stay with me.”

Jenny opens her eyes and tries to focus on Ivy’s voice. She groggily says, “Ivy?”

“Yes, Jenny, it’s me. Maizey’s safe. He can’t hurt her. No, he can’t ever hurt her.”

“Promise?”

“You got to stay still.”

There is the sound of a distant ambulance. The ambulance is coming.

Jenny looks to Carlos. “You’ll take care of Maizey?”

Carlos strokes her cheek gently. “Yes.”

Jenny starts to cry from the pain. “My head, my head.”

Ivy says, “You hit your head on the bench.”

“It hurts so much.”

“You got to try and keep your eyes open. Keep looking at me or Carlos until the ambulance comes.” Jenny has shut her eyes again. Carlos looks up and sees the EMTs running over with the stretcher.

Mullins pulls him away.

She says, “There will be plenty of time for me to question you later. Right now, I’m going to allow you to go in the ambulance with Jenny to the hospital.” She nods to the man. “You got the box?” He nods.

She looks at Carlos with a hard police stare and says, “Is there anything else anywhere?”

“No, this is it. This is everything we got.”

“Okay, Mr. Peña. I’ll follow up with you later today at the hospital. Don’t worry, we’ll take good care of Maizey and your wife. No one is in danger. In fact,” she motions to the other officer holding the box, “if I recall correctly, some of the things in that box will make everyone safer.”

Carlos says to Special Agent Mullins, “You’re really Ivy?” She doesn’t say anything. She just rolls up her sleeve to show him the distinctive snake bite marks on her arm.

Carlos crosses himself because it’s a miracle. Everything might just work out.

The man and the woman are coming right toward us. The man is wearing a jacket and there is a gun holstered on his belt. Maria sees them at the same time as me. She pushes me down and stands in front of me. She must have seen the gun too.

The woman motions to the man to go to where my mom and Carlos are. She holds her hand up, and then shows the FBI on her jacket.

All I can think of is my mom. I go to twist to see where the man went and I hear Carlos yell to call 911, and see my mom next to the bench on the ground. I go to stand up but the woman says to Maria, "Stay here. I'm FBI and I have medical training. Please stay here until the ambulance comes."

Maria nods and says, "Maizey, we need to listen to her."

"Okay," I say, but my eyes are fixed on my mother. She's lying on her back. The woman is close to her, probably talking to her. I can't see whether she's awake or not. Maria takes me by the shoulders and we watch. Just watch. I see the man take some sort of box that Carlos has dug up. The woman is talking to Carlos and he's nodding. He crosses himself. I hear the ambulance before I see it. Everything's in slow motion. They take my mom and Carlos in the ambulance.

It's so quiet once the ambulance leaves. Maria and I wait for the FBI to come over. Maria is tense. I can feel it. I just want to go home. I start to cry again. The woman directs the man to bring the car around. He has the box in his hand.

She comes around to us. She looks at Maria. She looks at me.

She says to Maria, "I'm Special Agent Cathy Mullins of the FBI." She extends her hand. "I'm on a special task force investigating human trafficking and illegal drug smuggling. We have been investigating recent activity related to the cold case of Harmony Farms."

"I want to tell you that none of you are under arrest. I want to assure you that anything that happened surrounding Ms. Morales's and Mr. Peña's involvement with Harmony Farms is not punishable by law."

I say maybe a little too loud, "What's Harmony Farms?"

Special Agent Mullins looks at Maria. Maria shakes her head.

Mullins says, "There'll be plenty of time for that later. Maizey, do you have any questions for me?"

My head hurts. I want to explode.

"Can I see my mom?"

"Of course, let me check with the other officer to see what hospital she's been taken to. Do you think you could drive your car, Mrs. Peña?"

"Yes, I think I'm able to drive."

Mullins points her head to the other car. "Why don't you lock it up? It should be fine here until either you or Mr. Peña can come to pick it up. Mrs. Peña, may I speak to you privately?"

"Of course."

Adult stuff again. Right now, I'm just tired so I don't give fuss or try to eavesdrop.

They walk a little ways away from me. Special Agent Mullins says "Off the record," and I can't hear the rest but I see her roll up her sleeve and show Maria something.

Maria gasps and then crosses herself. She and Mullins hug.

They come back to the car, and Special Agent Mullins still has her sleeve up. I can see what she showed Maria. It's the same weird mark on her forearm my mom has. I don't understand. My mom always told me it was a weird snakebite she got once hiking in the mountains.

Agent Mullins sees me looking at the mark and rolls down her sleeve.

Maria is more relaxed now. She's almost smiling.

The other officer comes over and says my mom has been taken to Memorial Hospital on Ocean Drive.

Mullins says, "Why don't you follow me?"

Maria says, "Okay." We get into the car.

I look at Maria, and I say, "Why does that FBI lady have the same mark on her arm as my mom in the same spot?"

"There'll be plenty of time for that later."

Everyone saying the same thing. I'm a little frustrated when Maria starts the car and pulls out behind Special Agent Mullins.

"Later." That's all everyone is saying to me.

"Maizey."

I start to cry, "Maria, I'm scared and tired. I don't know what is happening. Will my mom be okay? What did Carlos and my mom do that the FBI is here?"

"Your mom and Carlos did nothing but protect you from a dangerous man. They did it because they love you so much."

I try to let that sink in.

Maria continues, "Be strong right now. Later, you'll get all the answers to your questions. Your mom needs you."

I start to cry again. "Maria, is she going to be okay?"

"I don't know. I don't know, Maizey, but she's back with the doctors so I guess all we can do is pray."

We pull up to the hospital, and soon I'll know about what is going on with my mom and later I'll find out everything else. I walk into the ER and a guy is leaning against the door. He looks like Beto. I think, *God, please don't take Beto from me and help my mom get better*.

Chapter Twenty-Seven
Maizey's Journal

Friday, February 7, 1986

A lot has happened since Monday. First off, I got a counselor: Sharon Mason. The hospital and Carlos + Maria have been keeping me talking, but sometimes I don't want to. So Sharon says I should write down any thoughts or feelings I have in this journal. I don't have to share it with anyone if I don't want to.

I haven't been back in Phoenix since last week. I haven't talked to Jenna or Beto.

I'm really afraid to talk to Beto. Carlos and Maria say if he's a good guy, he'll be good to me. I want him so badly to be a good guy, but what if he isn't?

Next week is the dance so I gotta tell him what's going on in case he wants to take someone else. I guess I'd understand if he did.

My mom is still in the hospital. I go every day to see her, but she's still in the coma like before. The doctors are worried about her because they found she had at least two other head injuries from a long time ago, maybe from when she was a kid. Her hitting her head on the bench has made everything worse. I don't know what to think about my mom. It's really hard for me to go in there and see her. I get upset with myself because we had that fight, and I just want things to be back to normal.

I want her to get out of the hospital and come back to the apartment. I wouldn't yell or do anything to upset her.

Every day, I sit in her room and listen to the beeping of machines and I wonder if she'll ever wake up. That's when Sharon came in to talk to me. She told me it was normal to feel sad, and even mad. She gave me this journal and told me to write down my thoughts and feelings.

Carlos has been so upset because he's had to go back to Yuma to go to work but Maria has been staying with me here. It's easy to be with her. I still don't know what I think of all of the other stuff too. There's just too much.

I haven't told Sharon about all the other stuff with the FBI and Harmony Farms. I barely understand it myself. The FBI lady, Special Agent Mullins, is Cathy Mullins who my mom knew as Ivy at Harmony Farms. She was the one who delivered me? It's weird so weird to meet that person. She was able to tell me a little about

Harmony Farms and the marks on their forearms. I'm sure there more she's not saying and I'm kind of glad 'cause with everything else I don't know if I could handle it.

Everyone keeps saying that everything my mom had done was to protect me. Protect me from this dangerous guy, the Gardener. My whole life my mom has been living a lie. She's not Jenny Morales. She's not Hispanic. She's not from California. She's Jenny La Chance. She's French Canadian. She's from Vermont. So who does that make me? It's all messed up! Do I have any relatives there? Will anyone come and try to take me back to Vermont? I don't want to go to Vermont.

I want to stay with Maria and Carlos. I want my life back with Beto and Jenna.

I want to go to the Valentine's dance. I want Beto to be my Prince Charming and live happily ever after.

Maria says there's a letter for me that my mom wrote to explain everything about before she met Carlos at Woodstock. It's at their house in Yuma and I can read it whenever I want. I asked her if she or Carlos ever read it, and she said no, it was private and not her story to tell. She never really talked to my mom about "the before times" because there was so much else to do.

She explained how we just came to her and Carlos after escaping Harmony Farms. She said my mom was so stressed about the Gardener finding me and her. She had some papers and money she'd stolen. Carlos had some seeds and a report from a friend that said they were growing drugs that made people black out.

Carlos and my mom found the graveyard in California and decided to bury all the stuff in case they needed it later. Well, it's later. Just sooner than they thought.

My mom was so afraid that the Gardener would come and take me back to Harmony Farms because he forged my birth certificate to say he was the dad. So they were going to tell me when I was eighteen and he couldn't get me.

All of this. All of this is too much.

I want my mom to wake up so I can ask her, Why did she do what she did?

I want my mom to wake up because I want to.

I want to yell at her. Okay, I said it.

I want to yell at her, why? Why? Why did you not tell me the truth?

The truth is, I think my mom isn't really brave.

Carlos says she is. Cathy says she is. I think she's…

I think she's good at getting people to help her because they feel sorry for her. Oh God, I'm sorry, Mom. But it's true. The machines are still beeping. Her eyes aren't open. She doesn't want to face reality.

Okay, I'm starting to get mad now. I have to face all of this reality without you.

Without you. I don't get how you get to just lie there and not deal with this, and I have to stress out over everything?

Who am I?

Where am I going to live?

What am I going to do?

It's too much, Mom!

If I had something to slam I'd do it. maybe that would wake you up.

Oh shit, I said I wouldn't do anything if she just came back to the apartment. But I slammed the door the last time. That was probably the last thing she heard me do.

I'm sorry, Mom. I didn't mean any of it.

I hate this. All of it.

Monday, February 10

I am back in Phoenix. I am sitting in my bedroom. Everything looks the same.

It's weird to be back here without my mom. Carlos and Maria dropped me off, and Lisa is staying with me at night until we can figure out what to do.

Mom is still in the hospital in California. She hasn't woken up, even as they start taking her off the meds.

I know that's not a good thing, because I overheard one of the nurses say to Maria in the hallway the words "brain damage." Adults still think they can protect me by not saying things, but I can tell they are worried. It's the way they look at the chart and the beeping machines.

I think the only adult who gets me is Cathy Mullins. She's been to the hospital a couple of times to check on my mom, and she'll sit and talk to me. She must have had some sort of training at this 'cause she's super good at it. I feel comfortable with her. Carlos, who is my guardian at the moment, told her she had permission to say whatever she wants to me. He told me that she would have more answers about your mom and the Gardener than he would. So, she comes in and we talk.

We'll mostly talk and I listen. She told me about when I was born. She told me how she and my mom escaped and got the Gardener and Lily arrested.

She told me she decided to be an FBI agent after Lily was let out because of some stupid rule. She really wanted to get Lily back in jail and help other girls too.

I can hear Lisa doing what she calls putzing around the kitchen. She rearranged all the cabinets, so I can't find anything anymore. She says she'll stay out of my room, but I think I better keep this journal with me all the time. She seems like a snoop.

Maria and I talked about what I should say to Jenna and Beto. I kinda wanted to tell them everything and I kinda wanted to say nothing about it because I didn't want to answer questions. Maria said it was up to me.

Jenna came over the minute she saw the car this afternoon. I think Maria must have called her mom, because she was on her best behavior. She was so glad to see me and she said that Beto would be too. She said she and Damien were tight now. She barely looked at any other guy, well, except Marcus. “Well, you know Marcus,” she said, and she fanned herself.

I laughed. I hadn’t laughed in a long while. Jenna said, “Let me look at you, your makeup is a mess. Let me touch it up.” She does the whole bit and I look in the mirror, it’s an improvement. She says “I say tomorrow night we do face masks! Maybe even get Lisa to do it.” Now this made me laugh. I said okay.

I told Jenna that I was nervous about going to school tomorrow, but she said that I shouldn’t worry, and that I got her, Beto, Damien, and the Jones brothers.

I thought to myself, “The Jones brothers?” Jenna was trying to make the story better by mentioning them; I groaned and said to her that I couldn’t believe that.

“Well, they said they were sorry about your mom and she was always nice to them,” Jenna told me, “so anyone who messes with you will have to mess with them.”

Weird. Jenna says she thought so too.

Sharon the counselor told me to write everything I can remember down. Like if I was explaining it to someone else, so if I want to talk about it, I remember it. Since I may not see her again.

Carlos and Maria are working to try and move my mom to a hospital in Yuma. It's too hard for her to be in San Diego and there's something about insurance. I don't understand. No one's saying anything to me about what is going to happen.

I know there are a lot of things that are complicated, like legal things.

Carlos says not to worry about that right now. He's starting to be silly with me again, I think it is the twins. They give him no peace since he's been back, Carla makes him practice every day for the show wearing the tutu. When I said something about Beto, he started to whistle "Maizey and Beto Sitting in a Tree." I think my face must have turned red because Maria smacked him in the arm. Carlos just shrugged and winked at me.

Sharon said if I have something hard to write, I should write all kinds of other stuff first, and then the last part will be easier.

Beto. Beto Beto.

I called Beto's house, but his mom said that he was away for the weekend. Some camping weekend thing with his cousins, she said that he'd get back later tonight. I told her that he could call me if he wanted to. I gave her my number. I said "Maizey, just Maizey." Weird, I just could not say my last name. 'Cause it's not my real last name.

Well, it's almost 9:30 pm and Beto hasn't called. I guess I'll just have to see him at school tomorrow in Chem class. God, I'm so nervous no not nervous petrified. He won't like me anymore.

10 pm:
Oh my God, I just got off the phone with Beto. He's going to pick me up tomorrow so I don't have to take the bus. I didn't even have to say anything about the dance. He said that if I wasn't up for the Valentine's dance, his mom said I could come over to his house for dinner and a movie. I was nervous, but when I asked him if he still want to go to the dance, he said yes! I made sure to say "Me too." He told me he was sorry about my mom. I said "Thanks, Beto." It was really sweet. We laughed for a bit, but then he said was really tired from sleeping in a tent. "I'll pick you up at 7. Okay?"

Okay, good night Beto. Good night Maizey. See you in the morning.

I get Beto to myself before school.

I hope I can fall asleep.

Tuesday, February 11, 1986
I kissed Beto! I mean, he kissed me. A real kiss, not just a peck. It happened, it really happened! He held my hand too, a lot. Like in between classes so everyone could see!

Some of the track guys slapped him on the back. My face didn't even turn red.

I can't stop smiling.

This is how my day started. Lisa was up with a full breakfast ready. I nibbled at a few things, but I was too nervous to eat. Jenna came over and I told her that Beto was picking me up. She hugged me and said to have fun.

I waited outside with her until I saw Beto's car. He waved to me and he came around to open the door. I'll have to tell Carlos that. He'd like to know that. The bus came so we had a minute in the car by ourselves before he started.

Beto looked at me. I looked at him. I remember every detail so clearly. He turned to me and said, "I haven't been able to think about anything other than you, I know it's stupid, Maizey."

I said, "It's not stupid."

"I've been really worried about you 'cause of what happened to your mom. I'm sorry."

"It's okay, Beto. My mom, well, she's in the hospital and the doctors are taking care of her."

"Are you okay?"

"Kinda. I don't know what will make me feel better."

Beto looked at me after I said that, and moved closer. My heart stopped. He took his hand and put it under my chin. He brushed his finger along my face. I could not stop looking into those deep brown eyes.

He tipped his head and looked like he was going to say something, but instead, he put his lips on mine. Gently.

My hands moved up to the back of his neck and he opened his mouth and really kissed me. It felt like a second but I wanted it to go on forever.

After he pulled away, he said to me, "I wanted to do that for a long time. Was it okay?"

I looked at him like melted ice cream. I said back to him, "It was perfect."

After that, he shook himself and put the key in the ignition, and said that we had better get to school. He kept his hand on my knee as we drove to school. He asked me when we got there if we could get together after school. I told him I didn't know yet, so he asked me what my schedule was today. I told him, and he asked me if I could write it out for him in Chem class so that he could see me between classes!

That's how it went all day. Jenna was feeling a little left out 'cause I barely saw her all day and she was dying to know what happened with Beto. I was happy to have Beto with me in the hall, 'cause I could hear some of the girls whispering behind my back.

During lunch period, I had to meet with the principal. He said he was sorry about my mom and that he'd spoken with the teachers to arrange tutoring sessions to catch up. He said he would call Carlos to arrange all the rest.

I was starving by the time the last class was out. Beto came and found me in the hallway outside the classroom.

"Are you going to Chorus?"

I said, "Yeah but I'm kinda hungry 'cause I missed my lunch block. I'm going to walk down to the vending machines."

He took my hand and said, "Okay, let's go." We got down there, and he asked me what I wanted, before buying us a Coke and some chips. We sat down at the picnic table side by side. When he put his arm around me, I felt safe for the first time in a long time. He laughed a bit. I looked at him, wondering if I did something wrong, but he saw my face and asked me, "Maizey, is this our first date?"

"I don't know?"

"I can do way better than this. I hope you'll let me take you out soon. Maybe even before the dance?"

"I'd like that."

He said nothing, but kissed me again ON THE LIPS.

He ran his fingers through his hair, kinda like Carlos does, and said, "I gotta get to practice. Do you want a ride home? I can wait."

I told him, "No, Jenna and I can take the late bus." Then he asked if he could call me tonight. "Sure?" I said, and he gave me a quick peck before he ran off to the locker room.

I didn't have much time to think about anything 'cause Jenna appeared. We had some time before Chorus, so Jenna made me tell her the story of today at least three times.

I'm glad to write in this journal, 'cause by the third time Jenna's kinda changing things, and I want to have the official record of my first Beto kiss when I'm older.

The rest of the night, I was thinking only of Beto. I mean in the in-between times.

Carlos called and said he'll be at the school tomorrow to sign some papers. He said they are moving my mom to another hospital this weekend. They finally got the insurance stuff figured out.

While on the phone, he said that I don't have to come to Yuma this weekend, and when I asked why, he just started to whistle "Maizey and Beto," and brought up the Valentine's Dance. Maria started griping at him in Spanish then, and he said "Okay, okay. Here's Maria," and handed the phone over to her.

Maria told me to pay no mind to him.

"Do you need anything for the dance?"

"No, Jenna and I are going to get ready together. She's got more than enough stuff."

"It's good to have a friend like that."

"Yeah. Jenna's a good friend."

Since it's my journal, I can write what I want. I don't have to write anything I don't. I don't have to write about my mom today.

This day was the best day of my life.

Beto called to say good night. We talked for a little bit, really about nothing. I just like the sound of his voice.

I like that it was the last voice I heard before I go to sleep.

Good night journal.

Saturday, February 15, 1986
Yesterday was the best night of my life. I have to pinch myself. It really happened.

All of it really happened. I don't want to get out of bed because I'm afraid I was dreaming, but then I look over and see the corsage on the side table and I know it was all real.

I think I might be in_____with Beto… I don't want to say it, because I don't want to jinx it.

Me, Jenna, Damien, and Beto went together. Damien borrowed his brother's Caddy, so Beto and I sat in the back. Jenna's mom took pictures of us. I can't wait for Jenna to bring them to Fotomat so I can see them. She promised she'd do it today.

Beto said I was the most beautiful girl he'd ever seen and gave me a corsage. I never felt so happy, like, from the inside.

It just kept getting better. Beto was always by my side. Touching me, like holding my hand or putting his arm around me. I thought I'd explode when we had our first slow dance.

He whispered in my ear while we danced. "I'm so glad you said you'd come to the dance with me." He kissed my neck and it sent shivers down my spine. "Me too," I said, and he held me so close to him that I could hear his heartbeat.

We must have danced every dance. The King and Queen Committee, which picks the king and queen of the dance, chose me and Beto to be crowned! We even beat out Marcus and that

Loreinda. Beto put the tiara on me, and I did feel like a princess.

Most of the girls came over and said I looked so pretty in the teal dress. Most of them were wearing red or pink, so it made me stand out.

Mr. Alvarez was one of the chaperones, and he even came over to us. He shook Beto's hand, and said that I looked beautiful. Like a shining star. Leave it to him to come up with a science reference.

After the dance, Beto and I sat in the back. He kissed me even more than once but he whispered, "I want to do this with you, but not with them there," as he nodded to Jenna and Damien. Jenna was sitting so close to Damien that you'd think she was driving the car.

"Everything right back there?" Damien asked as he looked at Beto through the rearview mirror. Beto said, "Yeah, man."

Damien continued, "I got to get this car back to my brother or he'll kill me. Sorry. I can't drive up past the hill."

The hill was where the kids went to make out. I'd never been there.

Beto said, "Another time," and he squeezed my hand. I saw Jenna put her head on Damien's shoulder and he threw his arm around her.

Damien dropped off me and Jenna right before the midnight curfew. He walked her up to her door. Jenna's dad (who's a truck driver) was home and looked at his watch.

Beto walked up to my door and said to me, "Thank you, Maizey. Thank you. I really...... you." His words stopped short because Lisa opened the door.

"Oh, I'm sorry. I'm glad it's you. I was getting worried."

We looked at each other and he hugged me.

I looked into his deep brown eyes and said, "Good night, Beto."

"Good night, Maizey."

He skipped. I mean it, skipped down to the car. I watched the red headlights turn out of the parking lot. When Lisa asked if I had a good time, I said yes. She said, "He looks like a nice boy."

I got into my room and hopped under the covers. I am not going to let anything, not anything, keep me from thinking about this night. I pushed all the other thoughts away and fall into a dreamlike sleep until I woke up this morning.

Lisa was clanging pots and pans in the kitchen. I looked at the clock, and I saw it was nearly noon. She probably had been up for a long while.

Beto told me he has to go off today to his cousin's house again to help with something, so he might not be able to call me today.

I know that I have to call Maria and Carlos today. I know there are things that they want to talk about. I just don't want to do it yet. I knew that Jenna isn't doing anything today, so we planned to go to the mall. We don't really care about shopping, we just want to be alone to talk about last night.

The only one who is missing today is…my mom. She's missing this. She's missing all of it. Now I want to cry. NO NO NO!

I won't let it make me cry today. I know it is selfish, and I know I *shouldn't* be selfish. But I can't help myself.

I think I might call Cathy Mullins tomorrow. Maybe I could meet with her sometime soon. I know she lives somewhere near San Diego. She said I could call her if I want.

It's messed up. I'm the happiest I've ever been and the saddest I've ever been and the maddest I've ever been.

Lisa is rapping on the door. Bye for now.

Chapter Twenty-Eight

May 28, 1986

Carlos hated the feel of the starched shirt against his skin. It made him sweat and it was itchy. He kept pushing it away from his neck. This was the second time in the last month that he had to put on his suit and tie. He was happy that he was able to still fit into the "monkey suit." Carla had heard him call it that and made him do monkey sounds. He was grateful for that thought because he was very nervous about today.

At least this time, he did not feel like he was in the hot seat. Last week, he had been subpoenaed by a grand jury. He had a lawyer appointed to him. The lawyer told him that he was just to answer the questions they asked, and told him not to give them (the Feds) any more than that. He thought it odd that a lawyer would say that, so he was very nervous and guarded when he walked into the grand jury room.

He was surprised to see that there were only about twenty people there, besides the prosecutors. He thought he'd be in court. He had to raise his right hand and tell the truth. The prosecutor said the same thing to him – "Only answer the questions I ask, and if you want your attorney at any time, we can stop."

Then the part that made him queasy: "Anything you say here can be used against you."

Carlos settled in for the questioning. He was surprised when nothing was mentioned about him forging Jenny's Social Security card. He knew that he was there to answer questions about Lily and Jenny's time at Harmony Farms.

He had felt for sure that somehow the questions would turn back to him, and that he would have to answer them.

Carlos did his best to recall the time he went to Harmony Farms; what he saw and what he took. The attorney held up in evidence the test results of the seeds and old plants he had collected that day and hidden them under the bench in La Plaza. The attorney asked him to describe to the court why he and Jennifer La Chance, "who you knew as Jennifer Morales," had buried the items. Carlos explained that Jenny was terrified that the Gardener and Lily would come after her and her daughter. She had stolen some things when she escaped with another girl from the farm. She wanted to keep things in case she needed to come forward or after her daughter turned eighteen.

The attorney asked, “Why did you feel the need to dig up these items now?”

Carlos continued, “She got something in the mail, I think. That started it, then she got into that car accident and her memory was confused. She checked herself out of the hospital.”

“Mr. Peña, did you see the package?”

“Only bits and pieces. Because Gregg, that’s my mechanic, brought the stuff from her damaged car to my house. I recognized some of the things.”

“Did you see anything else that would make you suspect someone was trying to contact her or scare her?”

“Yes, there was a man in a black sedan that seemed to be watching her apartment, and maybe even following me and her daughter. But the most important thing is that I found a fake rattlesnake in her bed.”

“Mr. Peña, is there a significance to a rattlesnake?”

“Yes, someone had put it in her bed. Jenny was terrified of rattlesnakes because of something they would do at Harmony Farms. Jenny had showed me the mark on her forearm where he made the snake bite her.”

“And ‘he’ is…?”

“*He* is the Gardener.”

“So, someone broke into the apartment to place the rattlesnake to scare Jenny, to do what?”

“Give back the money, I guess.”

"Mr. Peña, have you ever heard the name Lily, aka Rita Caldwell?"

"Yes, I have heard that name; I even met her on that day that I went to Harmony Farms."

"How would you describe Lily's involvement at Harmony Farms?"

"I would say she was in charge."

"Why would you say that?"

"She looked to me to be giving the orders, and she didn't look drugged out. Juan, who worked at the farm nearby, told me she was in charge."

"Other than that day, did you ever have any other contact with Lily or the Gardener, aka Mark Goddell?"

"No, I have not."

"To the best of your knowledge, did Ms. La Chance ever have any further contact with either of them?"

"No, I don't think so."

When Carlos heard the lawyer say, "You may step down for the witness stand. Thank you for coming today and giving your testimony in front of the grand jury," he thought he'd scream "Yahoo!" Instead he walked as quickly as he could out of the room to the lobby. His lawyer was there and told him he was free to go, and that he'd contact him if the case went to trial.

Maria walked over to him, concerned. "You okay?"

"I think so." Carlos thought to himself that day that *Jenny* should have been there giving testimony. She should have been the one, not him, but Jenny could not do it.

Today, Maria, Carlos, Maizey, Carla, and Maggie were at the family court in Yuma. Today was a big day for all of them. Maizey was going to be officially adopted by Carlos and Maria, and change her name to Maizey Peña.

Cathy Mullins had helped to petition the court to straighten out Maizey's birth certificate, and she had some pull, so things moved fast. Cathy had emphasized to the court that Maizey, who was going to be a senior in high school, wanted to get a job and apply to college. These things were complicated by her lack of a real birth certificate and her mother's fake ID. It would make everything easier for Maizey if everything could be changed now as a minor, and then try to fix it later. The judge had talked to Maizey, and since she was willing to go along with the plan, he agreed.

So, here they were, here as a family to make it official. Cathy Mullins had gotten the day off from the FBI to come too. She and Maizey had been talking over the last few months. Maizey said she could understand why her mom liked her. She was easy to talk to. Carlos was relieved that she had someone to talk to besides Maria about her mom. Right now, Carlos couldn't get down about Jenny. He had to be upbeat for everyone.

Carla was trying to rope him into going to Chuck E. Cheese afterward to celebrate. She said she knew it wasn't a monkey (like in his suit) but instead a mouse, but that was close enough for her. Maizey went along with it because she could see how excited her new little sister was. Carlos hadn't fully committed to any trip, but the twins had started calling Maizey their sister as soon as Maria told them the plan.

They stood in front of the judge, and he asked Maizey if she was sure she wanted to do this. She asked Carlos and Maria if they were sure. The judge was about to read his declaration when Carla chimed in. "Excuse me, what about us?"

The judge smiled and looked up over his glasses. He said, looking at his papers, "You must be Carla Peña, and this is your sister Maggie?"

"Yes, sir."

"Would you like to come up here and talk to me?"

Carlos gave her a look and Maria whispered something in her ear.

"If it's okay with your parents, would you like to approach the bench?"

"Yes," Carla said and grabbed her sister's hand.

Carla went up to the judge and they spoke quietly. The judge was smiling, so Carlos was wondering just what Carla was up to.

The judge said to the twins, "You may return to your seats."

The judge looked up and said, "It has come to the attention of this court that the location of the celebration of Maizey Peña's adoption has not yet been confirmed. Mr. Peña, I understand that Chuck E. Cheese is still on the table."

"Yes, Your Honor."

"So, before I declare Maizey Morales Maizey Peña, I need to confirm the location of the celebration proposed by your daughters."

"Your Honor, Chuck E. Cheese it is."

Carla put her thumbs up at the judge.

The judge declared Maizey's adoption final, and they could go down the hall and get the paperwork. As they were leaving, the judge looked at them and said, "Mr. and Mrs. Peña, good luck with everything." Carlos felt a strong sense of relief if Carla's questioning was going to be the worst thing he'd have to deal with from now on. Nothing was going to happen to Maizey. Maizey was his daughter now forever.

The OT brought me a new calendar today. This one had pictures of New England. I could read the words under the photograph to see the location. It was supposed to help me remember. I flipped through the whole thing, but nothing.

I looked at the Vermont photo of colorful trees in October and wondered why I would ever leave such a beautiful place compared to the empty landscape of the desert.

The doctor came in, I think it was yesterday. He told me that I was making slow and steady progress. He asked me how I felt, if I had any headaches or if my vision was blurry. I said no to both, as far as I could remember.

I can read letters and numbers now, especially numbers. The OT told me that I used to be an accountant's assistant, so I worked with numbers all day. I asked her for a notebook so I could practice my figures. Sometimes, I find it comforting to just do the math. No matter how many ways you add together two plus two, it's always four. The answer is always the same question. Life isn't like that.

I know that Maizey's birthday is coming up. How can she be a teenager?

Carlos told me she was going to be sixteen. How can I not remember any of those years? Once in a while, there'll be something like a fog rolling in, and I try hard to get it, but it drifts away. They say that is common for people who have banged their head too many times, causing amnesia and memory loss.

Ivy has been in to see me here at this place. She looks older than I remember, but her voice is the same. We talk about Harmony Farms. Even though I don't want to remember that part of my life, I do. I do remember being there and escaping the Gardener.

It's strange that Ivy is an FBI agent. Carlos told me that she helped a lot with Maizey when we had the meeting about me not being able to take care of her.

Carlos told me that even if she was going to be adopted by him and Maria, she would always be my daughter. Maizey wanted me to know that.

Maizey has only come a couple of times. She's in another city, Phoenix. I'm in Yuma.

Carlos said that she missed a lot of school after the accident and had things to make up, but that I would be very proud of her. Ivy said the same thing, that she was a really smart girl and had a good head on her shoulders.

I asked the OT if next week's outing could be to Woolworth's so I could get Maizey a gift for her birthday. She said, "Sure, let's write it on your calendar." She gave me a pen and I wrote it on the day she said.

The OT asked me if I want to go into the day room with some of the other patients; they have a new puzzle on the table and *General Hospital* would be on soon.

I asked her about Robert Scorpio, she said, "Ah, that you remember!" I say, "Who could forget him?" We laugh, but I feel like we have had this conversation before. She wheels me into the larger room and says, "Do you want to try the puzzle today?"

I say sure. I see that it's a picture of an entrance to a covered bridge and some maple trees in the background. Someone else has already started working on the puzzle. I say to her, pointing to the puzzle, "This is in Grafton. I have been here with Johnny."

"Really? Tell me more."

"I know I was there with Johnny. I can see him walking on the bridge." I point to the picture on the box. I know she wants more, but I don't want to lose the picture in my mind of Johnny. So I say, "That's it."

"Well, I'll leave you to it."

"Can I pull this apart and start again?"

"Sure."

I break apart the puzzle on the table. I start at the beginning, putting the pieces back together.

May 21, 1986

Yesterday was my sweet sixteenth birthday. Carlos said I would have a party and oh, I did. He even rented a hall. Everyone from school was there. It kinda was a birthday party/going away party, because I'm moving to Yuma after school gets out.

I wasn't sure if I wanted everyone to know my new name yet. Carlos and Maria said it was up to me. I asked Beto and Jenna, and they said no one needs to know that. Jenna said to me, "You'll be out of Moon Valley High School soon anyway."

I think they are right, so I just addressed the invitation as a party for "Maizey's 16th."

Jenna was all in my face for getting the right outfit, so we've been to the mall at least five times. If I'm not spending time with her, I'm with Beto.

Beto and I were tight. I told him everything. Everything about the FBI and my mom. I didn't even tell Jenna, because I think she wouldn't be able to have something not leak out. Beto said he wouldn't tell anyone, and I believe him. I trust him. Carlos gave him a talk, Beto said. Carlos wouldn't tell me what they talked about, but Beto said it was okay because he was just looking out for me, as I was his daughter now. I wasn't used to having a real dad.

I guess if I had to have a dad, I'd pick Carlos, so I'm glad he picked me.

It's been hard without my mom in the apartment. Next weekend, I'm going to be cleaning out all the stuff with Maria and leaving Phoenix for Yuma.

I feel weird about it, but Cathy said that it would be good to have a fresh start in Yuma; even if it's only for one year (my senior year of HS). She's helping me get all my academic stuff for college readiness. Carlos and Maria are grateful, because neither of them have gone to college. Carlos and I agreed that I should go to the University of Arizona in Phoenix because I'll still be seventeen in my first year. I hadn't realized that when I skipped second grade, it would make a difference. But I'm happy about that; it's made everything easier. Beto and I will graduate next year. He's only applied to the University of Arizona too. He wants to run track, and he thinks they have a pretty good team. I'm so happy we'll be together. We are kinda together already. We haven't gotten that far but I think about it a lot. He does too.

Maria can tell we're in love. She says to go slow, because "you've had so much else going on." I know she is right, but some days, I have to pull away because it's like an explosion in my heart. Jenna doesn't know how I have self-control with Beto. She says she and Damien are hot and heavy. Beto laughs, 'cause he says that's not what Damien told him, but he says they're definitely super close. Beto says he'll wait for me forever, and when I look into those deep brown eyes I believe him.

I haven't brought Beto to meet my mom yet. The nurse said that maybe he could come when Carlos and Maria are there. I don't know. I know this is selfish, but I want to keep my two lives separate. Now that I'm Maizey Peña.

I should not just leave my mom, but I have to.

Cathy said that my mom will catch up to me when she can. She has a way of explaining things. "She is driving in the slow lane because she can't go any faster and you're in the fast lane. Eventually, you'll come to a red light and you'll stop together side by side."

I miss her. I mean, the old her. I'm not as angry and confused as I was. I kinda get what happened to her at Woodstock and in California. I don't want to know everything, 'cause everything is where all the bad stuff is and all the stuff that my mom doesn't want to remember.

One day, I'm going to go to Vermont. Cathy said she'd help look up and see if there was any record of family, or where my mom lived. I don't think just yet, but one day. One day I want to know about Johnny Ambrose too. One day Beto and I will go tobogganing and drink hot chocolate with marshmallows as my mother and Johnny did.

Epilogue

May 13, 1988

Harry liked the way the ocean breeze hit him in the face as he lay in the hammock. He never thought that siding with the Feds would have worked out so well for him. He'd been in Cabo San Luca for about a year now. He'd found a place, and got himself a girl. The FBI had come down to Mexico only once to get him to do an interview on tape about what he did for Crazy God and that chick Lily. He was happy to be out of that mess, because the money wouldn't have been there and he would have probably wound back up in the slammer.

He shut his eyes and thought, *Man, this is the life. I ain't gonna mess this up for no one.*

Cathy sighed. She'd almost forgotten to send her mom some flowers on Mother's Day. She was relieved when her sister reminded her that they were going to take her out next week for lunch. She'd had a lot on her plate the last few months. First, the Gardener was found dead in the prison yard by one of the guards. He'd been bitten by a rattler, and the antidote had been missing from the clinic. There'd been an initial investigation, but nothing turned up; so he was buried in the prison grave, and that was that. Somehow, Cathy knew the publicity of his case had reached inside the prison walls and, well, those guys just take care of stuff.

Cathy felt that the Gardener's death helped push Lily to make a plea deal with the D.A. She was relieved because she'd tracked down a couple of the girls from Harmony Farms who were willing to testify against her, but now they wouldn't have to go through that ordeal. Just paperwork on her end now. Cathy was very satisfied that Lily would get what she deserved: an extended prison term in federal prison.

Cathy and Jenny were planning their next move. Cathy had gotten a transfer to the Phoenix office, and had found a three-bedroom house they could share once Jenny was given the okay to be released from long-term care. Cathy had not figured that her own relationship with Maizey would mean as much to her as it did.

She liked being considered an "auntie" and helping her with stuff. She had often felt adrift, but now that the Gardener was dead and Lily was going to prison, she felt she could finally get on with her life – and it didn't hurt that she'd met a nice doctor at Jenny's rehab. Who knows? She might be a mother one day herself.

Jenny looked out the plate glass window of the rehab. She'd been waiting for Maizey and Beto to come and take her to dinner. They had already been over to Beto's mom's place for lunch.

Jenny was thankful for all of the people that she had in her life, but most especially Maizey. Maizey still loved her after all. It took Jenny about a year of full-time therapy to start to remember Harmony Farms and East L.A. There were still pockets of memory loss around the accident and Vermont.

She did remember Johnny, and she did remember her mother. She struggled with what to tell Maizey about her mother because some of the things weren't good. Maria reminded her that she had written a letter for Maizey to read on her eighteenth birthday. Jenny thought that Maizey would want to read it, but Maizey said she actually did not; well, not until her mom could remember more about Vermont.

Jenny was excited to be moving in with Cathy next month. Cathy had rented a three-bedroom house for them to live in, right in Phoenix. She helped Maizey, especially with all the legal and college things. Jenny was proud of Maizey. A college girl, maybe even a lawyer one day, and it looked to her that Beto might be the one. She looked at Beto the way Jenny remembered looking at Johnny.

Maizey and Beto were in the car headed to her mom at the rehab center. She had gotten some flowers at the grocery store for her room. Her mom had always liked flowers; she loved every flower, except for gardenias. Maizey understood everything now from Cathy and Carlos, and even some of the other girls at Harmony Farms (Rose and Jasmine). Maizey had pieced together her mom's life. It was weird for her to think of her mom as the same age as her now, going through all those things. Everyone kept saying it was a different time. Maizey knew that was just an expression used by grown-ups who didn't want to explain their younger behavior. She didn't focus on who her dad was. She had Carlos, and she had Beto. That was all that mattered to her.

Maizey's eighteenth birthday was next week. She really wanted to go away with Beto for the weekend, but she was afraid to say anything to Carlos. She asked Maria, who said she would talk to him. She and Beto had planned to go down to Tucson and stay in a fancy hotel. Beto wanted their first time to be really special. Maizey was a little scared, but she was so in love with Beto that she couldn't focus on her classes. She almost flunked an exam because she was daydreaming about her weekend with Beto.

Maizey had decided that the past was the past, and other than wanting to see the fall trees, and maybe snow, she didn't care about Vermont. She had the family she needed right here In Arizona, and she knew that one day she'd be Mrs. Beto, Esquire, if she studied hard and followed her heart.

Carlos went alone this time. He usually brought the girls and Maria, but today was different. He needed to be alone. He got a spa day planned for them, and off they went to get massages and their nails done.

He could hardly believe that Maizey would be eighteen next week. Even though she was going to be an adult, he felt possessive of her. He was proud of the way she'd handled the situation with her mom. He knew he could not take all the credit for her moving forward. There was Maria, Cathy, and of course, Beto.

He had had a good feeling about Beto since the beginning, and it was obvious to everybody that he loved Maizey, and that she loved him too. So he wasn't surprised when Maria asked him about Maizey wanting to go away with him for the weekend to celebrate her eighteenth birthday. He gave him a dad talk, but really he knew Maizey wouldn't be a girl for much longer. He gave Beto credit for waiting and wanting to make the night special for Maizey.

He wondered to himself if the twins would find someone as good and as kind as Beto. Maggie maybe, but Carla was already giving the boys in her class the business.

He wanted to go alone because he had news to share and it was special.

He had no problem crossing the border into Mexico this time. He had had an issue only once, trying to get back into the US. He was so grateful that Maria had pushed him to get the citizenship done.

The cemetery was small, but it was right behind the church in San Carlos. He had found some cousins that knew where it was. He and Maria had come down before and purchased the plot to bury his mother's ashes with her people.

Carlos spent the money to get a headstone and put both his mother's and sister's names on it.

He bent down and saw the candles burning. He had paid the caretaker to put new candles up on the holidays and around the date of the fire – the date he lost his mom.

He couldn't believe that it would be eighteen years tomorrow. He crossed himself, and he replaced the candles. One for his mom, one for his sister. And he took out a new candle: one for the baby on the way. He talked to his mother like she was there sitting next to him. He joked with her that he hoped the new baby would be a boy. Carlos thought the wind answered him back, and he could hear his mother praying and lighting all the candles in heaven, because he'd need it if the baby was anything like him.

Carlos touched his heart and felt his mother right there.

The End

Acknowledgements

The story of Jenny started in one place and ended in another. It began with an entirely different premise but in the end, the characters told their story. I just wrote it down.

If it wasn't for my daughter Mairead getting an unknown package, I never would have started this writing journey. So thanks, Mairead, for the inspiration.

It's one thing to have a story idea and another to see it to completion.

I am very fortunate to have my friend Jo and our beach walks where we sorted out the characters, especially in the beginning! Thank you for being a sounding board.

My friend Kathleen loves to lunch and talk. Your insights and encouragement kept me on track. Jenny and the gang, thank you!

My friends Eileen and Maureen who made sure the hospital scenes were medically possible. Thank you!

My son Derek, who copy-edited and got the techie thing right. He sold me on an iPad and I overcame my dread of typing. Thanks for giving me confidence in technology.

Taylor, who volunteered to be the beta reader and was the first person to actually read the story without any background. Thank you for your feedback and time!

Abi, who designed the book cover. Thank you for taking my concept and turning into a great design.

To the rest of my friends who expressed enthusiasm and encouragement and quieted my self-doubt during this process. Thank you!

And most especially my husband Patrick, who listened and gave me loads of ideas and the space for me to write I am eternally grateful.

I could not have done it without any of you.

Abi Eneman can be reached for art commissions at aceofsketch@gmail.com

Eliza Murphy, a sometime poet and amateur historian, is a true crime addict who loves to solve a good mystery. She lives with her husband on the Southern Maine coast. They serve a cat called Cornelia, and offer a B&B experience to their two twenty-something children. This is her first novel.

FB: facebook.com/elizamurphyauthor

IG: @elizamurphyauthor